Snuffed Out

Snuffed Out

A MAGIC CANDLE SHOP MYSTERY

Valona Jones

CROOKED
LANE

NEW YORK

Copyright © 2023 by Margaret Toussaint

All rights reserved.

Published in the United States by Crooked Lane Books, an imprint of The Quick Brown Fox & Company LLC.

Crooked Lane Books and its logo are trademarks of The Quick Brown Fox & Company LLC.

Library of Congress Catalog-in-Publication data available upon request.

ISBN (hardcover): 978-1-63910-205-1
ISBN (ebook): 978-1-63910-206-8

Cover illustration by Mary Ann Lasher

Printed in the United States.

www.crookedlanebooks.com

Crooked Lane Books
34 West 27th St., 10th Floor
New York, NY 10001

First Edition: January 2023

10 9 8 7 6 5 4 3 2 1

For Craig

Chapter One

Another inventory label perfectly inked with fancy letters and tied with jute twine to my newest fall-scented pillar candle. I closed my eyes, feeling the swell of soft chamber music resonate in my bones while the heady aromas of ginger, pumpkin, and apple candles filled me with pure joy.

I'm Tabby Winslow, and the energy in our family shop feels just right to me: inviting, peaceful, and invigorating. Our hand-crafted candles grace many a home here in Savannah and in far-off places. Often, customers try to pigeonhole the scents perfuming the shop air. I mentioned three aromas earlier, but if I walked two feet, I'd be breathing citrus-scented air; further on are candles with floral, musk, and beachy notes, to name a few.

Most days, including today, a group of students from the art college hang out on the cushioned wicker furniture in our book nook. They love the shop's eclectic vibe and use our place as their home away from home.

The Book and Candle Shop has become a must-see tourist destination, but for me, this place, and the apartment above, where I've lived my entire life, is home. You see, the natural energy of this location nourishes my family's secret power to manipulate energy. Like food and nutrient consumption, if you expend energy you must refill your tank, so a restorative place like this one is necessary for our survival.

Before Mom passed two months ago, she told my twin and me that there were other energetics in our region and elsewhere, but we've never met them. Mom claimed they weren't all nice people, and we were better off staying under the radar.

In the shop-adjacent stillroom, I pour candles of every hue and fragrance, from pillars to tapers, to votives. They fill the nooks and crannies on our brick walls, industrial shelves, and table displays. Interspersed between candles are whimsical statues of mythical creatures and pirates, books about Savannah, lotions, creams, soaps, lip balms, wind chimes, lush potted plants, and more. It is common for people to walk in, inhale deeply, and gaze at the explosion of color in wonder. Sometimes we have to invite them to come in further so that others may enter.

"Red sky at morning," Gerard Smith, our shop clerk, muttered.

Lost in my musings, I glanced up from my calligraphy to see him scurrying behind the shop counter as if it were full body armor. I clearly remember dawn today had been clouded out. Perhaps I'd misheard. "What?"

"Warned you," he said.

The front door chimed, and Blithe McAdam sailed in on a strong headwind, jaw clenched, and thinly groomed eyebrows beetled together, her tiny dog gazing out at us from the opening of her pet tote. Her sequined black blouse glinted with dark reflections.

I stilled as Gerard's comment became clear. He'd recited a line from an ancient mariner rhyme, which is followed by "sailors take warning." The pen I held fell from my hands, clattering on the display shelf.

For a woman in her early thirties, Blithe carried herself like a society matron of old—the ones born with silver spoons in their mouths, the ones who expected you to jump to serve their every whim. Full disclosure: she'd been born into such a family and was a trust-fund kid, all of which made her haughty attitude cut like a knife, knowing she could buy and sell our shop over lunch.

The woman's gaze locked on me like an infrared beam. I edged out of her line of sight, but she tracked me with sniper precision. My sister's frequent snarky lament—"you're only hurting yourself"—when I refused to use my paranormal abilities echoed in my head. I could manipulate energy as adroitly as my sister, but the last time I'd pushed energy defensively, I'd lost control. I shook off Sage's Cassandra-like prophecy and squared my shoulders against Hurricane Blithe.

"Charlatans! You people gypped me," Blithe yelled as she stomped over to me.

Our shop cats darted to the back room. Nothing wrong with Harley and Luna's fight-or-flight instincts. Blithe's stormy approach roiled the air in a way that had me wanting to escape too. As a new shopkeeper, I'd discovered customers weren't always rational. This woman crossed the sanity line more than most.

If I'd heeded the warning, I could've slipped away before she arrived. Instead, I had to endure her negativity storm. As far as I knew, Blithe was not an energetic like us. Instead, she was radiating her outrage broadly, the same as many people could do. Trying to infuse positive energy into the room, I offered her a friendly greeting, a strategy that often had defused her in recent weeks. "Good day, Ms. McAdam. How may we help you?"

Two browsing customers bolted through the door while another held up her phone as if she were a reporter about to film a six o'clock news segment.

Great. Just what we needed on social media—a recording of this angry woman. She wasn't my favorite person by any means, but I'd survived worse things than upset customers.

"I'll shut this place down so you can't swindle another soul," Blithe continued, shaking a bony finger at me. "I'll have your business license. Alderman Rashad Vernon is on my speed dial, and he'll hear about this. You can bet your defective candles on that."

I wouldn't bet on anything she said. My throat tightened at the hostility striking my aura's electromagnetic field. Her strong emotions rolled toward me like a chain of storm-churned ocean waves. *Not now.* I'd give anything not to be Tabby Winslow, a floundering energetic.

Concerned for my safety, I sent an SOS message to my sister on our silent twin-link. As Blithe attacked, my aura's positive energy deflected most of the bad stuff. It took total focus to maintain my harmonic balance without attacking her in return. I'd made that mistake before and nearly killed someone. I groped for a handhold as nausea set in because of the continued barrage. If I tossed my cookies on Blithe's shoes, would she leave?

Fabric rustled behind me, indicating my twin had joined us. Thank goodness. Sage thought nothing of using her innate abilities at any time. In moments, she would neutralize the negativity roiling around Blithe. Civilians, as in people without the ability to push back, didn't stand much chance against us.

Blithe's negativity stemmed from strong anger and scattered diffusely. In contrast, an energetic could emit a highly focused beam with pinpoint accuracy. Not an even match given how adroitly Sage and I could use our entire energy field to weaponize energy, but I selfishly welcomed the forthcoming respite Sage would bring.

I'd once been as carefree as my twin and wielded my paranormal talents automatically. Not anymore. Ever since my horrible mistake, I now stood in the camp of fairness, and since we knew no other energetics besides us, that meant I kept my protective currents on lockdown. I retreated a step and folded my arms to admire Sage's prowess.

"Ms. McAdam," Sage said when the woman paused, "let me address your concerns. You claim our candles didn't meet your needs. In what way did they fail?"

Blithe twitched around to glare at Sage. "They look like your aromatherapy candles and burn like them, but they didn't touch my headache."

Negativity pulsed relentlessly in the room. If this attack kept up for much longer, Blithe wouldn't be the only person here with a headache. With such an unstable person nearby, I wavered between restoring my equilibrium and watching her like I would a rattlesnake.

"There is a medical disclaimer on all of our aromatherapy products." Sage released a burst of crystalline current, and Blithe shrank into herself. Sage eased up and gentled her tone. "How can I make this right for you? Would you like replacement candles?"

Because of Sage's dampening efforts, the over-the-top tension around me ebbed to a more normal level. Relieved, I closed my eyes and focused on love and light. Especially light. Bright sunbeams, golden sunsets, light shot through a prism into rainbow hues. From these inspiring images I drew power, grace, and centeredness.

Pure light pulsed inside me, filling me with inner radiance. The negative ion assault faded, and I was glad for the reprieve. Best of all, I was no longer in danger of lashing out and losing it altogether. Blithe's odds of surviving this encounter increased by one hundred percent.

"Don't want your stinking candles. My head is killing me. That's what's wrong," Blithe cried out, clutching her temples in a flash of midnight sequins. The tiny, short-haired dog with a white coat whined at the outburst from her person. "Those candles didn't ease my pain. You peddle false hope here. You're quacks— that's what you are, trying to be so cool in your boutique shop. I caught you con artists peddling snake oil. McAdams don't cotton to cheaters."

"We will refund your money, ma'am," Sage said with just the right splash of cheer. "And we'll take the unused candles off your hands too."

Blithe sniffed and wrung her hands repeatedly. "Nothing left of those candles. I burnt them to the quick, hoping against hope they would produce a miracle. My head is pounding so loud surely you can hear it."

"We appreciate customer feedback, and we're sorry your experience was unsatisfactory." Sage turned to Gerard. "Give her a full refund."

He opened his mouth to protest but quickly closed it. Sage must've zapped him with her icer currents because he increased his pace. A micro-pulse of her freezing energy usually inspired briskness, while a larger pulse incited dread, horror, and ultimately death. Gerard's caramel-colored fingers darted over the register's touch screen, and the cash drawer opened. Quickly, he counted the money, closed the drawer, and shoved the bills at Sage.

"Ms. McAdam, I'm sorry you were dissatisfied," my sister continued smoothly, money in hand. "Your well-being matters to us. In addition to a refund, may I also offer you a complementary bottle of hand lotion?"

Blithe's gaze homed in on the premium products we sold. "The kind with rose water?"

Sage's hand moved away from the economical peppermint-infused lotion we made and instead selected the requested product crafted by one of our consignors. "Absolutely."

Blithe cracked a sly smile, grabbed both offerings, and stuffed them in her large tote with her dog, who protested the tighter quarters with a mournful yelp. "I appreciate the refund and the lotion, but I'm still telling everyone you're scam artists."

Sage moved lightning fast and blocked the woman's exit. *Uh-oh,* I thought. She'd never done this before. I feared for Blithe's safety and moved forward to flank my sister, ready to intervene or assist as needed.

"We recommend you seek medical attention for those headaches," Sage said as our energy fields synergized.

Blithe made a dismissive motion with her hand. "Bah. Doctors are quacks too. They can't figure out why it feels like drums are pounding inside my head. The Book and Candle Shop was my last hope, and now even that's gone."

With that, Blithe changed course to avoid Sage, clipping me on the shoulder as she passed. Her dog yipped in protest. I reeled from the nasty bzzt-sting of her pulsing aura, and because of our proximity, Sage felt it too. She shot a blast of energy at our assailant, pushing Blithe out of our shop.

The glass door closed, and silence descended. Because of our close proximity, Sage's still-raging fury coursed through me. She'd used *that* tone of voice to speak with our incensed customer, her ultra-nice one that sounded like it could render butter. Except it was laced with anger. Blithe hadn't reacted to the undertones. All she'd wanted was to be made whole again.

On the surface, Sage had bent over backward for Blithe. She'd calmed the customer with a full refund and offered a gift for the woman's inconvenience. But she'd pushed the woman out of the shop with our combined extrasensory abilities. When Big Sis was this wired, she needed to metaphorically open the pressure relief valve.

While Sage regrouped, my gut pinged with knowing, because Blithe McAdam was a walking disaster. What would happen when she berated the wrong person? Few people could subdue outbursts of emotions like an ice-bringer. She'd been lucky Sage intentionally chilled her bad vibes. Heck, we'd all been lucky. No telling what damage Blithe might've caused here unchecked. At the very least, her seething energy could have infected everyone in the shop.

Been there, done that.

Gerard made a motion of hurling an invisible softball of energy toward the door. "Good riddance, witch. Never cross our doorstep again."

I smiled inwardly as I disengaged from my twin and joined our clerk. Gerard could sell sand to a sailor, but he had no idea about the Winslow family secrets. It worked better that way.

"That was very odd," I said, sagging against the counter. The intangible currents in the shop dropped slowly from the red zone to a yellow one, though the ugly stain of Blithe shadowed the room.

Sage pushed close, invading my personal space again. "Catch me up, Sis."

Conscious of the customers browsing in our book nook, I nodded toward the stillroom. By unspoken agreement we walked there to talk privately. Instantly, the wholesome energy of the chandlery, the tidy jars in soldier-straight rows, shelved candles, and the fragrant drying herbs in the robin's egg–blue room eased my stress.

When we were alone, Sage asked, "Did you follow Auntie O's exact recipe for the candles?"

"Of course."

"What gives then?" Sage drifted closer and showered me with wintry sensations.

The energy chill tickled my funny bone and felt refreshingly familiar at the same time. In response, I pushed back lightly with my energy to let her know I was okay. It was our twin version of I'm-okay-are-you-okay. "Blithe McAdam is a repeat customer. She came in weekly for the last two months."

Sage stared out the alley window before answering. "Her declining health is not our fault."

Through the doorway, I saw Gerard square up products on the nearest sales counter. His OCD compulsion for neatness was a reason he was the weekday face of our business. He was also the grandson of one my aunt's good friends. With his Shemar Moore good looks and his propensity to flirt with everyone, including me, our sales tripled during his shifts. Thank goodness I'd finally gotten him to stop calling me "hon." I wasn't interested in him that way.

Oops—I'd forgotten to answer Sage. "She conned us, not the other way around."

Sage studied me, her sharp gaze itching under my skin, along with her intangible request to share my energy. "Any reason this time was different?"

I couldn't deny her request. She'd defended me, and it was only right to help her recharge. I moved closer, allowing our auras to touch for the transfer. As for the answer to her question, that was harder to say since it meant somehow I hadn't held up my end of the bargain we'd made.

I took a deep breath. "We ran out of Auntie O's candles. These were my first batch."

"If you followed the exact recipe in the candlemaker book, why were they different?" my sister persisted. "We need to stop this from happening again. We can't stay in business if money flows the wrong way from the cash register."

I drew myself up to my full height, though Sage had me by an inch. Because we were fraternal twins, our physical characteristics were different. For starters, she always wore her witchy black hair unfettered, while I kept my dirty-blonde hair in a ponytail. "It's a mystery why mine didn't provide relief. I'll contact Auntie O tonight. She's at work now."

"You do that. I wish she hadn't moved to Florida. This family is stronger together." She thrust her palm my way. "Don't say her relocation was driven by the weather. Our Savannah winters are mild."

"She wanted a change of scenery," Gerard said from the threshold, reminding me our conversation wasn't private.

Despite Gerard and Sage being an item once upon a time, he'd been a Book and Candle Shop employee for over two years now. We Winslow sisters had inherited Gerard, along with the shop, four months ago, two months after our mom passed and Aunt Oralee Colvin left the family business. Sage and I had been peripherally involved in the shop since we were old enough to see over the sales counter. We'd always known the shop below our apartment would be ours one day. Our grandmother and her sister had run it, then Marjoram (our mom) and Oralee ran it. Now it was our turn.

It stung that I'd messed up something important with our signature aromatherapy candles.

"I'll sort out the candle issue," I promised. "You focus on our book nook inventory and product consignments, and keep the online orders processing. I can't manage this place without you— not with my muzzy head for numbers."

Sage's fierce expression softened, and the chilly storm in the stillroom faded. "My candles are never as nice looking as yours. I need you too, Sis."

Gerard cleared his throat. "Now that we're all a happy family again, who needs fresh coffee?"

Sage and I raised our hands. "Be right back with java for all from Southern Tea," he said.

When we were alone, Sage patted my shoulder. "You okay?"

"Blithe's accusation hurt my pride. Gerard could've been more direct about trouble arriving, but he chose to be clever. I ignored his chatter until Blithe stood in the shop spewing her poison."

Sage shook her head. "Isn't it past time you put this fairness nonsense aside and accept who you are? I hate seeing you so bottled up."

"Following my moral code keeps everyone safe. I almost killed someone, in case you forgot."

We stared at each other for the longest time. Fueling my side of the stare was the appalling possibility of my ability causing me to be locked away and preventing me from touching my family ever again. That isolation would destroy me.

"You're not going anywhere, Sis," Sage said. "You have my word on that. I have your back, same as you have mine. But you're living half a life. I hate that for you."

"Since the incident, I've struggled in difficult situations. I freely admit that, but I'm still productive, functioning, and free to come and go as I please. Far as I'm concerned, it's a decent trade."

"Oh, for heaven's sakes. You're no meek pigeon. You're a fierce eagle and meant to fly unfettered. Don't fear being caged, Tabs, you're already in one of your own design. If you don't do something about it soon, I will."

Chapter Two

S age and I enjoy listening to music, but my twin totally adores rock and roll. She sings along with her favorites and can't be still when rock is playing. I enjoy listening to all kinds of tunes, but as a card-carrying introvert, I prefer meditative instrumental pieces in the evenings so I can relax and unwind.

Tonight Sage was frolicking with up-tempo melodies when I climbed the stairs from the store, so I donned ear protection to hear myself think. After eating the vegan lasagna Sage had prepared, I slipped downstairs to the stillroom behind our shop, with our black cats, Harley and Luna, padding silently behind me. I cued music through my phone, and soon classical notes lilted around me.

Drifting through the room, I savored the delightful scent of dried herbs and loved the look of my pretty candles on the shelf, ready to be sold. Or not. I took one down and studied it. They looked and smelled like my aunt's candles. Why hadn't this batch helped Blithe? If only candles could talk. I shelved the candle and wandered over to the essential oil drawer. I opened the peppermint bottle to dab a bit on my temples to ease a fledgling headache.

My sister's threat to do something about the mental lockdown of my energetic talent rattled me. Could she counteract my safety measures if I'd placed the block? Oh, how I wished Mom were here to answer that question. However, I had another lifeline. Aunt Oralee was a close second, and she was alive and kicking.

I settled onto a stool beneath the drying herbs, silenced the audio stream from my app, and called her. We chatted about this, that, and the other until Aunt Oralee finally said, "What's going on, Tabby?"

Bass reverb leaked through the old ceiling. I thought of Sage dancing with abandon upstairs, willing herself into the soul of each number. Dance therapy relieved her tension, same as the soft acoustic sets did for me. We had our differences, but the similarities we shared were many, same as Mom and Oralee.

A deep breath of the herbal air helped center me. After a moment, I said, "A repeat customer came in today, furious because the last aromatherapy candles she bought here didn't help. We gave her a refund and comped her some lotion, but we don't want to have that happen again. You graciously left us with such a deep inventory of candles that we only just ran out and began selling the ones I made. The most likely conclusion is that I messed up my candles."

"That is unfortunate. Did you follow the recipe, dear?"

Her question jarred me to my feet, and I paced the room. "Followed it to the letter. The aromatherapy candles are still our shop's bestseller. Anyway, said customer was livid. She made threats right and left about the poor quality of our products and threatened to use her connection to get our business license pulled. Her outburst terrified us and our other customers."

"How awful, for her and for you girls. That candle recipe never failed us before. Let me think." Silence ebbed and swelled on the line until she finally said, "The only other thing that occurs to me is mindset. Were you in a healing frame of mind when you created them?"

As I circled the tidy workbench, I thought back to making candles last week. "Can't say that I was. Gerard and Sage were going at it like pit bulls over expanding our bookshop area. Gerard is clueless because of the mild hypnosis she's used on him to help him forget she was in Europe with him, and he thinks he's doing what's best for the shop because he's our best salesman. Anyway, Sage insists we add a monthly author feature and hold a reception for them, to draw more locals to the shop. Gerald says books are a harder sell to tourists, and they don't turn over fast enough to keep the lights on. I agree with both, but they wouldn't budge. Their negativity triggered my fight-or-flight mode, so I puttered around in the stillroom for a bit to simmer down, and then I started on the candles."

"No one else entered the room while you were making them?"

"Nope. Just me."

"This isn't your fault, dear. It's mine. I'm so sorry. Mindset is so automatic to me now, I forgot to pass that tip on. When making therapeutic candles, thoughts, words, and deeds matter."

Harley crouched like a toad beside the candles I'd made. Luna perched on the stool I'd vacated. Their eyes followed me in silent accusation. "You lost me."

"Intentions matter. When performing an act of creation, it's important to feel as if you've just come from a yoga class. Be radiant, relaxed, and full of vitality."

It took me a moment to gather myself. "I met none of those criteria that day."

"Thought so. Anyone can craft perfectly beautiful candles, but to give them that extra zip, a Winslow must consciously infuse them with her calm, healing energy."

"It can't be added after the fact?"

"No. The effect would be superficial at best."

"Ack. It sounds like I tracked bad energy all over the room before I made a dozen candles that day. Can I melt them down and reuse the materials?"

"Theoretically, yes, but efficacy-wise, no. Throw them out. Start over in the right frame of mind."

I could already hear Sage's loud objection to the hit to our bottom line. "We can't afford expensive mistakes. But if good energy isn't instilled in the creation process, customers won't appreciate the candles. What a disaster."

"It's a learning curve, dear."

"I hear you, and I will definitely be effusive with the next batch. I wish that were the only reason I called." I stopped pacing to clear my throat, and my toes curled under. "Moving on to my next item, Sage says it's time I dusted off my energy talent. Further, she threatened to remove the mental block I placed on my abilities. Can she do that?"

Edgy silence filled the line. "May I remind you," Auntie O said, "that Sage's talents are off the charts. Usually, wards must be removed by the person who placed them, but the rules might be different for you two since you are twins. It is possible but unlikely."

I shook my head. "I don't want her inside my head any more than she already is."

"Then you'd best remove the block promptly." A doorbell chimed through the line. "Gotta run. My pickle ball group is here. Get your intentions in order before you make more candles."

Chapter Three

On Saturday afternoon, two days later, I staffed the shop by myself and filled the airwaves with soft music. With downtown Savannah a noted tourist destination, our family kept the shop open every day. Sage wanted us to develop a higher income stream before we added another employee, though we needed to hire someone. In the interim, I worked Saturdays, and she took Sundays in addition to our weekday shifts.

After each round of customers, I straightened stock, aligned our eclectic collection of books related to Savannah, pinched off brown fronds on our front-window fern pots, which were interspersed with fanciful sculptures of dragons, pirates, and more. The cats stayed closer than usual today, which suggested a brewing storm. To ward off trouble, I tinkled our special wind chimes, pleased with the harmonic notes.

Foot traffic through the shop slowed at about one thirty, and by three, I was counting the moments until five, when I could lock up. Or I was until two cops breezed through my front door.

Detectives Sharmila Belfor and Chase Nowry were a salt-and-pepper pair, him the iodized white salt and her the spicy black pepper. A few years ago the city and county had conjoined their police forces, but recently they'd become separate entities again. No official reason was given, but I suspected there'd been too many cooks in the kitchen. That never worked out.

I'd met the city detectives last month when they dropped by in relation to a burglary at the wine shop down the street. That situation resolved quickly, and I hoped for the same outcome to their Bristol Street visit today. "Good afternoon, Detectives," I said. "How may I help you?"

"We're investigating a homicide, ma'am," Detective Nowry said, easing onto the padded stool by the counter, his expression grim. His deeply lined face attested to his years of service as a law enforcement officer.

His words shook me, and my fevered imagination took flight, imagining a horrific end to someone I knew. I braced my arms on the sales counter and made myself ask, "Who died?"

"Blithe McAdam."

Buzzing sounded in my ears, as if I'd landed in a beehive. Blithe. She wasn't a nice person, but I wouldn't wish homicide on anyone.

"Ms. Winslow," Detective Nowry asked, "what can you tell us about this woman?"

"I knew her. She bought candles here from time to time."

Detective Belfor leaned in. "And hand cream?"

"Uh. Yes. The lotion. Um. My sister gave her the lotion on Thursday."

His head cocked to the side, parrot-wise. "She didn't purchase it?"

"Well, no." I didn't like the way he studied me, as if I were a bug in his private insect collection. Harley left his cozy basket on the floor and jumped onto the stool behind the counter, startling me. Feeling like I was under a magnifying glass, I scooped the cat in my arms, to use as my shield.

"Ms. Winslow, is there something you're not saying?"

Harley's contented purr steadied me. "Blithe McAdam suffered from severe headaches. When she couldn't find pain relief in the traditional medical community, she tried our aromatherapy candles. She bought sets of candles every week for several weeks, but this week she said our candles didn't help. Sage gave her a full refund and the lotion."

"Any heated words exchanged?"

I gave them my best shopkeeper smile. "The customer is always right. We addressed her concerns, and she left. That was the end of our conversation."

"Come now, Ms. Winslow," Detective Belfor said. "The victim was a disagreeable woman. I'm sure there's more to the story."

"We want our customers to be happy, Detectives. She arrived upset, and we eased her concern. She departed in a better frame of mind. What more can I say?"

"Did you see her after Thursday?"

"No, I did not."

"Did your coworkers see her?"

"Not that I know of. If you don't believe me, check our security footage." I pointed to the camera behind the counter. From long usage, I knew the lens captured the sales counter and the front door.

They observed me with their laser-focused cop vision, and I was delighted to have Harley to help me through this. My turn to pose a question. "How'd she die?"

"A blow to the head," Detective Belfor said. "You know anyone who had a beef with her? Someone who hated her enough to kill her?"

Blithe was a difficult person, but it was one thing to dislike her and quite another to end her life. "No."

"Are you certain?" Detective Nowry asked. "Perhaps someone who despised her. Are you protecting someone? A coworker, perhaps?"

My chin rose with my indignation. "No one I know would do such a thing."

"What about her friends or family?"

"She's a customer. We aren't best friends with our customers. Shopkeepers are friendly for business reasons."

"Interesting," Nowry said, "but you didn't answer my question. What about her family and friends?"

Good grief. He wouldn't stop with the questions. I'd have to share something, or he'd never leave. "We both grew up in Savannah, so I've known of her since I was a kid, even though she's five years older than me. She's from old Savannah money and lived in a big house on a square. Silver-spoon-in-her-mouth upbringing. Her parents are deceased. There's an alleged half brother somewhere, I believe. I can't recall his first name. He is older than Blithe, so maybe fortyish now. His last name was a TV show."

Nowry wrote furiously on a palm-sized notepad. "He's an actor?"

"Don't know, as I never knew him or knew where he lived." I tapped my temple trying to recall the man's name. I hadn't thought of that guy since high school. "Started with a D . . . Darby, Dallas, Doogie . . . No—I got it. Dawson's Creek. His last name is Dawson."

"Anything else?"

"There were rumors about him."

"And?"

"I don't spread gossip."

"It could be helpful to the case."

If only I could close my eyes and blink these cops away. "He grew up hard and disagreeable. Mouthy cuss, as I recall. People predicted he'd turn out bad, and if that happened, you should have a file on him. That's all I know about him."

"What about Blithe's friends?" Belfor asked.

I shrugged. "Can't help you there."

"Surely she had friends."

My smile felt like a grimace. Harley stopped purring until I petted him again. "If you'd spent five minutes with Blithe, you'd know she was . . . difficult. Her family money bought her a handful of acquaintances for a while, but not even money can gloss over a lifetime of rudeness and a sour disposition. I don't know where she moved after she lost the big house, but her neighbors at either place should know more about people in her life. Did you speak to them?"

"We did," Belfor continued. "Your statement corroborates theirs."

I didn't respond. Nowry tapped his notebook on the glass countertop. The cops exchanged glances, and then Belfor scanned the entire sales floor, much like a hungry lioness at a watering hole.

"You mind if we look around?" Belfor asked, eying my stillroom.

That predatory gleam in her eye concerned me. I'd answered their questions. I did not need to keep helping them do their job. "I do mind. I've answered your questions and cooperated. If you want to do more than browse the merchandise displayed in the store, you need a search warrant."

"As has been stated, the victim was disagreeable," the female cop countered. "Since we can't rule out people yet, everyone who knew her is a person of interest, including you, your sister, and your shop clerk."

The doorbell chimed as a customer entered the shop. Harley squirmed out of my arms and thudded on the gleaming wooden floor. I waved cheerfully to my customer. "Be with you in a minute."

I glared at the detectives. "Now, if there's nothing else, I have a customer to serve."

Detective Belfor jerked a thumb toward our high-end consignment products. "Okay if I try the tester of the product Ms. McAdam received?"

I shrugged. "Knock yourself out."

Judging from their odd expressions, that had been a dumb thing to say, seeing as how someone had knocked Blithe into the next life. I started to correct myself but stopped. No point in digging a deeper hole. I pressed my lips together instead.

"A word of advice, ma'am," Nowry said as he sniffed one of our lightly scented Sea and Sand candles. "Don't leave town any time soon."

Chapter Four

The customer from Macon, Georgia, adored aromatherapy candles. She bought one of every blended scent. Thank goodness I'd already pulled and discarded that bad batch. I made polite inquiries about her general health, and she assured me she was the picture of wellness. It would be a snap for me to verify her claim by checking her aura, but that would mean opening my personal Pandora's box.

No way, no how.

Last time I opened that door, with a purpose, someone got hurt.

In any event, she walked out with four aromatherapy candles, body spray, three kinds of lotion, and Terrance Zepke's *The Quirky Tourist Guide to Savannah*. For good measure, I slipped our business card into her handled bag.

Once she left, I realized both cats were staring at me. "What?" I asked.

Cats could be very Zen and open to the universe when they wanted to be. This wasn't one of those times. They expected me to do something right this very second. Waves of cat intensity bombarded me as if mealtime were ten minutes late.

"All right. I'll call Sage." A glance at my watch revealed it was half past four. "Better yet, I'll close early. I'd rather discuss the cop visit with her in person."

However, by the time I watered the ferns in the front window and the potted herbs in the stillroom, emptied the trash, ran the vacuum, and closed out the register, it was five before I hit the stairs. No rock music wafted under the door. No mouth-watering aroma of dinner stirred my taste buds. In fact, there was no sign of Sage in our modest living quarters. I grabbed a quick sandwich, fed the cats, and browsed through a craft supply catalog to await her return.

At five thirty, the time I'd normally be bopping up the stairs, I heard her moving around in her room. The bedroom door I'd left open was shut now, so I knocked on it. "Sage?"

"Give me a minute," she said.

I paced the hall as I waited. How'd she get past me? The question clunked around in my head like a square wheel. Auntie O constantly reminded me Sage's paranormal abilities were strong. Her icer talent was undeniable, especially after she perfected it on us. Well, mostly on me.

Mom finally made her stop tormenting me, and Sage soon turned into a vigilante against schoolyard bullies. The upshot of this was that kids steered clear of us. Still did for that matter.

Luna padded in, mewing for a treat, with Sage hard on her heels. "You're home early," Sage said. "And something's wrong. What happened?"

I repelled the questing energy she sent my way. "Blithe McAdam is what happened. Two cops came by this afternoon." I summoned a calming breath to deliver the bad news. "She's dead."

"I see." Sage didn't blink in the edgy silence that followed. Her rapt gaze reminded me of a lizard in a staring contest. "Natural cause or something else?"

"The latter. The cops asked questions and glared at me, like you're doing right now."

Blithe shrugged off my remark. "You held to the code?"

Our personal policy was to say as little as possible to authorities and never, ever mention our extra gears. "Yeah, but so what? They said we are suspects. Because of the hand cream you gave to Blithe."

Sage's jaw dropped. "The lotion killed her?"

"No, nothing like that, but it led them straight to our door."

"Just like the good old days." Sage shook her head and sighed. "Always start with the freaks when something bad happens. Just because our hidden energy talent makes some non-sensitives uneasy, we're blamed for more than our fair share of bad stuff. Once people have that 'off' feeling about us lodged in their gut, no amount of logic will counteract that fear response."

I hated that we didn't get a fair shake. We manipulate our energy fields, the very same energy everyone is born with. It wasn't our fault others evolved with an extrasensory blindness. Not our fault either that we didn't fit socially accepted norms. "*Freak* implies there's something wrong. We're normal for us."

"Keep thinking like that, Sis, and we'll both land in jail. How can we protect ourselves? I could tune the shop's energy so cops are too uncomfortable to enter, but they could still capture us if we ventured outside the shop. Scratch that plan. We can't hide in here for the rest of our lives."

"A cop-repelling barrier would only make them go elsewhere temporarily if they brushed into it, and would draw unwanted attention to our shop, so we need a better plan, one that flies under the radar. We can't rely on them to get this right. We have to get involved."

"Detective time?"

"I don't see another choice. Trust Blithe McAdam to screw us in life and death."

Sage scooped up Luna and paced the combined living room and kitchen. Mom called this area her Great Room, but it was a small, dual-purpose space. The road ahead for us looked dangerous, twisted, and energy draining. Focusing on murder would have serious repercussions to our well-being.

"I say we let ourselves into her place tonight," Sage said.

Her suggestion caused my heart to stutter for a moment. "It's a crime scene."

Sage grinned for all she was worth. "Luckily, my sister can sneak in without being seen."

Chapter Five

"You knew?" My skin prickled. I'd never told anyone I could disappear. "You never said a word."

Luna squirmed and jumped down. Sage sat in the rocking chair across from me. "Family motto: Don't share everything you know. Sometimes you vanished in the shadows as you slept in our room. I've known for years you can hide in plain sight."

"You kept my secret all this time?"

"Sure. Not like you don't know a few of my deep dark secrets. Far as I'm concerned what happens in these walls stays in these walls. No need to give anyone extra ammunition to use against us."

By now prejudice should be a thing of the past, but psychological principles showed that people clump together in like kind. That left us outliers twisting alone in the wind.

Both cats jumped from the back of the sofa, where I sat, and landed on the coffee table, in neutral territory, as if they intended to referee our conversation. I hope neither one pounced on me with claws out, so I kept an eye out for feline hijinks. "I see you remember that college psychology class."

"Right. I knew college wasn't for me, and that class proved it, though I did like my accounting class. You remember what Mom said when I finished that semester?"

Mom had said a lot at the time. She'd expected us to be the first generation in the family to have college degrees. I'd at least earned a two-year associate degree at Georgia Southern, so I hadn't disappointed her as much as Sage. "Refresh my memory."

"She said we can't change who we are. Our journey is figuring out how to use our extrasensory abilities for good, without inciting notice, because people will always be haters."

"Mom was good at saying the right thing to boost our spirits. She always praised our efforts."

My thoughts drifted to Mom's good energy, which still enhanced our home, and back to Sage, who rocked and watched me as if I'd missed something important. Her big reveal about my secret . . . maybe my invisibility talent wasn't as special as I'd thought. "Can you go invisible too?" I asked.

"Sadly, no. But it would be cool to spy on people that way. Not in a creepy way, of course, but to see if they're talking about you, or if they were up to no good. Your skill set fits nicely with our plan to discover who killed Blithe. You can eavesdrop on suspects and learn their secrets. You're lucky to have that skill."

"Thanks, I guess." I'd never considered luck a factor. My thoughts veered more to the unlucky side of the coin. While we were airing personal matters, I should ask Sage about her reverse Houdini act. "How'd you get to your room this afternoon? You weren't there when I came up from the store early. I checked."

"Nothing as cool as your invisibility. Figured out I can climb up and down the bricks from my second-story window. It faces the alley, so no one is likely to notice."

There was no soft ground in the alley. A slip would land Sage on concrete or in the dumpster. "Sounds dangerous. Why not use the doorway?"

"I like to have options. Never know when I might need an escape route. You should try it too. Oh wait—you've got invisibility. You can walk out the door without anyone noticing."

This wasn't the first time she'd pushed me toward wholeness, and it wouldn't be the last. "I don't use that ability indiscriminately. I can't even access it unless I withdraw the mental block, and I won't do that. I lost control last time."

"Time to get over that mistake. The person lived, not that he deserved such good fortune. It's been fifteen years. You're a different person now. *To whom much has been given, much shall be required.*"

I snorted, startling Harley into hopping onto the sofa and padding over. He curled up next to me, and I savored his good vibes. "Fine time for you to quote the Bible."

Sage spread her arms wide as angel wings. "I am a child of the universe, and I'm open to all ideas."

"Good for you. I'm not open to hurting others. It was cavalier thinking and emotional insecurity that got me cornered in the first place. When or if I ever decide to access my Winslow extra gears is my decision. It's wrong to invade someone's privacy by going invisible. It was okay to use that power when I stayed out too late and sneaked back in. However, now that I have a better idea of personal boundaries, I'd enforce a code if I ever tried it again. Like I could use it to escape from danger, but not for personal gain. Unless I cloak myself in shadows, invisibility causes a heavy energy drain. The longer I'm invisible in daylight, the more recharge I need."

"I believe you can handle your extra gears now. We know where this homicide investigation is likely to go. The cops came here first because Blithe had some of our shop's products in her home. Nothing deadly about that hand cream, and I sincerely doubt that plastic bottle was the murder weapon. Did they visit her grocery store or hair salon? I doubt it. They came here because we're different, and different means dangerous to them. It's been that way through the ages. When something goes wrong, the 'normals' blame the people who color outside the lines."

"Police investigations often single out loners and minorities." I sighed out my frustration because we *were* dangerous, and their distrust of us was justified. "Even if I risk using my hiding ability, I can't walk through walls like a ghost. The door must be open for me to enter."

Sage grinned. "I can arrange that."

I ignored her remark about doors and invisibility. "An investigation will draw more attention to our interest in solving this case. I have a better idea than sneaking into Blithe's house. I'll bake a batch of cookies for Quig in the morning. That'll get me in his door, and perhaps he'll share something from the autopsy that'll help us."

"Are you sure you want to encourage him? He's been sweet on you for a long time."

"Quig has his own agenda, but so what? Everyone has an agenda if you think about it. I'm not concerned about fanning the flames of our friendship."

My twin gave me a sly look. "So you won't add anything extra to the cookies?"

My eyebrows rose of their own volition, and I laughed out loud. "Didn't say that."

Chapter Six

"You could make a fortune selling these cookies. Why not add a mini café to the book corner of your shop?" Quig stopped to inhale another cookie, light glinting off his dark, rimmed glasses. "I love these coconut macaroons, and you know it. As an intelligent person, I surmise you came here with this delicious bribe because you have an ulterior motive."

Contrary to what I'd told Sage, I hadn't spiked the cookies to have any specific emotional effect on our Bristol Street neighbor, Dr. Octavian Henry Quigsly IV. With Quig, I knew who I was working with. He wanted to please me, and my pleasing him first usually had the desired effect of him granting my request.

Even so, his Renaissance man physique and Clark Kent good looks were very easy on my eyes. "No café in our future. Baking is not our lane. You're correct about my visit here. I need something. What'll it take to earn a favor?" I asked, secretly hoping my cookies had already sealed the deal.

"Go out with me."

That wasn't unexpected, given our new secret, but I wouldn't be another of his women he flaunted around town, even if I cared for him. "That wouldn't be fair to you. I'm married to The Book and Candle Shop right now. No time for a relationship." Sad that my cookie strategy failed, I retreated, but before I got out the door, Quig latched onto my hand, drew me inside, closed the door, and directed me to a tall bar chair at his granite-topped kitchen island.

Unlike the soft colors and padded chairs at our place, Quig's over-the-shop apartment had an industrial look, with straight lines and a palette dominated by charcoal gray and black. If I lived here, I'd add throw pillows everywhere and install handles on the flush cabinets.

He poured two glasses of milk in pewter cups for us and offered me a macaroon. "As it happens, I need a plus-one for an upcoming fundraiser. No strings attached. Will you do me the honor?"

The man had a Who's Who list of Savannah socialites in his phone contact list, and I'd lay even money that any of those women would've been thrilled to be his gala date. With his laid-back personality, huggable frame, and family money, he could have any woman he desired. I never understood why he'd fixated on me.

However, our interests aligned today. Agreeing to go with him would seal our bargain. "Okay. When is it?"

"End of next week. Black-tie affair. I've been meaning to call you about it, but I didn't want to get shut down. So I'm happy you're here, and we both have something we need from each other."

Black-tie events meant fancy dresses. Fortunately, our family kept a closet full of formal black gowns and impossible shoes. They never went out of style. "I have calendar availability, but let's be perfectly clear here. We go as friends. There are no extra perks involved in the deal."

He studied me intently, his eyes veiled behind those glasses. "Agreed. Now what did I trade my soul for?"

"Information about Blithe McAdam. The police came to our shop and grilled me about her. She bought our candles, and somehow we are now murder suspects. Information is power, and from where I'm sitting, you've got what we need."

"I performed her autopsy, if that's what you're asking."

I nodded. "The cops said she died from a blow to the head. What was the murder weapon?"

"Now we're in forbidden territory. Can you rephrase the question?"

I smiled, getting into the spirit of things. "Were there indications from the wound about the object's size or type?"

His head gave the slightest nod.

Encouraged, I continued this twenty-questions-like game. "Would you say the pattern was consistent with a hammer?"

He stared at me without moving, which I took as a negative response. "A fireplace poker?"

No response. I named off several other items commonly used as weapons on crime TV shows, before I happened on *baseball bat*, to which his lips twitched.

That was the answer. Someone beaned Blithe with a bat. Neither Sage nor I owned a bat. If the cops searched our place, we would pass with flying colors. Good to know. Meanwhile, I had a chance to get more info from Quig.

I cleared my throat softly. "Since Blithe came to our shop with migraine troubles, I wonder if you saw any biological indication of what caused her trouble?"

"There were no remarkable medical findings besides head trauma."

Not the answer I wanted. Darn men for being so direct. I tried another angle. "What about stomach contents? What was her last meal?"

"Confidential information."

"Hmm. This is hard."

He waved the cookie tin at me. "Have another cookie. Treats make everything better."

Good advice. I accepted another cookie and munched on it, trying to get him to open to me. "Any unusual scars, tattoos, or mended bones?"

"Yes."

"Are they relevant?"

He shrugged, so I went through the list individually until he made a nod for mended bones. "Which bone?"

"Suffice it to say she didn't have two good legs to stand on."

"Was the injury recent?"

"It happened a few years ago. I remember her being on crutches at a charity gala, making it public knowledge."

"Gotcha." That looked like all I'd get out of him about the autopsy. "Blithe threatened to sic City Alderman Rashad Vernon on us, to have him pull our business license."

The change in Quig happened as quick as a flash of light. Strong energy pulsed around him, and his voice softened. "Did she now?"

He wasn't an energetic like me, but sometimes I wondered what he was. I'd always felt comfortable around him because his energy felt familiar. "She claimed they were friends, and he would do her bidding."

Quig barked out a rusty laugh. "Not hardly. Rashad considered her his nemesis. He wouldn't grant her a favor unless she agreed to leave him alone."

I drew in a deep breath. "I'm relieved to hear that. So very relieved, as Sage and I haven't quite gotten the knack of running the store like Mom and Auntie O did. We can't afford extra stress while we're learning the ropes."

"You need anything, you call me," Quig said. "Most city and county officials owe me favors. I can smooth any pesky red tape associated with running a business in our district."

"Thanks. You don't know what a relief it is to have you as a lifeline."

"We're friends and neighbors." His voice gentled. "Of course I'd help you."

Drat. Now his energy flared in the sensual zone. I needed to keep this conversation on a professional footing. Maybe he remembered something else about Blithe from when we were kids. Sage and I had gone to public school, but Quig and Blithe had attended private school through eighth grade. "How long have you known Blithe?"

"Hard to say, exactly. She was four grades ahead of me."

"Can you ever remember liking her?"

He gave a wry grin. "Not my type."

"What is your type?" I covered my mouth as soon as I realized I'd voiced my private thought. Heat steamed from my face.

Quig escorted me to his door. "You know the answer to that question."

Yeah. Aside from his inexplicable interest in me, his interest ran to that black book of revolving socialites. My shoulders sagged. Everything I knew about Quig suggested he had deep waters, and yet his shallow dating style indicated a different nature. "Thanks for your help."

"Anytime, sunshine."

Chapter Seven

Gerard didn't show when we opened on Monday morning. It was the alternate Monday, meaning it was my day off, and I'd intended to spend my free time working on our undercover investigation. Instead, I manned the cash register and restocked our shelves. Sage kept muttering we should go check on Gerard. I assumed he was running late. After all, everybody had an off day now and then. Gerard would turn up sooner or later.

As the morning hours ticked by with both of us in the shop, I had to admit she was right. It wasn't like Gerard to be a no-show. Calls to his phone went unanswered. After our lunch rush, we flicked the "Open" sign to "Closed," grabbed his spare key from the register, and took off to his place. It wasn't within walking distance, so Sage got her car from the garage, and we went to a modest stucco home on the west side of town.

I'd never been to his place before, but as we drove to the suburbs, it occurred to me that our employee lived in newer lodgings than we did. Did he have other financial resources? We'd continued paying him the same wage he'd received from Mom and Auntie O. Sage and I weren't drawing much more than him from the business, and it was tight for us to cover our living expenses.

First thing we noticed was his white-on-white VW Cabriolet parked at his house. Sage and I hurried up the steps. Thoughts of him being too sick to move bounced in my head.

Sage unlocked the door and we barged in, careful not to touch anything with our bare hands. "Gerard!" we both called. No answer. The place was so quiet I could hear the glass jars vibrating against each other in his refrigerator.

I dialed his phone again, not sure if I wanted it to ring here or not, but I had to know. No ringing occurred. This place felt like a tomb. "He's not here," I said. "There's no sign of a struggle. Everything is OCD neat, as if only Gerard touched his stuff."

"This isn't like him to disappear," Sage said, chewing her thumbnail. "He's so responsible."

"Maybe he met someone over the weekend and is shacked up across town."

"No way. He would've called if he couldn't make it."

"Should we call the police?"

Sage shrugged. "We don't know how long he's been missing."

Shoot. I was primed for action. "I can call the area hospitals."

"Do that," Sage said. "I'll snoop in his bedroom and bathroom."

It didn't take long to call St. Joseph's, Candler, and Memorial hospitals. Gerard wasn't at any of those places. I called the morgue. He wasn't there either.

"His matching suitcase set, electric toothbrush, and shaving kit are here," Sage said. "He didn't take a trip, and it looks like someone else—possibly an older woman, by the clothes in the closet—lives here too. No one is home."

"He isn't a hospital patient or in the morgue. With his personal hygiene items and car here, I fear for his safety. The likelihood of his losing track of this much time isn't feasible, given his compulsive nature. He got snatched."

"Maybe. Let's get out of here. I want to check something else."

We left, making sure to wipe the doorknob clear of our prints.

Back in the car, Sage searched a popular video application. "Oh no!" She shoved the phone my way, and there was Blithe in our shop, making her dissatisfaction with our aromatherapy candles known. It was as if we were seeing a nightmare replay in the bright light of day. Like bad déjà vu, there at the end, Gerard called the woman a witch and ordered her never to cross our doorstep again.

Further, the video had over five thousand views. I groaned and smacked my head. "What a time for a video of the shop to go viral."

By government standards, Savannah's population of 146,000 placed it in the big-city category. However our city was a flotilla of small-town-like neighborhoods, all joined under the auspices of the City of the Dead. I glanced at my twin, who appeared deep in thought. "You thinking what I'm thinking?"

"We're tagging Brindle Platt." Sage tossed her phone in her purse and shifted her car into drive. "Gerard needs a lawyer."

*　*　*

The secretary for Cranford, Aldrich, and Platt ushered us into Platt's office. I didn't see him at first—only a set of darkly clad legs running up his wall behind his desk in the shaded room. "The Winslow sisters are here to see you, Mr. Platt," the assistant said, clicking on the overhead light.

The knees bent and came down. Brindle's head popped up. Though a bit red-faced, the man hadn't aged a day since I met him. After hugs all the way around, Brindle sat cross-legged on his desk. "What can I do for you ladies this afternoon?"

His physical flexibility wasn't lost on me, but I needed his mental flexibility. "Our employee, Gerard Smith, didn't report to work today. We used his spare key to enter his residence and do a wellness check. Gerard and his cell phone are missing, but his car is at home."

Brindle shrugged. "Sounds like a mission for the cops."

Sage rapped her fist on his desk. "We believe the cops have him."

The lawyer grinned. "Music to my ears. Catch me up."

Chapter Eight

The attorney suggested we return to open The Book and Candle Shop and proceed as if everything were normal while he checked to see if Gerard was being detained or questioned. Ha! As if anything felt normal with Gerard missing. We were leaping to conclusions concerning his whereabouts, but the more I thought about it, the more certain I was the cops had grabbed him. And for what? Since when was calling someone a name on par with deadly intent? If that were true, everyone in the world would be murderous.

Perversely, customers swarmed inside as soon as we unlocked the door. A group of overly made-up teenaged girls in heavy boots tromped over, to check out, with a package of our bestselling trio of herb-scented pillar candles and Georgia R. Byrd's *Haunted Savannah*. A dark-haired teen with multiple piercings glanced around and asked, "Where's the witch-pushing guy?"

"It's his day off," Sage said smoothly as she concluded their transaction. "Next time you shop here, you'll see him."

The teen nodded to us and her posse. "We wanna meet him. He's so cool the way he banished that witch from the shop. Will he teach us how to do that?"

Sage gave her the stink-eye with the sales receipt. "What do you have against witches?"

"They're mean," a skinny teen in the back said. "We want them to leave us alone."

I drew myself up to defend witches, who like us, had a different skill set than most people. Sage shot me a frosty look, letting me know she had this. I stood beside her, automatically linking our energy fields, and Sage showered the kids with good energy.

"Witches get a bad rap from TV and movies," Sage said. "Trust me, there are worse things in the world than witches. Be strong and bullies won't bother you."

The teens trooped out with their candles. I straightened the stack of tissue paper I'd used to wrap the candle purchase. "Where'd that pithy advice come from?"

Sage chewed on her lip for a moment. "I was in a similar situation once, until I learned how to deal with bullies. Think about it. We at least dressed like the other kids. Those girls have fostered their sense of otherness by their group's Goth-inspired style. We know how otherness affects normals. They shun it or try to cleanse it from their territory. I stood up to the kid bullying me, and word got around."

"Bullies called me names. *Dummy* was the worst." I hung my head. "That word eroded my confidence."

"Oh, Tabs, I'm sorry you suffered in silence." Sage gave me a big bear hug. "Think positive about the past, present, and future. You're in control of your life now. If you checked, I'm sure you'd be in control of your special talents. It's practically a guarantee."

"Practically?"

"Nothing is ever certain."

* * *

Brindle Platt herded Gerard inside the shop at closing time. "Phone cameras should be banned," Brindle said as he locked the door behind them. "Your customers who posted videos of Blithe McAdam leaving your shop did Gerard no favors."

"Are you okay, Gerard?" I hurried over to hug him, Sage fast on my heels for a group hug. "We were so worried."

"I'm better now," he said returning our embraces. "Thanks for sending Mr. Platt. His bulldog attitude got their attention right away."

"Well, of course," Sage said. "We wouldn't leave you there. Brindle's the best."

Our lawyer blushed and nodded, but his gaze riveted on Sage. "I did my part, but frankly, our firm's name carries weight, thanks to the clout of our senior partner, Barrett Brendon Cranford III."

"How long did they hold you, Gerard?" Sage asked.

"A patrol officer put me in his car when I came outside to leave for work this morning. It was like I suddenly entered another country. He drove me to the jail and stuck me in a holding pen for hours without my phone. Then they stuffed me in a tiny closet of a room and started grilling me about Blithe." Gerard shuddered. "It was beyond terrible. I plan to take three showers as soon as I get home."

"Did they charge you with a crime?" I asked.

"They insisted I killed Blithe, and then they told me how I did it. I denied everything, but it felt like the movie *Groundhog Day*. When one cop finished the accusation script, another officer started in with the same garbage. I understand how people cave and give them the answers they want during questioning. It was a nightmare."

"I made them stop questioning him," Brindle said. "Gerard and I conferred privately, and after that I answered their questions. They didn't like that. I insisted they charge him or release him. They left us sitting there for another hour, but he was released with the standard cautionary advice not to leave town."

"The cops grilled you because of a social media video?" I asked, folding my arms across my chest. Poor Gerard. I felt violated at the mental barrage and treatment he'd received.

"Yep," Gerard said. "I never want to go through that again. Can we get a phone scrambler for our shop?"

"Then your phone wouldn't work either."

"Those detectives didn't believe one word I said." Gerard's eyes glittered with emotion. "The whole thing made me doubt our freedom of speech. I wasn't angry before I was interrogated, but they kept asking me which sport I played. Sports? I told them repeatedly that I wasn't an athlete, that I'd never played sports. They implied I was a jock because my skin has color. I can't thank you enough for rescuing me, ladies."

"Think nothing of it. Sage and I will find out who did this, so that won't happen again."

"Good," Gerard said. "I've never been so happy to be klutzy and not to own any sports equipment before. I don't know if they searched my home, but if so, they didn't find any baseball equipment there."

I exchanged a glance with Sage. "We used your spare key to check your place after lunch when you didn't show up. No cops had been in there as of that time."

"No basis for a search warrant," Brindle said. "Given the victim's animosity toward others, there is a large pool of suspects. One thing I should mention. Detective Belfor said the victim's alleged half brother, Jurrell Dawson, is proactive on social media, and his tirades against your shop are nasty."

I fetched up against the counter, my knees trembling at the thought anyone might believe him. "Jurrell? He doesn't even know us."

"That guy has a mean streak," Brindle said. "My senior partner says he's been trouble since he hit puberty. Probably before that, but Jurrell's crassness and tenacious fervor weren't obvious until he went after people in public forums. I haven't seen his podcasts, but Belfor said he claims your aromatherapy products bewitched his half sister and rendered her defenseless."

"What?" Sage shrieked. "That's insane."

"We should sue him for slander," I said to Brindle. "Will you represent us?"

"While I don't turn down work, that may be unnecessary. This guy targets a different small business every week or so, belittling it and doing his best to shut it down. Someone else will be the flavor of the week soon."

"He's a cyberbully," Sage said. "Nobody objects to his tirades, so he keeps getting away with it. I won't stand for it."

Sage didn't issue threats lightly, and once she made up her mind, she followed through. Despite knowing her intolerant position on bullies, I worried she'd go after Jurrell Dawson. "What are you saying, Sis?"

"I'm saying Jurrell Dawson, like his sister, is ugly to people on purpose. If karma runs true to course, he'll get his comeuppance. Mark my words."

Chapter Nine

Sage went out to dinner and more with Brindle Platt that evening. Gerard was too shaken to go home, so he stayed the night at our place. He took three showers and borrowed a robe from me while his clothes washed and dried. Because of the differences in our size, my full-length robe hit him at mid-thigh and gaped across his chest. I fed him his favorite comfort foods of shrimp and cheese grits along with black-eyed pea and ham soup, all delivered from the Boar's Head restaurant. He ate his meal and half of mine, and we shared a slice of the restaurant's famous Jack Daniel's pecan pie, which was positively divine.

"I don't want to think about what happened today," Gerard said when dinner was done. "Let's do something fun. Like a fashion show."

I covered a burp with a hand over my mouth. "We just stuffed ourselves silly, and you want me to try on clothes?"

"Not just *any* clothes—the good stuff. I need to see sparkles and sequins and pretty girly things."

He remembered our family's stash of formal wear? It might help him relax since Gerard fancied himself an expert in woman's clothing. Maybe at some point during the evening he'd confide about his interrogation. "Brilliant idea. As it turns out, I need fancy attire soon."

"Hot date?" Gerard asked.

"Nothing like that. Quig needs a plus-one for a charity fundraiser. We're going as friends."

"He's yummy." His face glowed with happiness. "I'd date either one of you in a red-hot minute."

"No thanks. I'm having an all-consuming affair with the shop. Besides, you're like a brother to me, Gerard." Time for a distraction. "Let's take a look at those gowns."

From the back closet, Gerard withdrew a tea-length, off-the-shoulder gown with an A-line silhouette. It wasn't one I'd worn before, so I moved behind the dressing screen and put it on. Trying on clothes wasn't in my top-ten list—not even close—but Gerard was the perfect advisor for this.

His eyes lit with approval when he saw me in the gown. "So beautiful. Black becomes you, dear heart."

The chiffon skirt frothed around my legs as I bopped across the room. Something playful and fun sparkled in my insides, an inner radiance I hadn't felt in a long time, and I let it course through me unchecked. Sage was right about me opening my senses fully again: I needed to do it. This flouncy dress had me feeling years younger instead of my default old-soul mode.

I studied my image in the floor-length mirror. The bodice fit like a glove, but the low-cut front and off-the-shoulder treatment felt too racy for me. I tugged the front a smidge higher and barely recognized the sex kitten who grinned back at me. "It fits, but it's not quite right for a friends' date. My turn to select a gown."

And so it went, back and forth with picks, until Gerard handed me one that looked like a slender column. I fingered the delicate beaded and gold-thread-embellished overlay. "I adore this fabric, but it's long."

"Try it," Gerard urged. "It's elegantly classic without glitz."

"What the heck. I'll give it a go." I gathered the gown and slipped behind the screen to change.

Gerard moved near the mirror as I zipped myself into the gown. Hoisting the skirt in both hands, I stepped into a platform pump with a peep-toe, a six-inch slender heel, and a dainty ankle strap. The length was perfect.

I strutted over to the mirror. "What do you think?"

A soft breath came from my friend, followed by, "Oh-h-h."

I halted before the mirror. He was right about the gown's classic look. It totally suited me. The body-defining fabric emphasized my narrow waist and trim hips, while the V-neck plunge wasn't indecent. I released the skirt folds and slowly twirled before the mirror.

"This is the one," I said.

"Now that I see it on, those godet panels give you room for a sultry stride, and look at the way that narrow ruffle barely kisses the floor." He clapped his hands and then clasped them beneath his chin. "It's perfect. *You're* perfect. You look like a goddess."

"A goddess? I like that. But how will I walk in public in this?"

"Gather one side enough so you don't step on the gown. The men of the world are not ready to see your sexy feet in those shoes."

No one had ever remarked on my feet before, not even Quig. I hugged Gerard in my enthusiasm. "This outfit is growing on me."

He opened a drawer of clutch purses and handed me one. "Now. What about the hair?"

"Nothing elaborate. A sleek twist perhaps."

"It'll do." He raised his arms in a victory salute. "My work here is done. Let's watch romantic comedies until we fall asleep."

"Sure. I'll make popcorn."

During the second movie, Gerard said to me, "For the record, I would never beat anyone in the head with a baseball bat, not even someone as nasty as Blithe McAdam."

"I know you wouldn't. But I've often wondered why you had no patience with her."

He stiffened beside me on the couch. "She wasn't a nice person. She used people."

I nodded. "Everyone knew that."

"Duh. She cut me to pieces with her sharp tongue one day. Her attack was unprovoked and unwarranted. I kept saying to myself, 'The customer is always right,' but I wanted to claw her eyes out." He shuddered. "Good riddance to her."

"Did you tell the cops why you said those things on the video clip?"

"I'm not stupid. I told them she was rude, and I hoped she'd take her business elsewhere."

My breath hitched. Even I heard the difference in his voice when he spun that lie. "Did they believe you?"

"No." He dissolved in tears. "I am going to spend the rest of my life in prison if you can't save me."

Chapter Ten

The next morning Sage rolled in a little past eight, with a healthy glow to her pale skin. The shop cats padded at her heels as she entered our living quarters. It looked suspiciously like Sage was happy. I felt a twinge of guilt as I shoved Gerard out the door to go home for a morning shower before our workday began. He accessed a rideshare app on our landing.

Over coffee in our cozy kitchen, Sage leaned in, eyebrows pinched together. "So, I never thought I'd say this. You and *Gerard*?"

The cats threaded through my legs, sniffing. I reached for Harley and cuddled him close, but he wasn't having it and jumped down. He stalked away with a twitch of his tail and settled into his bowl of kibble.

I turned my attention back to Sage. "Not the way you think, but, Sis, you and *Brindle*?"

She beamed. "Yep. Bona fide sleepover with full benefits. That man is so flexible. You wouldn't believe the things he can do with his body."

I nearly dropped my jaw. It was so not like her to mention details. With such a deviation in character, I wondered what else I'd missed. "Is it serious?"

Sage gave a contented sigh. "I hope it goes somewhere, but given the number of variables, who knows?"

Her wry tone reminded me she spoke from experience. Every personal relationship to date had ended badly. Sage deserved happiness every day, not only in stolen moments. "I wish you and Brindle the best."

"Thanks. Now, about Gerard. I nearly fell out when I saw him in here. It looked awfully cozy to me."

"Just helping a friend. Poor guy was too upset to go anywhere after his police interrogation yesterday. I invited him to sleep on the sofa, and he jumped at the chance."

Sage rinsed out her personalized mug and placed it in the dish drain. "It's a wonder he didn't jump you."

I studied her closely as Harley stropped his tail across my bare legs. I picked him up and cuddled him close. "No need to be crude. Nothing intimate happened. However, I wish you wouldn't be so short with him all the time."

"He's lucky to have this job. Far as I'm concerned, that joker is living on borrowed time."

"We need him, Sage, unless you want to find a new place to live."

"It isn't something I do on purpose. I'm annoyed to have to work with him, and it shows. I'll never forget how he cheated on me when we were in Europe. You at least enjoy his company."

Harley's contented purr help soothe my ruffled feathers. "I do. We share many interests, so conversation between us is always easy. Do you feel guilty about being his boss?"

Not to be outdone, Sage gathered Luna into her arms. "Nope. Life is about survival of the fittest. Second place is not the position I want."

Me either. "What about last night? Did you and Brindle discuss the case?"

Sage must've squeezed Luna, because the cat yowled, leapt down, and padded to her empty food bowl. Sage took her time filling the dish.

"Well?" I asked. "What about the investigation?"

Sage circled the island putting space between us. "Brindle found out the cops interviewed patrons at the Moonlight Fishing Hole yesterday after they let Gerard go. They were doing a little fishing about our city alderman."

"Rashad Vernon is into bar scenes?"

"One of his childhood friends owns the Hole, and it's where Rashad goes to unwind. He's been overheard at the bar saying he'd kill Blithe if she didn't leave him alone. In any event, Brindle and his law firm's senior partner, Mr. Cranford, think the cops will question Rashad today about Blithe's death."

If the cops questioned everyone who ran afoul of Blithe, we'd be on the hot seat in due time. I couldn't stomach what Gerard had gone through at their hands, and was even more worried how I'd react to such bullying tactics. I'd never liked the assumption everyone was a suspect until their alibi proved otherwise. "They need to find the killer, not keep dragging innocent people into interrogation."

Sage snorted out a laugh and helped herself to our ginger snaps. "You saying Rashad Vernon is an innocent like Gerard? Come on—he's a politician."

My sister was certainly in a strange mood. Since when did happiness foster snarkiness? "I don't know anything about the alderman other than what we hear on the news. That's part of the problem. Look. The cops are stymied by Blithe's many enemies. We need to hurry the investigation along to keep Gerard out of harm's way, for his safety as well as ours."

"What are you proposing, Tabs?"

"You had the right idea earlier. Let's make an afterhours visit to Blithe's place tonight."

She jerked her thumb toward the sofa. "Agreed. Meanwhile, I'm doing a deep dive today on the social media presence of Blithe's half brother. I'll see who else Jurrell Dawson targeted, and maybe we can commiserate with them today to kickstart our investigation."

"I'll join you in that computer search. Two heads are better than one."

* * *

An hour later I pushed away from my laptop, rose from the sofa, and stretched like a cat. "I can't take any more of this man's vitriol. I thought Blithe was a negative person, but she shines like an optimist compared to her brother. Good grief! Everything I read was negative. Jurrell Dawson hated this, and he despised that. He couldn't summon up one nice thing to say in any of the ten business review blogs I read. If I were awarding rotten tomatoes, I'd give him a bushel basket full."

"The podcasts are more of the same," Sage said from the rocker, "though it appears he took a vehement dislike to the waitress over at the Southern Tea Shop. Says the woman refused to serve Blithe. I'm betting there's a story behind his remarks."

An idea popped into my head. "A cup of tea would hit the spot right about now."

"I'm coming with you," Sage said.

"Only if you let me do all the talking. If you start hissing like your cat, you'll scare Tansie off. She's a bit timid in demeanor."

"I do not hiss," Sage said.

"Right now you should consider purring and being agreeable."

With a quick word to Gerard, who was aligning local author books on a bookshelf, we darted across Bristol Street. As it was midmorning, several tables were open, and we snagged the one closest to the counter.

The vibe in here was eclectic on speed, from the ice cream café tables to the primary-colored floor tiles, to the smooth jazz in the background. A low rail of calico curtains gave a sense of privacy. And then there were the walls. Dine-in guests were encouraged to list all the displayed items on the wall that started with the letter *t*. If an entry had one hundred or more items correct, the person got their order on the house. I usually stalled out about fifty, so I gave up. Today I noticed tom-toms, a purple teapot, and a neon-splattered tennis racket. Our table held a miniature turquoise truck between the salt, pepper, and sugar dispensers.

Tansie Fuller bustled over. Since my last visit, she'd completed the series of tattoos covering both arms, tattoos that were displayed to advantage by her white tank top. "Hey, gals. Long time, no see. What'll you have? A peppermint tea and an Earl Grey with lemon, along with two brownies?"

"Sounds great. And a latte to go for Gerard." I chuckled at her amazing power of recall. "Your talents are wasted here, Tansie. With your incredible memory, you could be running the world."

She shook her head, and several tendrils of her autumn-colored hair slipped out of the topknot she had secured with two pencils. "As if I wanted to rule the world. Heck, it's hard enough to keep track of my life, much less everyone else's. Orders are easy to recall, and it's just as well life cut me some slack somewhere, you know?"

A group of three ladies entered and caught Tansie's attention. "I'll be right with you," she said, gesturing broadly. "Sit wherever you like."

Before she left, I cleared my throat. "Tansie, we hoped to speak with you about a personal matter, specifically about Jurrell Dawson."

A hot energy spike pulsed from the waitress. I flipped into my other-vision instinctively to deflect the dark currents shimmering in her cloudy aura. This woman felt animosity toward Blithe's brother. What was I doing? Omigod. I shut down my other-vision before I was tempted to lash out. Time stood still as I waited.

She huffed out a breath straight up her face, and her wispy bangs fluttered in the mini-breeze. "That snake in the grass. I'd grind him into dust with my heel if I could. Let me get this other party's order sorted out, and I'll be back. Even if we get busy, I want to talk to you about him."

As she scuttled to the table by the ottoman-sized tiger, I muttered to Sage. "We came to the right place."

"I wasn't expecting such an intensity from her. I registered anger, frustration, and yet there was something else underneath. Don't want to name it until we know more."

A grin filled my face. "Tansie is hiding something for sure."

"Let's hope she killed Blithe." Sage scanned the shop. "Look at these people here and on the street. Who are they? Where do they come from? They can't all be on vacation. Doesn't anyone work these days?"

"You see these strangers as slackers. I see them as potential customers for our shop. Something brought them to Savannah.

Maybe their spouses have a business trip here. Maybe they're visiting relatives. They aren't necessarily slackers. Just people out to enjoy the day."

Sage grimaced. "For an introvert, you spout a surprising amount of optimism."

And there it was: that niggle of competition. Sometimes it spurred us both to do more. Right now her criticism hurt. "Sage, I wish you wouldn't—"

Tansie plopped our mix-and-match teacups, teapots, and brownie plates on the table and slid into the chair beside me. "You got one minute, maybe two before Cook notices I'm not bustling around the tearoom. Go."

"We're on edge because the cops keep asking us questions about Blithe McAdam," Sage said. "Figure they might try to pin the murder on one of us. Also, we just found out Jurrell Dawson bashed our shop online in a breathtaking display of profanity. We need to know why that man is purposefully misdirecting the cops."

"Whoa. Didn't expect that," Tansie slouched in the chair like a teenager, visibly vulnerable and tightly wound. "Didn't know he'd targeted you two. His attack on the tea shop and on me was vicious and mean. Like brother, like sister."

"Now you've surprised me," I said, cradling my delicate teacup and trying to focus on her physical aspects. The sparkles and glimmers of her aura kept distracting me. Looked like she had a short circuit in her natural energy field. "I heard those two weren't close."

"They met here for tea twice a month, so they stayed in touch," Tansie said, shuddering for all she was worth. "When I hadn't seen them for a week or so, I dreaded coming to work. They were quite rude to me and always complained to the manager about slow service. I was afraid Barbara would fire me."

"What did they talk about?" Sage asked, pinching off a corner of a brownie. "Did you overhear anything we can use against Jurrell if the cops come after us again?"

"I stayed as far away from them as I could, so I didn't hear what they discussed." Tansie braced her tattoo-covered arms against her chest, more powerful spikes randomly glinting in her aura. "Jurrell's a miserable excuse for a human being, and I don't care who knows my opinion. He complained every time he came in here. Tea wasn't hot enough. Danishes tasted stale. Bathroom wasn't clean. Bull. He lied about everything and created the bathroom mess. The only thing that saved me that day was the boss had just used the sparkling clean unisex bathroom before Jurrell."

I considered that for a minute. No way would Blithe share the spotlight with anyone. "And Blithe let him claim center stage like that?"

"She egged him on, like he was running a footrace. I wanted to smash a cream pie in her face. I would've if we'd had any. The closest things we have are eclairs, and I darned sure wouldn't waste those on her."

"Ever notice them arguing?" Sage asked as she squeezed lemon in her tea.

Tansie tucked loose strands of wispy hair behind her ear, the errant sparks barely visible now. "Nope. They seemed compatible, and often Blithe slipped him an envelope. Sometimes he gave one to her."

"What kind of envelope?" I asked, intrigued.

"A brown one. About the size of a sheet of paper folded in half. And before you ask, I couldn't tell if anything was written on it. They were very secretive about the exchanges." Tansie cut her eyes to the service window and winced. "That's it for me. Gotta go. Rest assured I hated Jurrell and Blithe, but I didn't act on that hate."

As Tansie rushed off, I sipped my peppermint tea, allowing the comforting steam from the brew to fill my head. Blithe and Jurrell had been close. They'd exchanged secret messages in public. What was that all about?

"Did you sense it?" Sage asked, tearing off another bite of brownie. "When Tansie mentioned Jurrell, her anger piggybacked on another emotion."

"I missed it. The energy bursts in her aura distracted me. What'd you conclude?"

Sage savored another bite of brownie, then leveled a finger at our waitress. "That woman is scared to death of Jurrell Dawson."

"He's an out-of-control bully with a public platform," I said. "Wish we could stop him."

Once the words burst from my lips, I wanted to recall them. Sage stink-eyed me, and I bristled. "No. Not that way. Something legal and normal. Something that penalized him for his false characterization of so many Savannah businesses."

"Brindle would sue him for us, but it would be expensive, and from what I've seen of Jurrell Dawson, he isn't rolling in dough. It isn't cost-effective."

This was the part of being an adult I hated. Everything came with a price. There would be no tilting at windmills. My eyes drifted to the toy truck, and I wished it were full-sized and mine. "Wonder if he inherited Blithe's estate. He's her next of kin."

"Brindle could check to see if her will is on file with the county clerk. It would be interesting to know who benefits from her estate.

I never saw her driving a car. Her condo on East Starling Street should be worth at least half a million."

"Her will is a good avenue to pursue, but surely the cops did that. We need to find clues that lead away from us. Visiting her place and seeing her belongings will likely reveal different information."

"Agreed. I'll call Brindle and put him on finding the will." Sage checked her watch. "I've got errands to run. You good working with Gerard until mid-afternoon?"

"Sure."

Chapter Eleven

That night, Sage and I dressed in black for our top-secret mission at Blithe's condo. "How will we get in?" I asked, shoving thin gloves and a small flashlight in my back pockets. "Neither of us can pick a lock."

"Speak for yourself. I've been practicing. If I can't finagle the lock, I'll ask Brindle for another lockpicking lesson, and we'll try again later."

An odd skill set for a lawyer, but I saved that line of questioning for later. "What'd he say about Blithe's will? Did he find it?"

"Not yet. He was second chair for Mr. Cranford today."

"I see. Inquiring minds want to know if you're seeing him soon."

Sage's lips twitched as if she were carefully selecting her words. "Both of us are slammed during the week with work. We agreed to catch up with each other on the weekends."

Um-hmm. I suspected that was guy code for "you're not that important to me." From experience, I knew Sage wouldn't take that well. Best to move to the topic at hand. "You have a plan for our search?"

"My plan is to see what's there," Sage said. "We're interested in evidence that steers the blame away from you, me, and Gerard. Say, I wonder what happened to Blithe's little dog?"

Sage paused at the bottom of our alley steps to add, "Before you get any wild hairs about adopting an orphaned pet, let me remind you we've been a cat family for generations."

I chased after her, keeping my voice low. "Think about it. That dog lived in a toxic sea of negativity. He deserves a second chance. I hope Jurrell doesn't inherit the dog."

"Jurrell wouldn't keep it—he's too self-absorbed."

That rang true. "We could contact him about the dog."

"No way would he'd talk to us, not after he tore into our shop in those videos."

"We could smack him with a dose of karma if we taped the conversation and aired it to prove how vile he is."

"Let me sleep on that idea because it might backfire," Sage said. "I want to focus solely on Blithe tonight."

"Of course. We need to be sharp to stay under the radar." I shivered with excitement as we inched along the dark side of a building. "I wonder if Sherlock Holmes felt this edgy."

Sage groaned. "Holmes is a fictional character. Our situation is as real as it gets."

When Sage focused on an objective, she was all business. So I shut up. By tacit agreement, we cut through alleys and avoided any security cameras—hence the dark clothes and black ball caps. We crisscrossed the alley, sometimes dropping to our feet and army-crawling forward when there were security cameras. Given the toasty evening, it wasn't long before my clothes were sweat soaked and dirty.

Reality settled on my shoulders like a weighted blanket. Our breaking and entering would look bad if anyone found out, so we better not get caught. A car crept down the alley, and we crouched behind a dumpster so stinky my eyes watered. Something small ran over my foot. I used a microburst of energy to keep it moving along. Not really violating my anti-energy manipulation rules, just tending to self-preservation.

Finally, we reached Blithe's block on East Starling Street. Her back alley appeared deserted; I gazed at the jungle of garages and doorways. "Which one is hers?"

Sage pointed to one of the buildings. "It's second from the end of that one. I drove by earlier today to prepare for this. Crime scene tape is still up in front. Not sure if they taped the garage door in back."

"They should've," I said.

Sage stopped and gestured toward the door in question. "You see any yellow tape?"

"I don't. That's odd."

"Put on your gloves."

I grabbed mine from my back pockets. They were the blue nitrile kind we used for cleaning, and they hugged my hands like second skin. In the faint twilight, they cast an eerie glow.

"Tread as quietly as you can," Sage whispered in my ear. "No talking until we're done."

I nodded to show I understood. Step by step we crept closer to the access door beside the garage. About halfway, a bright light shined in the alley. Sage squatted. I did the same, holding my breath until the threat of discovery passed. Then we continued our silent trek. The windows of Blithe's place were dark.

Sage knelt beside the door and fiddled with the lock. The faint rasp of metal on metal seemed so loud. Would someone hear us and call the cops? To counteract that possibility, I envisioned us passing through this door without incident. Positive vibes were second nature to me, and I beamed them all around.

I caught the taint of food gone bad. Garbage, most likely, as we'd passed a dumpster behind the building. The more I breathed the noxious fumes, the more I wanted Sage to pick the lock so that I could breathe fresh air in the condo.

Sage beat the lock. I cheered inwardly at her new skill. She turned the handle, but the door didn't budge. It took both of us pushing and shoving to open the door enough for us to enter. One thing was certain as we stepped into a pile of debris on the floor. The rotten odor arose from Blithe's garage, not the dumpster. That wasn't all. Mildew and urine warred with the rotten food smell. The cloth face covering I wore did nothing to filter the stink.

"It's ripe in here," I managed as I tried to balance atop a stack of magazines.

Sage ignored me and shone her penlight around. Boxes and piles of items were everywhere. A sloped mound of plastic grocery bags occupied the nearest corner. We climbed over boxes and bags as best we could to discover the condo door was unlocked.

Cautiously, we entered her unit. A refrigerator crouched beside the wall, but I couldn't hear it humming. Starlight leaked through the over-the-sink window, bathing the room in thin light. I reached for the counter at hip level and encountered cold stone. Yep. Definitely the kitchen.

Sage moved to the window and shut the blind. She padded close again and whispered in my ear, "Keep your light below the window level. We'll search the kitchen first."

My penlight beam revealed counters cluttered with groceries and canned items, some containers empty, some full. I opened a drawer, and it was like opening a tube of compressed toy snakes. Papers slid over the sides and dropped on the littered floor.

Not a square inch of the stove top was visible. Cracker boxes and empty soda bottles abounded. I saw two dishtowels of indiscernible color. The sink and counter overflowed with dirty dishes. The under-the-counter garbage can added a rotting seafood smell to the near-toxic fumes.

I pulled up my shirt over my mask to help staunch the foul odor, so grossed out, I spoke without thinking. "This is intolerable. How'd she live like this?"

"Blithe was a hoarder," Sage said softly, a finger to her lips.

Crap. I'd spoken in a normal voice. Again. Some spy I was. I blinked to clear the tears from my eyes. This strange accumulation made sense as a hoarder's treasure trove. I spoke again, this time in our inaudible twin-speak. *"Sorry I messed up and spoke. Sis, it may be impossible to find anything in this mess. Further, one aromatherapy candle couldn't staunch this odor or this level of chaos. There might be nothing wrong with the candle Blithe bought from us."*

"Check the fridge," Sage replied in kind as she thumbed through a loosely stacked tower of unopened mail.

I opened the door carefully, unsure of what I might find. The interior light did not turn on, and the air inside felt warm to my face. A putrid stench wafted from the moldy cartons of carryout containers and spoiled, uncovered food. I shut the door quickly and glanced in the freezer. Only thing up there was an ice maker and a half-empty bottle of vodka.

"Fridge is off. Nothing in here that looks like evidence," I said. I glanced around for a pet feeding station and found none. *"No dog stuff. Where is it?"*

"You're obsessed with that dog," Sage said.

I moved a few items on the counter, and roaches skittered in every direction. Boy, was I glad I was wearing gloves. *"Not obsessed, just stating facts. This is a clue."*

"Maybe."

We trudged around a small island, and I struggled to keep my balance on the cluttered floor. No wonder this woman had been depressed. Who could function in such chaos?

"The cops had the same problem searching her place," Sage pointed out. *"Hard to know where to look when stuff is everywhere. Let's keep an eye out for tech equipment. Blithe probably had her cell phone close at hand, but if she had a computer, it may be hidden."*

We inched into the next room, conceivably the dining room since there was an overflowing table and chair set in the middle of the room. Every surface was stacked chest-high with boxes of clothing, toys, books, and shoes. Some items bore store tags, others looked like they'd been rescued from the trash.

I held the flashlight in my mouth and used both hands to sort through a box, but there was no space to move it to tackle the underneath box when I finished. *"What a disaster."* I felt bad for all the uncharitable thoughts I'd ever had about this woman.

"Agreed. Time for Plan B. Cut the flashlights and use our enhanced vision."

A five-alarm fire erupted in my gut. *"No. Not me."*

"Have it your way, scaredy-cat. I'll do the looking then. But since I'm doing twice the work, put your hand on my shoulder. I could use a power boost."

Translation: she wanted to burn my energy. Not fun, but less scary than the alternative. I complied, and the place plunged into darkness.

With the physical contact, I was aware of Sage turning to survey the room. When I used my extra sight before the disaster years ago, the view resembled a photography negative with a twist. Strong emotions left a stain, and that's what we were looking for.

"*See anything?*" I asked.

"*Everything is splashed with dark emotions. Blithe was a nervous wreck in addition to being crazy and mean.*"

"*Any area of the condo she visited repeatedly?*"

"*Not in this room. Let's check out the entire place. I see where she walked now, so that's a bonus.*"

She took off, and since the intact energy bond didn't allow me to move my hand, I lurched after her. "*Let me know before you do that again.*"

"*You wouldn't have a problem if you helped with the search.*"

I wouldn't let her goad me into using my talent, even though I recognized I'd been allowing small blasts of it through recently. I kept on my toes, anticipating her every step. Blithe's bedroom had fewer carboard boxes and higher mounds of clothes and shoes. Stacks of empty paper plates littered the bed. The badly stained sheets smelled locker-room gross.

There were no windows in the bathroom, so after Sage did a night vision sweep, we turned on our flashlights again. I tried the light switch on a whim. It didn't work. The sink mirror was broken in a way that looked like something weighty and softball sized had hit it.

I also tried the water. Nothing. "*That was fast. The power and the water are already turned off.*"

"*From the looks of things, they've been off for a while,*" Sage said, opening a sealed bucket in the bathroom, quickly closing it, and pinching her nostrils shut. "*That's rank.*"

The medicine cabinet brimmed with over-the-counter remedies for headaches. The inside of the cabinet was covered with multiple stickers that read, "I gave blood today." My gaze stopped on one item. Remembering the need for stealth, I spoke in twinspeak, *"What's with the pregnancy test kit?"*

"She wasn't much older than us, though she acted older," Sage said. *"Some women conceive into their late forties, some their fifties."*

"She had a boyfriend? And he was okay with her housekeeping?"

"Can't answer that, but I see no prescription meds and no means of birth control."

"Carry-out dining and a hoarding lifestyle must produce good health. Maybe we should all live like this."

"No way. We don't need this much stuff, and we don't want toxins in our bodies."

"Long as you do the cooking, I'm fine with that. Let's look at her bedroom with the flashlights. I have a sense something in there needs to be found."

"Do you now?"

Her question irked me. *"I didn't resurrect my talent. My intuition is nudging me."*

Sage nodded as she turned away, a big grin on her face. *"Awesome. This B and E is paying off in unexpected ways."*

I ignored her smugness and followed my gut to Blithe's tidy dresser. A fancy stand rested atop the bureau, and it was covered with hair. Blithe's hair. I retreated. "Ack!"

"What?" Sage said at full voice.

"Shh." I switched to twin-speak. *"Blithe wore a wig. It's right there."*

"Yep. That's her hair all right. Wonder why? Maybe your buddy Quig can shed some light on her hair status."

"*I'll ask him.*" I looked around again. "*There's no sign of a dog ever having lived here. No pet bowls, dog beds, dog toys—nothing. How is that possible?*"

"*Maybe whoever took the dog grabbed the gear as well.*"

"*Perhaps, but it strikes the wrong note with me.*"

"*You should follow up on that.*"

"*How?*"

"*Keep listening to your intuition, that's what. No point in wasting more time here. There's nothing to find.*"

"*Wait,*" I said. "*Look at her closet and dresser. Both are unexpectedly tidy when everything else is a mess. Now look at the floor, the bed, the chair. You can barely see any of them because of the junk.*"

"*You're right, Sherlock. What does it mean?*"

"*My intuition tells me Blithe hoarded for a long time. Maybe the root cause is a lack of love.*"

"*She substituted things for love?*" Sage asked.

I nodded. "*It's a theory. So, if we assume she can't stop hoarding, then these tidy areas are important to her. These clothes. That wig.*"

Sage walked over to the closet. "*These clothes look expensive. Blithe liked to keep up appearances.*"

"*That fits. She hoards stuff to take the place of parental love. She dresses nicely to show her status, and because she's no longer living on a square, she probably values her status more than almost anything.*"

"*I don't know, Sis. The bulk of the evidence is the huge mess everywhere.*"

Sage raised her hands. "*I'm sold on the theory. Makes perfect sense to me.*"

"*We'll probably never know.*" I followed her out of the room, my flashlight beam trained on the floor. "*I can't believe anyone lives like this.*"

"Not our problem. Same drill on the way home."

Immediately after we exited the garage, we were pinned by the beam of a large truck rolling down the alley. Neither of us moved, and I thought my heart might leap from my chest. When the truck kept going, I heaved a sigh of relief.

I glanced over at Sage, and she'd vanished. Oh no! I glanced down and couldn't see my body either. Some way, somehow I'd defensively rendered us invisible. The only good news was that I'd used shadows to conceal us for that short time, so the energy expended was minor.

"This is so rad," Sage whispered when the danger passed. "You have to teach me how to do this."

"Don't read anything into it. I didn't consciously use my ability. It kicked on automatically."

I shut it down and hurried after Sage, the noxious taint of Blithe's place infused in my hair and clothes. "Dibs on the shower," I said.

"We'll see," Sage answered as she went faster and faster.

As I dodged pools of light, security cameras, and emotional hotspots going home, my thoughts veered to my intuition. How was my blocked extra sensory perception working? Had Sage removed my mind block while we were linked?

Chapter Twelve

The next day, I left a call-me message on Quig's voicemail and made a batch of aromatherapy candles. I went exactly by Auntie O's recipe, and I consciously beamed good intentions and healing energy into the containers, wicks, wax, and essential oils as I worked. Though we had extreme heat for eight months of the year in Savannah, I preferred the malleable beeswax candles over the firmer organic soy ones. I liked the look and feel of them, even though the air temperature for most of the year rendered them soft and melty. For scents, I chose sandalwood, cypress, and violet.

As the scented wax heated, I savored the fresh woodsy scents, and my deep-seated tension drained away. For tourists, our top selling sizes of candles were the eight-ounce glass jars and the two-and-a-half-ounce tins, so that's what I made. I glued wicks to the bottom of the containers, wrapped the top of the wick around a thin dowel, and poured the wax.

The work energized me, and so I blended a second batch of coconut-and-pineapple-scented candles. Gerard paused in the doorway while I was cleaning up. "The entire shop smells amazing.

I've been selling candles right and left out here. You should make candles every day."

"Not sustainable to our bottom line, as Sage often points out. She won't be happy I made two batches today because now we need to restock before I make more."

"I vote we don't tell her," Gerard said.

"She'll figure it out after our monthly inventory. I wouldn't have made two batches today, except I had a feeling we needed this second batch more than the replacement batch. Maybe we'll have a bride in here this weekend, wanting the tins for wedding party favors."

"That'd be great."

The air between us was charged with expectation. I glanced up from cleaning to see him beaming from ear to ear. Curious. "Is there something else?"

"It's nice to hear you humming in here. You enjoy your work."

My smile went all the way to my eyes. "I love creating things in the stillroom. Now that Auntie O shared her secret ingredient with me, my candles will help people. I feel good, so the recipients of these candles will feel good."

"Excellent," Gerard said. "I want one from the first batch. That deep forest scent is divine."

I applied polish to the work counter and wiped it off. "You need aromatherapy?"

He stepped closer. "Ever since I was questioned for that woman's murder, I can't stop looking over my shoulder. The prospect of spending the rest of my life in prison keeps creeping into my thoughts."

I paused my cleanup routine to meet his gaze. "Relax. Sage and I are searching for the real killer so you can release those fears.

Also, good choice on your candle selection. You're welcome to one of those for your place, and we can burn one in the shop for good measure."

Gerard drew in a deep breath over the candles, waving the aroma toward his nose. He sighed contentedly. "Thanks. Any luck so far in your search?"

"Yeah, but not the good kind. We have more leads to follow, but everything takes time."

"I'm glad she's gone. Blithe McAdam was singularly the most difficult customer we ever had. She always made me feel like a worm. A clumsy worm."

I stored my polish and discarded the used paper towel. "I wonder what made her that way. Blithe was born to a wealthy family with every advantage. But if she had bad health, all bets are off. Disease is no respecter of persons and can ruin even an angelic personality."

"Don't fob me off with excuses for her bad behavior. I know the root cause of her problems. Money can't buy everything, but if you're used to money and run out, that's a huge problem. I mentioned Blithe to a friend last night over drinks, and he said she'd run up a big tab at his store because her cards were declined. She was broke."

It was on the tip of my tongue to mention she had a house crammed full of stuff, but then Gerard would know we'd snooped inside her house. "Interesting," is what I said. "I wonder if the detectives are aware of all the money she owed."

"Wouldn't hurt to mention it to them. Why don't you call them?"

I didn't like the idea of talking to those detectives any more than he did. "You could tell them."

"Nope. Not interested in talking to cops ever again. I hear their voices in my nightmares as it is."

I nodded my understanding. "You'll get past this. Before you know it, this experience will fade, and you'll feel like yourself again soon."

"Funny you would mention my memory," Gerard said. "I remember my childhood like it was yesterday. High school and the one semester I tried college are firmly etched in my mind. After that I have gaps in my memories. Europe is mostly a blur."

"That's . . . odd," I said, wondering what Sage might've done to him. "What is that about?"

"Don't know. Must be some life trauma life I'm blocking. You know anything I should know?"

"In the two-plus years we've been acquainted, you've been of sound mind and body."

"Thank goodness for that. What about before I came here? Have I ever mentioned that?"

"Not so much. What do you remember about Europe?"

"I did my own tour abroad, catching trains across Europe and working in restaurants when I ran out of money. When I wanted to come home to Savannah and couldn't afford it, a kind person paid my airfare."

I smiled brightly. "Not so many gaps after all. You probably remember more from your life than I do. These days I stay so busy I don't seem to lay down long-term memories."

"Whatever." Gerard shrugged. "I love working in this shop, but I feel like there's something else I should be doing."

"Sounds like you skipped most of college."

"Not interested in that. Too much book learning for me. I prefer to form my own opinions, chart my own course."

A teasing mood came over me. "Like a boat captain?"

He shuddered. "No way. Seasickness is the pits. How could you forget me spewing all over your last car after that one ferry ride?"

"Trust me, I'll never forget that, but the charting-your-course reference you made suggested you wanted to be on the high seas."

"I used a metaphor, and yeah, this college dropout knows what they are. Trust me, my feet are firmly planted on the ground from here on out."

The shop's door chimed. Gerard returned to the salesfloor to work his own magic, and I stored my candle supplies. Thinking of messes put me in mind of Blithe's place. How'd she become a hoarder? Why hadn't she talked to a therapist about it?

The therapist possibility darted into my mind as I soaped my pouring pot and filled it with very hot water. Gerard had mentioned Blithe owed money all over town. Sounded like she couldn't afford psychotherapy, and her pride wouldn't let her go to any place offering free help.

"You ready?" Quig asked.

Chapter Thirteen

I yelped at the sound of his voice and turned off the water. "Quig! You startled me half to death."

He waggled his eyebrows. "You wanted to talk, so here I am with carryout lunches for us to eat in the square."

I glanced at the bag he held. "Expedient as always. As it turns out, I just finished a batch of candles, and I'm starved."

"Perfect. Let's go."

"Sure. I need a few minutes upstairs first. You're welcome to wait here or in the shop if you like."

"No problem. Smells great in here."

I took that to mean he was okay with waiting. "Be right back." Regardless of his easy manner, I didn't want to keep Quig waiting more than a few minutes. A quick dash through the bathroom, and I was ready to go.

"Here I am," I announced when he didn't turn to approach me.

"These are amazing," he said, turning at last, his expression dreamy. "It smells like you captured the essence of summer in this candle."

"Glad you like it, and I want you to have one as a thank-you for lunch. Shall we go to the square?"

"Right." He gestured for me to go first.

With his height advantage, Quig could see the top of my head. Why hadn't I thought to run a brush through my hair? No telling how many strands of hair had come lose from my ponytail. Oh well, too late now.

We made small talk as we threaded our way through the busy sidewalks. As it turned out, the benches at Johnson Square were occupied, so Quig placed the lunch bag on the fountain wall, and we sat there. I drew in a deep breath, glad to be away from everything right now, glad to feel the sunshine on my face.

"You should do that more often," Quig said, handing me a veggie wrap and a bottle of water.

"How'd you know my order?"

"Simple. I asked Tansie. One thing I've always wanted to ask you and haven't: Is Tabby short for Tabitha?"

"No. Mom named me after the strong building material popularized in the 1800s. Tabby used in construction is a mix of—"

"Sand, oyster shell, and lime," Quig stated, interrupting me. "She named you after a wall?"

"She named me after something that had great meaning to her."

His brows beetled. I could almost see the gears turning in his head. He was a bulldog once he got locked on a subject. I'd better take control of the conversation. "Now, the reason I called is that Sage and I learned Blithe wore a wig. We wondered if it was due to a medical issue or merely a personal preference."

"Her scalp was buzzed when I examined her. Nothing in her medical record suggested she'd undergone chemo. I observed no evidence of a skin condition on her scalp. Not many Caucasian women shave their heads, so I'm led to believe she didn't like her real hair. Why are you interested in her hair?"

No help on the wig angle. Might as well ask the other medical question. "This may sound strange, but was she pregnant?"

"No. Why do you ask?"

I waited until a woman with two frisky dogs on leashes passed by. "We wondered if she was seeing someone."

"If she had a boyfriend, it wasn't public knowledge."

"Rats. I was so hoping we'd found a lead. The only other thing we discovered about Blithe is that she owes money all over town, but I'm sure the cops found that out already. Also, her little dog, Boo Boo. What happened to it?"

He paused, his water bottle halfway to his mouth. "She had a dog? That's not in her file. There's no record of Animal Control being called either."

"She carried that white chihuahua in a pet tote bag every-where she went. If the dog wasn't there when the cops arrived, they wouldn't know she had one, that is, unless the pet bowls were present."

Quig finished his BLT wrap and stared at the slowed car traf-fic around the square. "What's your point?"

"I'm trying to figure out who killed Blithe."

"You didn't hear me say this, but sometimes people who can't cope with life, they either consciously or subconsciously put them-selves in harm's way. I believe Blithe was one of those people. The few adult interactions I had with her indicated she was bitter and miserable. She appeared well groomed, but I know better."

I drew in a quick breath. "That's an odd thing to say."

"Her living situation was . . . primitive to say the least."

His understatement made me laugh. "Nothing like roughing it in a condo."

"No laughing matter. She was a hoarder, and from what I observed, she's lucky she didn't die of food poisoning or worse."

My lips twitched. I wanted to say something, but I couldn't without giving away our little breaking and entering.

"I know you went in there," Quig said in a barely audible voice, tapping his steepled fingers. "No way you could've known about the pregnancy test or the wig without being inside her place."

Fear stuck, blinding me like a thick curtain of Spanish moss. I pushed through it. "You can't tell anyone."

"I'm your friend," he said. "Never forget that. We swapped a few secrets, so we're bound by those secrets."

"Okay." I dared to breathe again. "I'm not used to trusting people outside my family."

"You can always trust me, Tabby. We go way back."

"Are you counting how you used to carry me around when we were kids?"

"It was the only thing I could do. Your tiny legs wouldn't allow you to keep up."

"True confession. Sometimes I got tired of running to catch up, and let you carry me."

"I know." He grinned. "It worked out for both of us."

I shook my head. "Why'd you want to carry around a little kid anyway?"

"One day you'll understand. One day soon."

As I pondered his words, I noticed people hurrying past us. Sirens warbled in the distance. Quig stood, and I followed. "What is it?" I asked, knowing he could see over the top of most people.

"People are running from our block of attached buildings."

I scrambled to stand atop the fountain wall, a move that made me taller than Quig. Trouble was that the only thing I could see were tree branches. I went to step down, wobbled, and would've taken a swim if Quig hadn't snagged me in midair.

He grinned and nuzzled my hair before he set me down. "Just like old times."

Chapter Fourteen

We were within a block of the shop when police officers cut short our mad dash. "Turn around. Seek cover," the tall one said. "Bomb threat."

"Where?" I asked, dreading the answer.

The cop named the address of The Book and Candle Shop. I turned to Quig, mute with horror. He scooped me into his arms and ran, charging down the sidewalk. His habit of picking me up was the impetus I needed to unfreeze. I pushed at his chest. "Put me down."

"Not taking a chance you'll be in harm's way."

"This is embarrassing. I can run. Where are you taking me?"

His breathing wasn't even labored as we rounded another corner. "Where I know we'll be safe. The morgue. It's one-story and has weathered over a decade of hurricanes. It'll withstand a bomb blast too."

"Wait. Go back. I have two cats in my shop. And Gerard. And maybe Sage."

"The officers will evacuate everyone. The cats too. Then they'll check the entire block for a bomb."

"Can they search our property without a warrant?"

"Yes, for matters of public safety."

Not what I wanted to hear. I didn't like strangers touching my things, judging my belongings. I didn't want my home and business to blow up either. "Glad I made up my bed this morning."

Quig strangled out a laugh. "I didn't."

"You don't make your bed?"

"Why? I'm getting back in tonight."

"Do you pick up your clothes?"

"Mostly. What's this about?"

"Sorry to be so personal. Everything always looks shipshape in your living room and kitchen."

"I'm a guy. If not for my mother, my whole house would be as messy as the bedroom. But I do have home training. I mean, you wouldn't hold an unmade bed against me, would ya?"

"None of my business." *It could be my business.* That thought flashed neon bright in my head, and I panicked. We were several blocks away from where we'd started running, and the morgue was in the next block. I'd had enough of being carried. Why'd he carry me anyway? Was he trying to prove how manly he was?

I arched my back, twisted my torso, and kicked out with my legs. A second later I stood flatfooted on the ground, Quig scratched his head beside me. "How'd you do that? Why?"

"I hope those questions keep you occupied for the next hour."

"You're not coming with me?"

"I will but under my own power."

He nodded in approval. "Feisty. I like that."

"Look, *friend*, I appreciate your concern for me, but I need to check on my sister, Gerard, and the cats."

"Sure, once we're safely sheltered inside the morgue. If a bomb explodes, we might still be in range of projectiles."

I hadn't thought of that. "Good grief." I trotted after him like a pup as he picked up the pace. By the time we arrived, my lungs burned, my calves throbbed, and my side hitched from so much aerobic activity. Only pride kept me standing tall when I wanted to bend over double.

Quig, darn his hide, took one look at me and grinned. "You made it."

"Why'd you go so fast?" I somehow managed to say between gulps of air.

"You were running, so I ran."

My chest heaved as I gulped air. "To keep up with you. Running isn't my thing."

His expression sobered. "You should've said something."

And let him get the best of me? No way I would ever quit a challenge. Then another thought occurred. He wanted to verbally spar to take my mind off my shorter strides and poor physical fitness. I shot him my best stink-eye.

"You're all right, Short Stuff. Come on." He latched onto my hand and dragged me into the low-slung morgue.

I was too busy staying on my feet and mouth-breathing to put up a fuss. People we passed in the hall shot us a few pointed looks. I ignored them. So did Quig.

He locked the door behind us. "You're safe here."

"I need to call Sage to make sure she's okay." I was proud of how even my voice sounded given how dry my throat felt.

"Cell phones don't work in here." Quig pulled two electrolyte drinks from a small undercounter fridge. "Sit. Drink."

That explained why there was often such a lag time when he finally responded to voicemail messages I left him. Despite his curt commands, I sat and drank because that's what my body needed. The orange beverage hit the spot. I paced my drinking so that I didn't guzzle the whole thing at once.

Quig sat on the counter near me, taking his time with his drink. The disinfectant smells hit me next. I'd met Quig down here before when he called to do lunch, but I'd never spent much time looking around. Everything was tidy to a fault. The flat surfaces gleamed, the glass on the upper cabinets looked spit-shined. The floors appeared to be brand new.

Maybe he needed to be sloppy at home because he was full-blown OCD in here. "You said cell phones don't work here. May I use your landline phone?"

"Sure."

Using his landline, I tried both Gerard and Sage's cell numbers. Neither picked up, so I left messages saying I hoped they were all right and that I was safe with Quig. I also sent a twin-speak message to Sage saying I was okay and asking for her to respond. She did not reply.

"What do we do next?" I asked.

"We wait." He chuffed out a breath and finished his drink. "I'll get a sitrep once things calm down. I'm concerned a bomb threat was called in for your shop. That's not good."

It more than concerned me, but I didn't want to examine the why of it yet. I couldn't, not with strangers pouring through my private spaces. I needed a new topic. The bottle in my hand was a good place to start. "I don't recognize this brand of drink, but it's quite good."

"I special-order it. Glad it's working for you. Thought it might help."

A quick self-check assured me I'd never felt better. I nodded over at the wall of vaults. "Are those all occupied?"

"Only the ones with white cards on the outside," Quig said.

I drifted over to the wall, curious about his work. "How long do you keep bodies here?"

"Until they're claimed or we cremate the remains to make room for more bodies. In a larger city, there are over a hundred and fifty deaths a day. We're not that busy, though during the height of the pandemic we brought in refrigerated trucks to hold the dead. I had three assistant coroners at that time. Those were tough days."

"Yes."

One vault card stopped me. "You've still got Blithe McAdam? It's been a few days. Why didn't her half brother claim her body or make arrangements for her funeral?"

"Why indeed?"

Another strangeness in the woman's life. If I ended up dead in the morgue, my twin and aunt would claim me right away. "Is it possible for me to see her body?"

"You're not related to her and you're not a cop, so the official answer is no."

"Is there an unofficial answer?"

He joined me in front of Blithe's compartment. "It would be unprofessional of me and might even get me fired. Besides, have you ever seen a deceased person before?"

"My mom."

"Of course. But this is different. Blithe died violently, and the back of her head is bashed in. Don't want you to pass out or have nightmares."

My fingernails curled into my palms. "I won't."

"Swear you won't tell anyone."

"I swear."

"Here we go." He opened the latch, then slid Blithe out partway.

The smell of death brought tears to my eyes. Blithe McAdam's skin was tight across her fresh-scrubbed face. The alabaster skin tone made it hard to recognize her. "If I saw her on the street like this I wouldn't recognize her. Without her life force, she resembles a mannikin. That spark of animation does so much for a person."

"You all right? Not going to faint on me are you?"

"I'm good. Her natural hair's the same color as her wig, though she kept it very short."

"It was probably easier to wear the wig than to worry about styling her hair every day."

"The front of her head looks fine."

"Yes, and you do not need to see the back of it." He rolled the body inside the cold unit and shut the door.

"Q? You there?" a scratchy voice asked.

"Here we go. Answers." He strode to his desk and seized a portable radio unit. "This is Q. Go ahead."

"No bomb in the building. An item of interest was seized from the candle and book shop. We think it's the murder weapon from the McAdam homicide."

"Anything else?"

"Cops are looking for the Winslow sisters. They have the shop clerk in custody."

"Where was the weapon found?" Quig asked.

"A weird room that resembled a kitchen."

"Thanks. Q out."

He put the radio unit down and turned to me. "You need a lawyer."

"The building's okay? No bomb? My family is okay?"

"Yes to all three."

"Who called it in? Why would anyone think we'd have a bomb at the candle shop?"

"That's a police matter. Also, they believe they found Blithe's murder weapon. In the stillroom. This is bad, Tabby. You need a lawyer."

The air temperature suddenly felt ice cold. I trembled against the chill. "I don't understand. I don't own a baseball bat. My attorney is Brindle Platt, only he's representing Gerard now."

"There's a conflict of interest since you are both suspects. Gonna hook you up with my guy, Herbert R. Ellis, right now."

I didn't recognize his name. My suspicions mounted as Quig punched up the number from memory on his office phone. "Is he one of those slip-and-fall guys?"

"He's a discreet criminal attorney who was top in his class at UGA."

"Is he expensive?"

Quig gathered our empty drink bottles and rinsed them in the sink. "Very. But he'll make sure you don't spend a moment in jail."

"That's good because I don't know how they found anything connected to Blithe's murder in our shop, and especially not my stillroom. I keep that place spotless at all times."

"I'm not saying you knew it was there. Could've been placed there to frame you."

Someone framed me? The day tanked from bad to worse. "Why me?"

Quig held up a finger as he left a voicemail message for the lawyer, explaining the situation, and asked him to meet us at the police station as soon as possible before hanging up.

"Why not you?" Quig asked. "After that video with Gerard and Blithe went viral, your shop got all the foot traffic on your block, and most likely higher sales. Could be someone didn't like that. Or maybe whoever killed her realized leaving the weapon in your shop would take the heat off him or her."

"That's a rotten thing to do." I fumed silently, replaying the conversation in my head. "Wait a minute. Since when do *you* need a lawyer? The bodies that flow through these doors can't sue anyone."

"Oh, but their families can. Happens more than you'd think."

The weary tone of his voice surprised me. I tried to imagine my life without my friend Quig. Couldn't. Took me a long moment to respond. "You never mentioned being sued."

"Herbert is that good. None of the cases went to trial."

"I see." I also noted that Quig pronounced Herbert's name as if there were no final *r* and the name rhymed with *rabbit*.

My hands kept fisting, and I kept prying them open. "Why call him now? I've done nothing wrong. I don't believe in violence, and I certainly never touched anyone's bat. I don't like hurting people."

"I called Herbert because my intuition is very good. Sorry, Tabby. I can't stop this from happening. Once they take you into the interview room, don't say anything but 'lawyer' and his name. Got it?"

I barely had time to process his remark and nod before an insistent knock sounded at the locked door, along with "Police. Open up!"

Chapter Fifteen

This closet-sized room reeked of negative energy, fear, and desperation. Layers of misery coated the walls, ceiling, and floors. Given the level of bad vibes in here, even a non-sensitive would feel uneasy. It made me positively nauseous.

I glanced at the camera mounted near the ceiling. The green light flashed as the device recorded my every breath. They'd brought me straight to this room from the morgue. Was my sister hemmed up in this place too? And Gerard—where was he? What had happened to my cats after they were evacuated?

Per Quig's suggestion, I'd refused to speak without my lawyer present, and for that sin, I'd been abandoned in this hellhole. I rubbed my temples and continued pacing three strides in each direction, trying to summon a positive outlook. Knowing help was on the way kept me focused on my freedom.

It wasn't easy. Whispers of dark energy sparked and flared inside, begging to be released. If I went invisible, they would rush in here and I could walk out. That would yield immediate relief, but I wouldn't be able to explain my vanishing later. I buried the temptation as I had done repeatedly over the past fifteen years. This was not the time to embrace my differences.

When I'd counted my steps into the hundreds several times, the door finally opened. A dapper man about my height strutted in along with an ocean-fresh scent. His steady-eddy gaze behind those no-nonsense glasses and custom suit assured me that this was my lawyer.

"Thank you for coming, Mr. Ellis. I'm Tabby Winslow."

He nodded and glanced at the camera. I followed his gaze and saw the blinking light was dark. I released a shaky breath.

Mr. Ellis sat on the far side of the table and motioned me to sit across from him. He regarded me steadily. "I'll straighten this out in short order, Ms. Winslow."

"Thank you. Is my sister okay? What happened to Gerard Smith, our shop clerk, and my cats? Who called in the bomb threat?"

"The call was a hoax. No bomb was found, and the tip was anonymous from a burner phone. Everyone is okay. Your sister and Gerard are in other interview rooms. I apologize for the delay in my appearance. I demanded to see where the weapon was found, and they allowed it. The baseball bat was on the uppermost shelf over the door, behind dusty glassware, which still stood in place. The good news is the hiding place wasn't in plain sight."

My breath hitched, then words tumbled out as if a dam had broken. "I didn't kill Blithe McAdam. We don't own a baseball bat, and I don't know how that bat got there. I don't use that top shelf because I can't reach it without a ladder, and my aunt took our stepladder with her to Florida. That glassware belongs to my aunt."

"The cops are salivating over the bat. This is big for them and very bad for everyone in your shop. I overheard Detective Belfor say they couldn't pull a single print from the bat. However, the human tissue on the business end of the bat will likely prove it's the McAdam murder weapon."

Human tissue. Fingerprints. Murder weapon. My jaw gaped wide as he spoke. I tried to link those points and failed. I jumped out of my seat. "That can't be right."

"Take it easy. There *is* a silver lining here. I will argue the bat is inadmissible as evidence since it wasn't in plain sight. A bat clearly isn't a bomb. They should've gotten a warrant after noticing it there. Not following procedure is a no-no in the legal world."

His rationale sunk in as I clenched and unclenched my hands. He was as good as Quig promised, possibly better. "Please get me out of here. I hate confined spaces."

"No one likes them. That's why they make the rooms so small." He glanced around. "Usually they make them hot too. You're lucky."

Good grief. No wonder so much heavy emotion covered these surfaces. "I've never been questioned for a crime before. What should I expect?"

"I'll do the talking. You are not to say a word. Understand? Quig assured me that you would follow direction, no matter what insults or lies they spin. Paste a calm expression on your face and recite mantras or whatever centers you. If you do as I say, you'll be out of here in thirty minutes, guaranteed. They have to try to make you talk, but they don't have to succeed."

"Okay. I can do that."

"I'll signal for them to enter. Remember, stay calm. Don't believe a word they say. They often lie to suspects to get them to betray each other."

"Got it." And I did. With Herbert R. Ellis on my side, we breezed through the questions. Detectives Belfor and Nowry grew visibly agitated by my lawyer's repeated "No comment." The longer I sat there, the calmer I became, and a strange thing happened. The cops quit scowling. They didn't break into smiles, but the hostility in the room went from level ten to a one. The energy turned positive.

After one long pause, Herbert Ellis stated, "If there's nothing more, Detectives, my client is leaving."

"By all means," Detective Nowry said, rising and opening the door.

I sailed out of there in great spirits, full of hope and, surprisingly, joy. With warm sunshine on my face once we exited the building, I turned to my lawyer. "You're amazing. Thank you for helping me."

A car door opened. Quig loped over to us and caught my hand. "Everything okay?"

My grin stretched from ear to ear. "Yes. I'm so relieved."

"Good. Let's grab a late lunch." He glanced over at my attorney. "Want to join us?"

"Thanks, but I'm good. Need to head back to the office and prepare for a deposition in another case. You take care of Ms. Winslow. She's special."

Quig nodded and herded me into his Hummer. He drove to a nearby coffeeshop, where we grabbed sandwiches and coffee. With a full belly, I looked around the bustling room, feeling out of sync with reality. "I'm not sure what happened in there. The cops came into the room loaded for bear, and by the time it was over, they were tripping over themselves to be nice to us."

"Stranger things have happened," Quig said.

He didn't grasp the significance of what had happened. "I must not be telling this right. It was a seawater change. I was miserable, frightened, and alone. I lost hope I'd be walking out of there given the way they came at me like rabid wolves at first. And then, the more Mr. Ellis said, 'No comment,' the more my anxiety vanished. The calmer I got, the more peaceful the room became. It was a kumbaya moment for everyone."

"That's good."

"But looking back, it doesn't seem natural or possible. I'm curious what happened."

"You got out of there unscathed, thanks to Herbert. That's the takeaway."

"Odd advice, coming from someone with an inquisitive mind. I need to understand this."

Quig shrugged. "The universe cut you some major slack. Accept it. Please. Nothing to be gained by asking questions."

Now that I was safe and relaxed, I realized how selfish I'd been. My stomach roiled that I'd forgotten about my sister and employee. "I hope Sage and Gerard are okay. Will Mr. Ellis represent my sister if she needs a lawyer?"

"Conflict of interest. She needs a different lawyer if she chooses to have one." Quig signaled for the check and became very busy with the bill. I got the message. Sit on my curiosity, or keep asking questions that he wouldn't answer. Or *couldn't* answer.

We walked to the parking lot and his black Hummer. I turned my face to the sun again and rejoiced in my freedom. I would never again take for granted the ability to draw in a fresh breath of air. "Can I go home now?"

"They released both sides of Bristol Street quickly once the bomb threat was debunked. Your shop has crime scene tape on the doorways, though I believe your residence upstairs is accessible from the alley stairs. My place was cleared."

Irritation flashed like heat lightning inside my gut. "How long can they close my shop? We have bills to pay."

"Rules are different when a crime is involved. According to what I've heard from friends on the force, the bomb squad finished quickly. The detectives swept in behind the bomb crew to search the stillroom. Herbert assures me they didn't follow procedure as no search warrant was filed or served. They'll release your residence soon if they haven't already. I imagine the same is true for the shop."

My frustration eased to a low simmer. Quig didn't deserve my sharp tongue. He'd helped me. I had better manners than this. "I'm grateful for your recommendation. Herbert Ellis walks softly but holds the line. The cops never got so much as a rise out of him."

"You don't want to see that guy angry. Not a pretty sight."

"Good to know." I squeezed his hand. "Thanks for all your help. I'd be sweating bullets in that room right about now, if not for you."

"Interesting visual, but I have something else in mind."

The smoking-hot look he shot me could've ignited a three-alarm fire. It's a mystery why my clothes didn't catch on fire. Okay, I hadn't been entirely honest with my twin, and I'd die if she found out. Quig and I were friends with benefits. Had been for a few weeks. And at this moment, I craved the physical outlet he offered.

I met his gaze with pure energy—white hot, flashing, and sparkling. "I was thinking the same thing."

He punched the accelerator. "My place."

Chapter Sixteen

A few hours later, the text from my sister read, *Where are you?* *With Quig. Are you okay?* I texted back. I guess she'd gotten tired of getting my twin-speak away message of "Not now. I'm too busy." We always responded to one another immediately unless we were with someone. For years she'd put me on hold when she was with a boyfriend. And now the tide had certainly turned.

Peachy. Come home. I need you.

Give me a few minutes. With a hooded gaze, Quig watched me dress, a charcoal-colored sheet draped across his lap. I knew he'd love to have me stay, and I wanted that too. But I needed to be with Sage, to hear how she'd handled her experience. "I have to go. Can't thank you enough for everything."

"Anytime. My door will always be open to you. Come back later if you like."

"Thanks for lunch too. You helped me relax so much I lost track of time—and of where Sage and Gerard were. I'm so glad she's free, and I hope the same is true for Gerard."

I gave him a quick kiss and hurried two doors down the alley to my place. Twilight had fallen while I was otherwise occupied.

I'd had a wonderful respite in a crappy day, but now I needed to hear how my sister had fared and learn Gerard's fate.

Sage opened the alley door and watched me mount the metal steps. "What happened to you?" she asked, her arms locked across her chest.

The cats churned at her feet. Harley started meowing when he saw me. Self-consciously, I smoothed hair away from my face, realizing too late it was a hot mess and that I'd left my ponytail holder at Quig's. "Blowing off steam. Didn't you get my text earlier?"

Sage glowered at me. "After the most traumatic incident of my life, I needed to see you with my own two eyes. How'd you bolt out of there so fast? Why didn't you wait for me?"

"I should've waited, but I couldn't stand to be near that cauldron of seething emotions after being confined for two hours. The walls pressed in on me, and I fought energy surges the whole time I was being held. I almost went invisible to escape. Battling my flight instinct drained me. I'm truly sorry for selfishly sending a text message and leaving, but once I discovered they didn't have a search warrant and the bat was seized improperly, I figured they would release you as well. Quig was there, and I left with him." I reached for my fluffy black cat and hugged him close. Harley rewarded me with a contented purr. "My new lawyer is a miracle worker."

"Come inside and tell me the whole story. Why didn't you use Brindle or another lawyer from our usual firm of Cranford, Aldrich, and Platt?"

As I entered the kitchen, the cat's soothing energy took the bite off Sage's militant mood. I shouldn't have been so self-indulgent when I broke free—not when they had my sister. In all fairness,

Quig had engineered my freedom and my calm, centered mood. "Quig said it would be a conflict of interest if I used Brindle. He asked his lawyer to help me."

"Which is why I didn't call Brindle and why I endured hours of torment. I couldn't stand being penned in that tiny room too."

I winced and guilt flooded in like a storm surge. "I hate them for holding you so long. You should've demanded a lawyer, Sage. I'll ask if Herbert has another partner in case this happens again. Before he came to the jail, he went to our shop, saw where the bat had been found, and noticed a procedural gaffe. His preemptive thinking helped all of us. Then he sat with me and answered every cop question. The only thing I said on record was requesting him as my attorney."

Sage slammed the door shut behind us. "Wait a second. Herbert as in Herbert R. Ellis?"

"That's the one."

My sister's slack-jawed expression surprised me. "How'd you . . .? I mean, what'd you . . .? How'd you even get his number? He's unlisted and only takes a few clients a year."

"Quig arranged it. Why so many questions?"

My sister gestured with both hands in large sweeping motions. "Because I thought they'd grilled you to well done, that's why. I was in there five hours, and I exercised extreme restraint not to do more than to blank out the camera from time to time. They said terrible things about us, about you. They said you implicated me in the crime."

My spine went ramrod straight. "I did no such thing. I told you I didn't say a word after my lawyer arrived. I would never implicate you in a crime, even if you did it."

Sage stomped over and sniffed me. "I knew you'd been with a man from the musky scent and your wild woman hair. You even smell like Quig. Are you sleeping with him now?"

Harley tensed at Sage's approach, jumped down from my arms, and scampered away. After the tensions of the day, I was in no mood to be grilled by anyone, not even my closest kin. "I'm a grown woman, and you aren't my mother. I don't interrogate you when you come home after a date."

"You went on a *date*? While I was rotting in jail?"

"That didn't come out right." I sighed. "We grabbed a bite to eat because I was starving and spent time together afterward. That's it. I couldn't face this place yet. Knowing they'd pawed through our closets and drawers, touched our possessions, and invaded my stillroom overwhelmed me. I needed a distraction—and time to recover."

Sage regarded me steadily. "While I am all for you dating, it galls me to say that Quig will break your heart into a million pieces. He isn't like us. He doesn't understand our needs. He's a player."

"Leave Quig out of this." I wasn't having *that* conversation right now. Besides, she was mistaken. I was an eyewitness to the fact he understood my needs perfectly. Time to talk about something else. "What about Gerard? Did they release him?"

"Brindle was unsuccessful in springing him. Gerard is being held for further questioning about Blithe McAdam's murder."

I sagged into the counter, the weight of the day once again heavy on my shoulders. "Poor Gerard. How can we get him out?"

"Prove someone else killed that dreadful woman."

"I saw her." The words I spoke were barely audible, a trick of sound Sage and I learned very early in life so our mom couldn't hear us talking. If cops planted listening devices in our home, they couldn't pick up words spoken so softy. "Her half brother didn't claim her body."

"You have my attention," Sage said in the same ultra-soft voice.

"Quig allowed me to see her corpse. You can't tell anyone, or he'll get fired."

"So?"

"She had the same color hair as that wig, albeit hers was closely cropped."

"Not that. The Winslow stuff."

I shook my head at the rotating topics, not wanting to discuss my fettered abilities either.

"Tabs, we need you at full capacity. Ditch that mental block on your extra gears. You must be the real you. We are in very big trouble. The cops questioned both of us today."

"I am a decent human being." The words shot out of my mouth like rapid-fire watermelon seeds, further disrupting the kitchen's normally serene atmosphere. "I am not a destroyer. I will not be that for anyone—not for you, not for our shop, and especially not for me."

"Your talent is more than that. You call it destructive. I call it protective. Besides, if you hadn't acted instinctively to shield your-self all those years ago, that man would've raped and killed you," Sage said, a tremor in her soft voice.

"I hear what you're saying, Sis, but it's been a long day for both of us. Emotions are running high, and our energy is running low. I promise you can bug me about the past and present later, but I can't go there right now." I stretched and studied the kitchen. "Doesn't look too bad in here," I said in a normal voice.

Sage matched my speaking volume. "I closed the cabinets and cleaned the fingerprint dust mess they left behind. I also stripped the beds, and our sheets are washing."

I yawned and covered my face. "Thanks for doing all that. I'm so tired I don't need sheets. I'll grab a blanket from the linen closet and call it good for tonight."

"I'm holding you to that promise to talk about everything tomorrow."

I started to leave, then stopped as I made a mental connection. "With Gerard out of commission, you and I will be running the shop together. Hence, we should get a good night's rest. Alternating days as lead? I'll take lead tomorrow."

"You do that. I need the entire day off after that negativity overdose. Unlike other people in this room, I didn't have a white knight swooping in to save me from danger and then treating me to a bout of lovemaking."

Guilt rode me hard. I had been hyper-focused on self-preservation. I'd barely spared a thought for her or Gerard once I was with Quig. I owed Sage—heck, I hadn't even offered to share my energy with her this evening. "Do whatever you need to clear your head. Mom always said it was important to keep our house in order. Her words seem particularly apt tonight."

"Our house *was* in order—that's why we're free and clear. The cops must've tricked Gerard somehow for him to still be there."

"We'll have to do something about that," I said.

"Not yet and certainly not tonight. I plan to go on the roof and howl at the moon."

That made me laugh, only I wasn't entirely sure if she was serious. Whatever. We were safe and in our home. We'd get it back to our level of clean tomorrow; of that I had no doubt. If the cops left electronic listening devices here, they'd be disposed of and destroyed in due time.

Nobody messed with the Winslows and got away with it.

Nobody.

Chapter Seventeen

Business was brisk the next morning. Something about bad news and disasters drew people, and while I was glad for the business, my heart was heavy for my confined employee. The front page of the Savannah paper displayed Gerard's mug shot. He looked miserable. Today must be a living hell for him. I couldn't imagine staying there overnight, and I'd never made it past the interview room. The actual jail cells must be drenched in dark emotions and negative energy.

Two TV reporters did live segments in front of The Book and Candle Shop. One braved the doors of the shop with her camera crew, and I gave them the boot. Students from the Savannah College of Art and Design, known locally as SCAD, and from the Georgia Southern at Armstrong campus filed into the shop by twos and threes and asked about Gerard. I smiled and said he'd be back to work soon. Somehow our guy had become a touchstone for these kids.

I sold out of the teacup candles and white tapers. Our lotions and soaps flew off the shelves too. Shoppers who bought our ghost books and guidebooks also picked up dragons and griffins. I emptied the carton of Brenda's Bees lip balm twice. During a lull in sales, I restocked the sales floor and wished Gerard were here doing his thing. He'd told me on multiple occasions that this job was his happy place. I finished eating my stash of nut bars and wished Sage would appear so I'd have a quick break to grab lunch.

After a while my stomach wouldn't stop grumbling. I locked the shop door, changed the door sign to a spare that read "Back in Ten Minutes," and trotted upstairs to eat and check on my sister. Harley and Luna snuggled on the sofa. Sage was gone. Not a trace of her. Didn't even look like she'd slept in her bed. I shot her a *Hope you're okay* text message, and immediately I felt her smile in my head. She was okay, at least, but elsewhere.

I made a quick PBJ sandwich, filled one of those clunky thermos-style cups with sweet tea, and stuffed my cross-body shoulder bag with apples and cookies to hold me through the entire afternoon shift. I also grabbed my phone charger.

Returning to the shop after that quick ten minutes, I had a queue of people awaiting my return. One of them was City Alderman Rashad Vernon, a man I considered a possibility for Blithe's killer.

I went with a light and breezy tone when he made a beeline for me. "Mr. Alderman, what can I do for you today?"

"I need a present for my wife's birthday. She loves the stuff in here."

Oh, Gerard, why aren't you here? You'd remember everything that woman ever purchased. But Gerard didn't magically appear— not that I believed that would happen. Pity, though.

"I'm happy to help in any way I can." I gestured to the tables and shelves of personal care and lifestyle items. "We offer many locally made products. What are her favorites?"

He shrugged, so I began a guessing game as I walked him around the shop. I steered him to our products first. "Does she ever burn candles?"

"Yes. They smell like forest and sea at the same time."

I grabbed the appropriate candle. "What kind of hand soap does she use?"

"The foamy kind. Often her hands smell like lemons."

We went around the shop until Mr. Vernon had tea, honey, lip balm, lotion, a facial, candles, and soap for his wife. "You gift wrap, right?" he asked.

"Certainly." Glad my other shoppers were still browsing, I drew out a large gift bag, fluffed tissue paper to line it, then swaddled each item individually in tissue paper. The top included more tissue, a cute tulle bow, and a complimentary birthday card.

"Sorry to hear about Gerard Smith, but he did the world a favor," the alderman said. "That McAdam woman was a menace to society. She hounded me at our meetings over every little thing. I won't miss her."

I'd been about to push his bag across the counter. Instead, I gripped it tighter. "First, Gerard didn't do it. Someone put that bat in our shop to frame us. Second, that poor woman was murdered. No matter how unpleasant she was, she didn't deserve that. Lastly, Blithe McAdam was one of your constituents. I'm surprised you aren't pushing for justice for her, urging the cops to control crime in the historic district and get the bad element off the street."

"Are you telling me how to do my job, Ms. Winslow?"

"I'm telling you as a constituent who voted for you that I expect more from you as my representative."

He wrested the bag from me. "I am doing my job. A suspect is in custody. The bad element *is* off the street."

"Gerard is innocent. He lost his temper with that woman once. That isn't a crime, no matter how many views that viral video received. I'm sure you've said worse about her at the Moonlight Fishing Hole."

Rashad leveled a long finger in my face. "That's gossip and hearsay, and I know for a fact you don't go there. You have no idea what I said."

He didn't cow me. I stood toe to toe with him. "The cops questioned you, so you're a suspect as well. Did *you* kill Blithe McAdam?"

"I am not a suspect. I have an alibi. If we're going there, what about you and your sister? Heard you took turns in that interview chair as well."

"We also had alibis. We were both at home during the time of the murder."

"How convenient."

"It's the truth."

"Everybody knows the Winslow family is . . ."

Energy surged and swirled within me. The hair on my arms lifted. "What are you saying?"

He got a hunted look in his eyes. "Eccentric. Your family isn't like other families."

I managed to hold onto my cool, though I nearly lost it. "Nothing wrong with my family, and even if we do a few things our own way, so what? Everyone's family has eccentricities. Even yours. You're circling the wrong oak tree."

He swore loudly. "Like an elephant, I don't forget slights and won't forget the blatant allegation you just made about me. Vernons are the epitome of normal."

I smiled through gritted teeth. "*Normal* is a subjective construct."

"You're playing with fire, missy. This is my district. You can't talk like that to me."

Never had I been happier to have our security camera. If something came of this elected official's threats, I had a video of him making them. Clearly we were talking at each other instead of communicating. Worse, he believed the derogatory gossip people spread about my family. Instead of continuing to defend myself, I said, "Have a blessed day."

"Watch your step, girl."

That did it. When he turned to exit, I directed a mental shove of energy at his knees, hitting him with so much juice he stumbled into the door and nearly fell.

I walked over, every bit the concerned shop owner. "Are you alright, Mr. Alderman?"

He swatted my hand away and straightened. "I'm fine."

"Be careful."

"Get away from me. I don't want your kind of help."

He was lucky I didn't knock him down again. "What kind of help would that be, Mr. Vernon?"

"You're all crazy in this shop."

I held the door for him, pleased at the plethora of phones taping his bumbling exit. "Thanks for visiting The Book and Candle Shop, Mr. Alderman."

He left and my other shoppers suddenly looked busy. Meanwhile, I stowed my gift-wrapping supplies. It was only later, when things had quieted down, that I realized what I'd done.

I'd used an energy blast on him. The realization chilled me to the bone. Someone could've been hurt, but Rashad Vernon survived with only his pride damaged. In anger, I'd pulsed a small current of energy his way, wanting him out of my sight. My precise level of control surprised and pleased me.

On a positive note, I felt certain a new video or two of him stumbling and swearing would surface online. You gotta love karma.

*　*　*

Sage showed up after closing time, looking like a cat that had drunk two bottles of cream. She carried a bag of Chinese carry-out. I was so happy to see her looking relaxed that I didn't chide her for abandoning me. The cats made a big fuss over her. I don't know if they could smell the seafood in the bag or if they truly missed my twin.

Once I finished my fortune cookie, I figured her grace period was over. "Where were you?"

"Out," Sage said, her nose going up. "I was out. I needed clarity, and I couldn't get it here."

"Clarity? About the bomb threat and our subsequent interrogations?"

"Clarity like you had with Quig. I needed to lose myself in passion and not think about life for a while. It's a good way to put distance between myself and a recent event, and it worked. I feel much better."

I couldn't deny her excuse. But still she'd shown little consideration for me by not even letting me know of her intended absence. "You stuck me with the shop all day."

"Feel free to stick me with the shop tomorrow."

I scowled at her. "I will."

"Did something else happen?" Sage asked all wide-eyed.

"City Alderman Rashad Vernon happened. He bought presents for his wife's birthday, and then he said Gerard did the world a favor by killing Blithe. He mashed all my hot buttons, so I dished it back in kind. Then he called our family crazy and said something snarky as he was leaving. I lost it and gave him a focused energy shove, even with a shop full of customers watching. He stumbled into the door, which I took to mean that I can control a low-level energy event, or else he'd be dead."

Sage radiated approval. "That's wonderful about your new-found level of control. Too bad you didn't knock Vernon on his keester or worse."

"Thought about it, but the witness problem wasn't one I could address."

Sage stroked the ragged edges of her fingernails. "He realize what happened?"

"Don't think so. No one was near him when he stumbled."

"He's good friends with the city inspectors. If he asked, they'd come in here and search until they found a reason to shut us down. We think we're in good shape, but with an old building, you never know what an inspection might find."

I hadn't thought about any of that. We couldn't afford those consequences. "Message received. I won't go after him unless we're alone and he needs to die."

"Great plan. Catch the dishes for me, Tabs. I'm due for a long soak in the tub." She paused after rising. "How'd we do on sales today?"

"Busy all day. Long as we stay out of trouble with city officials and don't get implicated for any other murders, we'll be in good shape this month."

Sage snorted. "Like that's going to happen."

Chapter Eighteen

Gerard was released Monday morning. He called me as soon as he was free. "I am feeling the sun on my face for the first time in twenty-four hours. As God is my witness, I will never so much as jaywalk for the rest of my life. I am out of jail."

"Yay!" I said, feeling a smidge guilty to still be puttering around the apartment when he'd been in a bad way. I'd heard Sage get breakfast earlier and clomp down the interior steps to open the shop. I put him on speakerphone so I could finish my makeup. "Glad you're out."

"Now you have to find the real killer," Gerard continued. "I never want to be behind bars again, and I hope I never need Brindle Platt again. You have any new leads to report?"

His sharp tone concerned me, but who was I to judge? Thanks to Quig's quick thinking, I hadn't spent the night in jail. "No new suspects or clues, though City Alderman Rashad Vernon stopped in here yesterday. He bought gifts for his wife's birthday and brought up Blithe's murder. He said you'd done the world a favor by killing her."

"I did no such thing," Gerard shouted. "I hope you set him straight on that."

I grinned at my reflection in the bathroom mirror. "I did and on a few other points as well. He called me pushy after he started an argument with me. I don't know if he has a problem with women or people in general, but either way he won't get my vote again."

"Mine either, though if the cops don't arrest somebody else, I am screwed. My lawyer said their case is based on circumstantial evidence."

"But probably not the bat." I relayed the information my lawyer found to him as I carried the phone to the closet and searched for shoes.

"Good to know, but I'm still feeling the police heat. I need your help."

His words made me wonder how many innocent people were in jail because of circumstantial evidence. I couldn't let that happen to my friend. "Gotcha. I will give it my all to find out who killed Blithe." I paused and cleared my throat softly. "You should take today off, okay?"

"I need to bathe for an hour to get this funk off me. Then I plan to pig out and shower again, whatever it takes to get this rank smell out of my nose. Once I'm me again, I'm taking a nap. I didn't sleep last night. Too afraid to close my eyes. So my answer to your question is yes, I'm taking a leave day. I'll be there tomorrow."

With that he hung up on me. As the display darkened, I renewed my pledge to save Gerard. He'd gotten a few lousy shakes in life, but I couldn't—no, I *wouldn't*—let him go to prison for a crime he didn't commit. In the kitchen, I poured the last of the coffee in a cup with ice and headed down the alley stairs. First stop on my rounds was Brindle Platt's office.

* * *

"Do you have an appointment?" the receptionist of Cranford, Aldrich, and Platt asked.

I couldn't help but notice that they had a beautiful new hire manning the gate to their inner sanctums. "I'm a client, and I need to see him. It won't take long."

"Mr. Platt had a family emergency over the weekend, and his schedule is full today," the blonde countered, giving me an additional setdown with her heavily mascaraed eyes. "Unless it's an urgent matter, I can fit you in two weeks from today."

"I won't take more than a few minutes of his time." Glad that I'd dressed for success with heels and a tight skirt and, yes, some cleavage showing, I pushed past the sputtering woman and into Brindle's office. I shut the door firmly behind me.

He glanced up in alarm, then beamed a sly smile my way and rose. "Tabby Winslow, to what do I owe the pleasure?"

I may have leaned forward a bit, flaunting myself to get his attention. "I need a moment of your time."

"Of course." He waved to the guest chair and came around to sit on the front edge of his desk. "What can I do for you today?"

I sat for politeness's sake, though I very much wanted to stand over him and get right in his face. "First thing is off the record. What are your intentions toward my sister?"

His hopeful expression shuttered. "My professional and personal relationships with Sage are none of your business."

"I know all about your *family emergency*, Brindle. Sage told me where she was on Friday evening and all day Saturday. It is unlike Sage to spend so much time with you, so I believe that something changed in your relationship. Or at least, she thinks something's changed. That's why I'm here. Though Sage acts like a tough cookie, she's not a one-night-stand kind of woman, and she's emotionally vulnerable. Which leads me back to my original question: What are your intentions with my sister?"

"Again, none of your business."

"Moving right along to question two, what evidence do the cops have against Gerard?"

"Well, ma'am, seeing as how you chose another firm to represent you, this aspect of your inquiry is a bona fide conflict of interest."

I'd expected his protest. Would he accept my explanation? "Quig encouraged me to use his lawyer. Said you couldn't represent me because you were already Gerard's attorney of record."

"He's right, but that doesn't mean your defection didn't hurt. You didn't so much as notify me of your intent, and I've represented your family for over ten years."

Yikes. He was upset with me. I hastened to explain further. "Sorry. I should've made that call, but everything happened so fast. Quig barely had spoken to his lawyer about representing me when the cops stormed the coroner's office and took me into custody. Then once I got out of the police interview, I was, uh, distracted for a few hours."

"Quig?"

"Yes. He made sure I didn't do anything rash."

Brindle gave me an all-over appraisal. "I'd be glad to counsel you and your sister next time. I have lots of clarity to offer."

Ooh, gross. I ignored his suggestion, feeling cheaper by the minute as he stared down my blouse. Was an intimate encounter with twins on his bucket list? So not happening. "Sage lit into me when I got home on Friday. Then she disappeared for a night and most of Saturday getting *clarity* from you. I ran the shop alone and fended off Alderman Vernon."

Brindle lifted his gaze to my face. "Doogie bothering you?"

It was common in certain circles to call the alderman a version of Doogie Howser, a TV character. "Yes. He outright said Winslows were crazy and implied we didn't know our place in this town. He said he ran the historic district. I took that as a threat."

"Talk to your new lawyer."

"He's only filling in temporarily while you're helping Gerard. You're the Winslow's lawyer. If he comes after our shop, it will affect Sage too."

"So noted."

His phone rang and I left, unsure if I'd made things better or worse. Brindle might not be faithful to Sage, but heck, I didn't know if Quig and I were exclusive either. There wasn't anyone else for me, but Quig hadn't called since I'd left his place on Friday. That lapse of communication created doubts about his intentions toward me.

Not one to languish in limbo, I made up my mind. Time to swing by the coroner's office. I sure hoped this visit had a different outcome.

Chapter Nineteen

The coroner's office was locked up tight as a tick when I arrived. I sent Quig a text message from outside the morgue: *Where are you?*

His typed reply was immediate. *Work meeting.*

Can I see you today?

Yes. Meet you at Southern Tea in an hour.

Despite my high heels and sleek skirt, I opted to walk home instead of calling for a ride. I wended my way through oak-shaded streets alternately lined with shops and homes, strolling among tourists and strangers. On a whim, I took a small detour and stood in front of Blithe McAdam's condo on East Starling Street. Her place seemed shrouded in shadows.

Blithe, what happened to you? The world was your oyster until it ate you up.

Just then the door of the end unit beside hers opened, and a harried-looking millennial exited. "This is private property," the person said.

The person appeared gender neutral in boots, jeans, a muscle tee, and a thick silver necklace. The hair was royal purple—what there was of the razor-short cut. Piercings on the face and ears and heavily tattooed arms completed the picture.

Unsure of this person's gender, I summoned my courage and walked toward him or her, extending my hand. "Hi. I'm Tabby Winslow. Your former neighbor used to shop at The Book and Candle Shop where I work. Do you know what happened to her small dog?"

The person's militant bearing eased slightly. "Eileen Hutson." Eileen shook my hand firmly. "That darned dog. He always pooped on my lawn, and Blithe encouraged him to do it. Good riddance to Boo Boo, I say."

Though Eileen shook hands like a man and had a deep voice, I assigned her a female pronoun because of her feminine name. "Oh dear. That sounds awful. Blithe must've been a difficult neighbor."

A dark cloud passed over her face. "You have no idea. I complained to our condo association about the dog poop. Their response was to install a security camera. I love all animals, but I had ugly thoughts about her pet for fouling my tiny lawn. She left it home alone often, and it barked nonstop until she returned. Yap-yap-yap. I can still hear the shrill sound."

"Not a good situation. It sounds like the dog wasn't well trained. Did the cops pick it up when they came for Blithe?"

"It wasn't inside. Hadn't been for days." Eileen jerked a thumb toward her condo building. "You'd think this new construction would have thick walls, but they're wafer thin. I heard her crying in there a lot. It creeped me out."

"She suffered from bad headaches, and they were getting worse. That's why she visited my shop, hoping our aromatherapy candles would help. She must've been miserable without Boo Boo to comfort her."

"I'm glad she's gone. I hope my next neighbor likes music and is pet-free."

A patch of blue sky opened in the clouds overhead. "Did the cops question you about her visitors?"

"I told them about her loudmouth half brother and the alderman."

A slight breeze would've knocked me over. "Alderman Rashad Vernon?"

Eileen nodded.

How odd. "He claimed she was a thorn in his side. She challenged his decisions on the city council."

"People are different in Savannah, that's for sure. The cops didn't believe he visited her. They even checked the new security camera in the back, but it isn't working. This place is a joke, but at least I don't have to put up with that trio's loud arguments anymore."

"They argued?"

"All the time. Every conversation ended in yelling."

"Could you hear what they were saying?"

"It was always about money."

I let that knock around in my head for a moment. "You told the police?"

"Sure did. I'm the one that found her. I noticed the open door. I started to close it because once mine blew open from the wind, but the odor inside her place made my eyes water. I called the cops."

Cops were suspicious of people who found bodies. "Was it bad?"

"They questioned me for a long time. I'd rate the experience between a root canal and a busted ankle." Suddenly sunshine blazed all around us, and Eileen immediately shielded her face from the sun. "Eek! I can't stay in the sun. I have to go."

I glanced at the time and realized I needed to hurry to make my lunch date with Quig. "Thank you for speaking with me, Eileen. Have a great day."

Eileen dashed inside. I speed-walked to the tea shop and parsed my findings as I went. Blithe routinely had two visitors, her half brother and the alderman. Heated words were exchanged, usually about money. The rumor mill had it that Blithe owed money all over town, but I'd seen the stacks upon stacks of horded items in her place. Her lifestyle puzzled me.

When I reached Southern Tea, Quig was seated, with two tall glasses of sweet tea on the table. He'd ordered two shrimp po' boys, and they arrived as I plopped into a chair.

"Thanks. This looks and smells great. How'd you beat me here?"

"My meeting let out earlier than expected, so I drove here and preordered our food. Thought if we expedited lunch we might have time for other things."

My pulse quickened. "Clarity?"

His gaze warmed. "Absolute clarity."

*　　*　　*

Afterward, I had a eureka moment. "This newfound clarity made me wonder how Blithe McAdam got around. Far as I know, she didn't own a car. She must've used a rideshare to run her errands. Further, given her disagreeable personality, she may have gotten crossways of a few operators."

"You think a driver killed her?" Quig asked, dark eyebrows rising.

I stretched like a cat beside him, feeling sated. "Who knows? I need to find those drivers. I'd like to keep picking up rocks to see what crawls out."

"Not many natural rocks on the coast. Too much sand," he said, absently drawing his fingers through my tangled shoulder-length hair. "Savannah has many catch-a-ride services. I bet each one has some twenty to fifty drivers."

"People are creatures of habit," I added, very sure of myself. "Blithe probably had one or two ride-hailing apps on her phone."

"A phone wasn't found with her, but she must've had one."

"Just saying her name to a customer service person might get a reaction. Blithe made quite an impression on folks. I'll know when I've found the right service."

"Sounds like a lot of work with little return."

"If I discover someone who hates Blithe, that person will have a strong motive to kill her. The cops will have to investigate, and then they'll leave Gerard, Sage, and me alone."

"Forget Blithe." He reached for me. "We have better things to discover."

Chapter Twenty

A rmed with righteous fervor, I called rideshare companies later that afternoon. It was impossible to connect with a real live person on the apps, so I had to make two lists: one of companies who answered the phone and another of companies I couldn't reach. An hour in, my head began to pound. After two hours of getting nowhere, I considered moving to Florida with Auntie O.

Then a miracle happened. An actual person answered at the Sand Gnat Express. I gave my name and explained I was helping a friend trace Blithe McAdam's last steps.

"She was our customer," the woman began, her tone guarded, "but unless it is a police matter, we don't share that information with anyone."

This must be the right service. I couldn't stay seated a second longer. I rose and paced the Great Room of our apartment. "Please. Something was different those last few days. Ms. McAdam wasn't herself. She blamed others for things that weren't their fault. She might have inadvertently upset the wrong person."

"You sound like a nice person, Ms. Winslow, and I know your aunt, Oralee. Her candles helped me through a rough patch in my life. This is off the record, and I'll deny our conversation if anyone asks. Ms. McAdam had run-ins with one of our drivers, and he's no longer with the company."

My intuition pinged. "Thank you so much. My aunt and I appreciate this small confidence. Please, if you could share the man's name, I'd be ever so grateful."

The line quieted until I could hear my own heartbeat. I wasn't sure if anyone was listening, except the connection remained open. My teeth clamped together. Just when I thought I should hang up, a whisper trickled across the line, followed by the disconnect sound.

I hurried to the table to write the name down before I forgot it: Luis Chickillo.

I checked the phone book. He wasn't listed. Anyone in the rideshare business had a mobile phone anyway. I ran his name and *Savannah* through an internet search engine, and one of those cellular directory sites came up with his number, if I'd only pay for it. What the heck, I thought, shelling out the fee. Seconds later I had the driver's mobile number.

When I dialed the number, it dumped my call into voicemail. I left a message asking him to return my call. Since it was my night to make supper, I pulled fresh veggies out of the fridge, to cook with pasta for dinner.

After chopping onions, celery, spinach, carrots, and broccoli and tossing them into a heated wok, I started the pasta water. Sage liked pasta cooked in chicken broth, but I'd forgotten to buy broth.

Once all was ready, I sat at the kitchen counter and called the animal pound. After someone answered, I asked, "I wondered if Blithe McAdam's tiny dog ended up at the pound. Blithe passed away recently, and no one knows what happened to her pet."

"What does it look like?" the woman asked.

"Boo Boo is a small dog with white fur and uppity ears, big bulging eyes, and very short hair. Blithe carried him in a tote bag."

"Sounds like a chihuahua. How long has the dog been missing?"

"Blithe died last week."

"Let me check."

The on-hold music consisted of multiple infomercials about pet care, pet vaccines, and the benefit of spaying and neutering. My eyes glazed over before the woman returned.

"Sorry to take so long. No white chihuahuas in residence, and none were recently adopted or fostered out. However, we have several of that breed are available for adoption if you're interested."

Not what I wanted to hear. "I'll think about it. Thanks."

Okay, so Blithe's dog wasn't at the pound. Possible options included the killer taking it, a concerned person rescuing the dog from the street and keeping it, or an unfortunate accident for the little dog. Of those choices, I hoped someone nice had taken him home.

To recap what I knew about our suspects and the investigation: The dog was missing, possibly left through Blithe's open front door. Her neighbor Eileen had discovered Blithe's body. The city alderman had been stalked by the victim, she'd made his professional life a living hell, and yet he had been a frequent guest in her home. Her relationship with her half brother, Jurrell, was fraught with arguments about money. Blithe's rideshare driver, Luis Chickillo, lost his job over a run-in with her. Last, Gerard's calling Blithe a witch in a viral video wasn't doing him any favors.

Harley sauntered over, meowing loudly. I checked that his bowl was full of food and freshened his water. I'd already cleaned the litter box this morning. That left affection. I scooped him into my arms and was rewarded with a contented purring sound. Despite my lack of progress on solving Blithe's murder, I felt better. Trust this kitty to know I needed comfort.

Sage came up from the shop, inhaled my veggie parmesan, muttered that she hated customers, and declared she needed a nap. Soon, I found myself alone again. If I called Quig, he'd think I was truly into him since we'd lunched together and *more* earlier today.

Restless, I dusted the apartment, wondering if I'd still be here and alone in fifty years. When I thought of the years spent concealing my not-so-normal qualities, it dawned on me that my future seemed less bright. Maybe Sage was right. I was grown up now. I had control of all my emotions and urges. There was no reason to believe I'd max out my abilities in self-defense again.

Night passed, morning came, and I sat at the kitchen table again, coffee mug in hand. It was my day to help in the shop, though Gerard would be the main staff person. With luck I could emote good intentions into a new batch of candles.

Or so I thought until loud pounding sounded at my door. I hurried to see who stood on the alley stairs and groaned. Not my lucky day after all. What did Detectives Nowry and Belfor want with me?

Chapter Twenty-One

I opened the door, heart in my throat. "Yes?"

"We'd like a word with you, Miss Winslow," Detective Nowry said.

My guard went up immediately. I did not invite them inside. "What's this about?"

"May we come in?"

I stood my ground, even though I was still in my nightgown. "After our last conversation, I am uncomfortable talking with you without my attorney present."

Detective Belfor groaned. "Told you this wouldn't work."

"We need to speak to you in private," Detective Nowry said. "We can do it here or at the station."

I didn't want to go to the station. "Talk. I'm listening."

"You sure you don't want to keep this private?"

"I'm sure I don't want you in my residence. Anyone in this alley is my neighbor or a city worker. I'm okay with them hearing whatever you have to say."

"So be it." Nowry tapped a notebook on his palm. "Do you know Ms. Roberta Green?"

"I don't recognize the name."

"She called to tell us you questioned her about one of her former rideshare drivers."

"I called many rideshare companies yesterday. No one I spoke to offered their names."

"Ms. Green owns Sand Gnat Express. She's afraid you might try to railroad a man who had a disagreement with Blithe McAdam. Specifically, Luis Chickillo."

I nodded. "I spoke with a woman at Sand Gnat Express, and she shared the man's name. So what? I called him once and left a message. That's all."

"You seem to think you're a cop. Why are you asking questions about our case?"

"I'm a concerned citizen. Y'all have a bead on Gerard, but Gerard isn't a danger to anyone. He wouldn't kill a flea."

Nowry growled. "How about a Sand Gnat? Luis Chickillo was badly beaten last night."

I gulped in air and clung to the door. Harley twined circles around my legs. "That's news to me." I reached down and scooped up Harley for comfort. "Gerard is not a violent man. He loves selling candles and lotions."

"Doesn't exclude violent tendencies. I've seen killers who loved their pets, for instance."

Since I was holding my pet, my cheeks stung at his words. "Are you implying I'm a killer?"

"We're fishing for answers, same as you. But we're trained in interrogation techniques and licensed to carry weapons. We've also been trained in pursuit and reading people. The bottom line is we're professional crime solvers—you are not. Your meddling could jeopardize our investigation. Stop, or we'll haul you into the interrogation room again. With your high-dollar lawyer."

Nothing helpful came to mind. I flashed a fake smile. "Have a nice day." With that, I closed the door firmly in their cop faces.

I turned around, and there stood Sage in shortie pajamas. "What was that?" she asked.

"The detectives complained about me asking questions."

"Tough for them. Last I checked this is a free country," Sage said. "You keep asking questions."

"I will because I don't want Gerard to go to prison. Somebody killed Blithe. We need to figure out who had the biggest motive. Yesterday, I located Luis Chickillo, a rideshare driver she probably got fired."

"Uh-oh," Sage said, directing me to the sofa. "I know that look."

"Several hours after his ex-boss shared his name, Luis got beaten up."

My twin shook her head. "They think *you* did that?"

"No, but I don't like the coincidence of what happened to Luis after I spoke with his boss, Ms. Roberta Green. She made a big deal of giving me his name, said she'd known Auntie O and that Auntie O had helped her. I don't see as how my call to his former employer got him beaten up."

"There are no coincidences." Sage chewed on her thumbnail for a moment. "Roberta Green. I know something about that name, only I can't call it to mind."

"While you're thinking on it, I have something else to confide. Yesterday, I spoke to Blithe's next door neighbor, Eileen Hutson. She discovered Blithe's body. I also learned Blithe's dog is missing. The neighbor said Blithe and her half brother often quarreled about money. Their loud voices traveled straight through the thin walls."

"My, you *have* been busy."

"There's more. Eileen stated Alderman Vernon frequently visited Blithe's condo. Even went so far as to say she thought they had an intimate relationship."

"Get out!" Sage drummed her fingers on the sofa. Both cats jumped up to investigate. "No wonder the cops are rattled. They realize you know what they know, only they must not know how to put the information together, or this case would be solved."

Harley wandered over and claimed my lap. "The information is solid, but each piece is an island. No bridges or causeways to connect them."

"What's our next move?"

"I'll visit the bar Vernon frequents, the Moonlight Fishing Hole. Thought I'd swing by this evening—after dinner, that is, if I'm not zonked from work. Thank goodness Gerard is back."

"You can say that again. Yesterday was busy-busy all day long. I prefer periods of solitude during the day. We need to move more product per hour and hire a second person. I hate being stuck on the sales floor by myself. One customer yesterday had strange energy. He seemed to feed off everyone's energy in the shop."

I had no trouble connecting what she implied. My hand stilled in Harley's fur. "An energy thief? In our shop?"

"Yeah. He would've thought he'd died and gone to heaven if you'd been there with all the positive energy you constantly radiate."

"Glad I wasn't present. Did you take his picture?"

"Tried to. He didn't show up on our security cameras either. He's got mega-talent to fuzz his appearance like that."

"Send him on his way if he comes in again. Moving on, let's coordinate our schedules. I'm in the shop with Gerard today. What are your plans?"

"I plan to ask Brindle for a favor. He can run Luis Chickillo through his system, find out if the man has a record, and discover his address. Then I'll meet you at the Moonlight during happy hour, say five thirty. Let's eat there as well. That way we'll catch the alderman if he arrives early or late."

"Good deal." I glanced at my watch. It was nearly time for the shop to open. "I need to get dressed and get downstairs."

"Me too!" Sage said. "Get dressed, that is, and I want to make sure what I wear gets Brindle's full attention."

I had a qualm, knowing Brindle might be playing the field. "Is your relationship with him serious?"

"No more serious than yours with Quig."

I jerked at her accusatory tone. Harley leapt off my lap, inadvertently clawing my thighs. "That's not fair! I've known Quig forever."

"The man has always been goo-goo eyes over you."

"You know?"

"Of course I know. I asked him to meet me for drinks a couple of times. He always begged off."

"Good." Oops, I hadn't meant to say that. "I mean having him and Brindle as special friends might be tough for you to balance."

"Nice try, but those dating attempts I made with Quig were a test. He passed with flying colors. Besides, your eyes sparkle when Quig's name is mentioned. Will you put the man out of his misery and date him?"

"Not possible for me to be more than friends with benefits with any man. Too much to hide. Besides, why risk losing a good friend?"

"Anything's possible. Depends how much energy you put into it. Try it, and if it doesn't work out, I still don't think Quig's going away."

"I'll keep things the way they are now. Friends with benefits suits me fine."

It occurred to me she'd used Quig as a distraction to keep me from realizing she hadn't said much about Brindle. "Nicely played, Sis. What's the real scoop with Brindle Platt?"

"Not a clue. We like each other well enough, but we each prefer independence to cohabitation. He likes to play the field, in any event."

She knew? Weird. "You're seeing him today, right?"

"Yes. So what?"

"Guys can take availability as exclusiveness. He might read more into this than you think."

Her aura pulsed with energy before she spoke. "Brindle and I have an adult understanding."

"You ever wonder why Dad left so quickly, and Auntie O never remarried?"

Sage shrugged. "Probably Mom and Auntie O were like us—too independent for their own good."

"Exactly. That's why I won't risk losing Quig."

Sage sighed out a long breath. "One of us has to reproduce, or the Winslow family line dies with us."

"Hadn't thought about that, but you should be our Mother Duck. You're more comfortable in your own skin."

"Good try. You have infinite patience and a guy that sticks to you no matter what. That's important for raising kids."

"Let's agree to disagree on this one."

Chapter
Twenty-Two

Right after I finished pouring aromatherapy candles that morning, Gerard called out from the shop, "Tabby, come here. You have to see this."

He sounded stressed, so I didn't even bother to remove my craft apron. The cats and I hurried to join him. "What is it?"

Gerard pointed to a commotion outside on our sidewalk. "That creep is trash-talking the shop and filming it. Probably streaming it online."

Though I didn't know the angry man personally, I recognized Jurrell Dawson from earlier hate videos he'd made about our business. "I'll ask him nicely to move, but let's be prudent. Please call the cops about a disturbance of the peace."

I folded my apron on the counter and hurried outside, and Jurrell immediately trained his cell phone camera on me. "Here's one of them now."

"One of what?" I asked, mashing a few buttons on my phone and videoing him.

"One of the lying, thieving, killing Winslows!" he shouted.

"Sir, please move along. You're creating a public disturbance," I said.

"It's a free country. You can't make me. Everyone deserves to know the truth about what happened to my sister."

Ignoring his incendiary remark, I zoomed in on his face, camera running. "The police will make you leave if you keep this up."

"You better not call the police if you know what's good for you," he growled, towering over me.

This man had a lot of nerve coming here and making these false accusations. I glared at him. "Sounds like a threat to me."

"It *is* a threat. You con artists peddle false hope in The Book and Candle Shop."

"We sell handmade personal care products, local crafts, aromatherapy candles, and books about Savannah. Your sister asked for and received a full refund when she was unhappy with one of our products. We also comped her a bottle of lotion and recommended she seek medical attention for her preexisting health issue."

"That's not what happened," he said. "You kept her money, made her headaches worse, and sent her home to die."

"I beg to differ, and there is a security video of what happened that day to corroborate my set of facts."

"Videos can be falsified."

His logic escaped me. "Then why are you out here making a ruckus and shooting a video?"

"I want proof in case anything bad happens to me."

"Like what? Like if the cops think you harmed your sister? I heard you two were closer than you claimed and that you argued all the time. You're her family, so you probably inherited her estate. I bet you took the dog too. Sounds like a motive to me."

"Stay out of my business. You don't know what you're talking about. First, I'd never take that rat dog. Second, she has no estate. Her will donated every penny to charity. Good thing, too, because she was about to be foreclosed on. She's broke. Ran through the family money ages ago. If it weren't for me 'loaning' her money every week, she'd have starved."

Two facts seemed obvious. The white chihuahua was still missing, and Jurrell Dawson got gypped on the inheritance.

"I'm glad you helped her," I said, meaning it. "Those headaches made her miserable."

"Don't tell me you liked dear old Sis."

"We were acquaintances, same relationship as I have with our other repeat customers. She regularly bought products from us that she did not return."

"That's not how I heard it."

"I'm speaking the truth. Everything I've said has been true."

"Bull. You're making this up for the camera."

My ears picked up the wail of an approaching siren. "I don't want the situation to escalate. Go home while you can."

"No way. Close this store, close this store," he chanted. A few others took up the refrain.

I edged toward the shop's front door and kept videoing. The blue emergency lights on the approaching vehicle were visible to me because of the direction I faced. I took a deep breath as Jurrell continued chanting and drowning out the sirens.

Suddenly he stopped. Listened. His face turned red, and he glowered at me. "You shouldn't have done that."

"I didn't do anything except shoot my own video of the spectacle you are making."

He lunged for my phone, and I retreated into my shop's doorway. "Not so fast, Jurrell. It's not only my camera you have to confiscate. Look how many other people taped you. Perhaps they're even livestreaming you to their social media platforms. You can't deny you are here slinging false accusations and inciting civil unrest. Too many witnesses."

At that, he grabbed my phone arm. Self-preservation overrode the safety blocks I'd erected after my accident. I aimed a pulse of current directly through the skin contact and twisted loose. The blast didn't faze him.

He snarled and came at me again. Quickly I tucked the phone in my bra and used both hands to block his advance. In self-defense, I shocked him again through every point of contact. He shrieked and sank to the sidewalk. "What did you do to me?"

Nowry and Belfor raced up the sidewalk. "What's going on here?"

"She's trying to kill me," Jurrell managed before he passed out.

The detectives looked at me. "What happened, Ms. Winslow?" Belfor demanded.

"Jurrell Dawson stood outside The Book and Candle Shop shouting slanderous remarks about our business that are lies. I came out and asked him to leave. He refused and chanted, 'Close this store' repeatedly. I have proof because I taped him on my phone. When he heard the sirens approaching, he attacked me, lost his balance, and fell."

Nowry called EMS and checked the man's pulse. Jurrell's chest rose and fell, so he was alive. Besides, it would've felt different if I'd maxed out the connection. Been there, done that.

"I'd like to see your video," Nowry said, extending his hand.

As Nowry watched the video, Belfor made her way through the crowd, collecting names and addresses of witnesses. For the few who'd witnessed the entire event, she took a complete statement and copied their videos in her police car.

I turned to go inside the shop, but Detective Nowry had other ideas. "Stay put."

Once the ambulance hauled Jurrell Dawson away, the crowd dissipated. Finally Detective Nowry reached the end of my video. "Okay. It happened as you said. He made a nuisance of himself, you asked him to leave, then he assaulted you. He'll be written up for disturbing the peace, and assault."

"Good. I want to file a restraining order against him."

"Probably wise at this point. The man is fixated on you. You must come to the station for the restraining order. You can ride with us."

Sounded like I didn't need a lawyer for that, and the offer for a ride sweetened the pot, as I no longer owned a car. I drew in a shaky breath. "Okay."

His eyes drilled into mine once I was seated in his vehicle. "While you're there, we'll talk more about this sham investigation you're conducting."

Chapter Twenty-Three

The interview room felt smaller this time, and it smelled grody, like a locker room. Obviously, they needed the healthful benefits of my aromatherapy candles. "I can explain."

"Your type always has explanations," Nowry said from across the table.

Despite my intention to cooperate, his comment rankled. "My *type*?"

"Yeah. You nosy parkers who think you can do police work because you've watched a TV show. Police work is not for amateurs. This is an ongoing investigation, and your questioning might cause a witness to change their story. What training do you have for interrogation?"

At least he was complaining about my snooping and not my energy takedown of Jurrell. I cut him some slack for that. "None."

"You have no business questioning my witnesses. Blithe McAdam's neighbor told me you spoke with her."

"About Blithe's dog—did she mention that part?"

"What dog?" Belfor came away from guarding the door and stopped behind her partner.

"Her white chihuahua named Boo Boo. It's missing. I called the pound and checked with her neighbor. I was concerned about the missing animal. Since when is that a crime?"

"How odd," Belfor stated. "No evidence of a dog in that place. No food or bowls."

"Probably smelled rank, though. I can't believe Blithe was with it enough to care consistently for her pet."

"There was a foul odor in the condo, but we didn't associate it with a pet."

Nowry swiveled his neck, like a camel, to glare at his partner before glaring at me. "If you had concerns about the missing animal, why not call us?"

"Every time I see you, it's unpleasant. You make me feel small and insignificant. You treat me like I'm guilty of a crime. If you want people to share information with you, consider polishing your manners."

"Can't catch crooks with manners. Police officers have to be tough."

"They can have compassion too. Years ago, I was assaulted in front of that store. Today a man attacked my business reputation and my body. In return, you insisted I come to the station and file paperwork, leaving my store short staffed and wasting my time."

"You don't want to press charges against him?"

"I do. I want to file that restraining order against Jurrell Dawson, so why put me in this sweat box? You dumped me in here to intimidate me."

"I don't like lippy females," Nowry said, "but you're not wrong. A lot of things don't fit in this McAdam case, and you and your shop are two of them. Didn't the wave of being a hippie pass about fifty years ago?"

"I'm not a hippie. I am a reputable businesswoman with an eye on the bottom line. We sell personal care products in our shop, same as any drug store or grocery store."

A knock sounded at the door. Belfor answered it. My new lawyer pushed his way inside. "Ms. Winslow, is there a problem here?"

Belfor grinned and raised her hands in surrender mode. "No problem, sir, none at all. Your client just gave us a verbal scolding."

Herbert R. Ellis set his briefcase on the table and leaned down to me. "Are you all right?"

His spearmint-scented breath was oddly comforting. "Yes. I came here to give a statement after being assaulted and to file an order of protection. Instead, I got grilled because I asked a neighbor about Blithe McAdam's missing dog, a pet these detectives didn't know existed."

"There you have it, detectives," Mr. Ellis said, towering over the lot of us, something of a miracle for a man my height. "My client is guilty of loving animals. She's here to fill out your paperwork, and then she's going home. Badgering her must cease immediately, or I will take it up with your superiors."

Nowry stood next to Belfor, and so I stood too. "While we're at it," my lawyer said in a honeyed tone, "I insist on concluding her visit in a better location."

Nowry nodded to Belfor. "Put them in the conference room and stay with them. I'll get the forms."

After Nowry trundled off, Belfor led us to a brighter, bigger room in the opposite direction. "You two made my day," Belfor said, gesturing for us to take our seats.

"How so?" Mr. Ellis asked, sitting directly across from her.

Belfor returned my cell phone. "It's not often someone calls us on our crap. Well played."

"Detective Nowry wasn't happy about it," I said, sitting beside my attorney.

Belfor shrugged. "Nowry is old school. That says it all."

Mr. Ellis fiddled with his briefcase, adjusted his glasses. Sure seemed like he was nervous about something. That didn't bode well for me.

"Everything else okay?" he asked Belfor.

Her eyes grew round, but she held her composure and said, "Everything is fine. Very fine."

Reading between the lines, Mr. Ellis had a thing for Belfor, and it appeared mutual. Hopefully, that might work in my favor.

Forms in hand, Nowry returned, stewing under a cloud of dark energy. I was glad he mumbled something about Belfor having babysitting duty and then left.

I wrote the statement of my interaction with Jurrell Dawson. Mr. Ellis filled out the restraining order against Dawson. We handed the completed paperwork to Detective Belfor and walked out of the building.

"How'd you know to come?" I asked him.

"Your shop guy called Quig, who called me in turn. You should've asked for me first, before they put you in their car."

"I thought I could handle it. They said it was about filling out the restraining order on Jurrell Dawson. Once I agreed and sat in their car, they changed the plan."

"Cops don't like to be shown up. Leave the investigation to them."

"Can't do that. They think my shop clerk committed murder because someone planted the baseball bat in our back room. You suggested earlier that the bat wasn't in plain sight, so they couldn't use it, and now it seems like they're not talking to anyone else about the case. Gerard can't go to prison for a crime he didn't commit."

"If your guy never touched the bat, it is merely circumstantial evidence."

"None of us touched it. We didn't even know it was there. Blithe's still dead, and her dog is missing. Doesn't seem like we've come very far at all."

"Canvas area veterinarians. Perhaps someone brought in a similar dog."

How curious. He was now urging me to continue asking questions. "Wouldn't that be police work?"

"Perhaps, but Nowry won't bother with a dog lead." His phone pinged, and he checked the display. "I'd offer to run you home, but I'm waiting on Sharmila."

"Who?"

"Detective Belfor. We're, uh, seeing each other socially."

A smile filled my face. "Good for you. I'll call a rideshare company for a lift."

He nodded to the man striding our way. "Never mind about that. Your ride is here."

Quig to the rescue. Wow. What were the odds?

Chapter
Twenty-Four

"There you are," Quig said, joining me outside the municipal building. He nodded to my lawyer. "Thanks, Herbert."

"Always glad to help out," Herbert R. Ellis said. A black sports-car pulled up to the curb and honked. "There's my ride. Catch you two later."

"I did not know they were a couple," I said to Quig as Mr. Ellis hurried off to join Detective Belfor.

"It's new for them, but they at least admit there's an attraction."

My back teeth clamped together at his droll tone. Trust Quig to use their relationship to pressure me about ours. I took a deep breath and remembered my manners. "First, thank you for calling Mr. Ellis. Everything changed for the better once he arrived."

"Herbert has that effect on people."

Much as I appreciated the lawyer's skill, his unknown fee worried me. "I don't know how much I owe him. All of my inheritance is tied up in the shop."

Quig's fingers closed over mine. "He'll be reasonable about it, or he'll answer to me."

Big bad Quig, taking care of me again. I could either be annoyed or be thankful for his protective instincts. Emotion welled inside as I squeezed his fingers in return. "Glad you're here. Can you give a gal a lift home?"

"Perhaps, if she'll do me the honor of sharing a pizza. Picked it up once I knew about your situation."

I couldn't miss the desire blazing in his brown eyes. Though I was tired, that smoldering look revved me up. If I went with him, we'd do more than share a meal. Turns out I was fine with that. "Sure. I'll text my sister and Gerard, so they won't worry."

He whisked me toward his Hummer. "Do that on the way. I've been sitting in pizza-flavored air for nearly an hour, and I'm starved."

We got belted in, and I appreciated what he meant about the aroma of his vehicle. Before I could mention it, he leaned over and drew me in for a kiss. "I'm not much on public displays of affection, but I can't wait a second longer."

When he finished, he studied me with narrowed eyes. "Something is different about you."

I was shielded again, but I hadn't had time to fully recharge after zapping Jurrell Dawson with an energy spear. Is that what he was noticing? Too bad I couldn't ask him directly. "It's exhausting to be in that hot seat. If you hadn't sent Mr. Ellis over, I'd still be inside. Once I eat and rest, I'll be good as new."

He looked like he might challenge me on that, but he held his peace and rolled out of the lot. It wasn't possible he detected my low energy level, was it? Otherwise, what did he mean about something being different?

The mystery of Quig was something to ponder another time. I texted Gerard and Sage that I was with Quig and would return later in the afternoon. I got a smiley face emoji in return from Gerard and *Again?* from Sage. What did she have against him? Maybe Quig knew.

"Did you cross swords with Sage?" I asked.

"Not that I know of, but your twin is always very protective of you."

That news caused me to blink. Sure, Sage, had looked out for me after The Incident, but had she always been running interference for me? I needed more information, and perhaps it was time to set some boundaries with her. I wasn't a complete weakling. "Did she say something to you?"

"Didn't have to. She glares every time she sees me. Always has. I don't take it personally."

"That's kind of you. I didn't know she did that. I'll speak to her about it."

He gave a low laugh. "Don't give her a hard time. She read me like a book from the start. I've always wanted to be with you."

"You are a good friend," I said to him. "The best."

"Remember that. I am positive your twin sister is irritated with me. She resents us spending so much time together."

I shifted uneasily in my leather seat. There was only so much I could tell Quig without risking our family secret. "My sister isn't my keeper. I'll remind her of that."

"Obviously, she thinks I'm a bad influence. I've never been one before, so let me know if I'm doing it right."

"I enjoy our time together—actually, more than enjoy—but I'm not ready to label it, and I'm grateful for the rescue just now. Those cops look at me like I'm a serial killer."

As he slowed for a horse-drawn carriage full of tourists, Quig laughed. The noise sounded so rusty, at first I didn't recognize it.

I smiled at his enjoyment. It was nice to see him loosen up too. When he quieted, I asked, "What's so funny about that?"

"Cops view everyone that way. It's their stock in trade. The scarier they appear and the more they grill someone, the more likely they are to get a confession."

"I don't want anything to do with them. Their aggressive manner in those tight quarters gives me nightmares. It would kill me if they put me in jail."

"We'll make sure it doesn't happen," Quig said as we stopped at the next light. "I want you to have a long and happy life."

"Shouldn't you be doing the Vulcan salute with that?" I made the iconic V-shaped sign with my right hand and said the appropriate words. "You know, 'Live long and—'"

"Yeah, I know." Quig cut me short with a smile of his own, his eyebrows waggling. He flashed the same sign back at me. "You're a Trekkie? How did I not know that about you?"

"Fun. I didn't know you were a fan either. Good intel for binge-TV nights. Especially fun for me because Sage is not a fan, and it's always a skirmish what we watch on TV at home."

"I was so glued to those shows! My folks thought I might hit the road for Hollywood and try out for the show. I would've been the first Quigsly in generations who wasn't a medical examiner."

"You love your job."

"I do. But if I'd found a way to be on the show, I might have chunked financial stability for fleeting glory. Besides, now I have another way to rile your sister."

"Be careful. Sage is a powder keg if she's pushed too far."

"She's your sister. Of course, I'll be careful."

We were almost back to his apartment, which was two doors down from my shop, when I noticed "For Sale" signs in two other shops on the block. "That's odd. I don't remember seeing those signs before. Wonder why they're selling out."

"Seems like there's a turnover on our entire street lately. Hard to believe the wine shop and the drug store are calling it quits. Thought sure they'd have to carry old man Kane out of here under protest, but he was the first to bow out."

"Sage and I aren't going anywhere," I said.

"Understood." His gaze swept my length. "Neither am I."

I stretched and gloried in the freedom to do so without feeling like a felon under a cop microscope. My stomach rumbled. "I am so hungry I could eat a horse."

"You'll have to settle for pizza," he said, turning off the motor. "And me."

Chapter
Twenty-Five

Later, I propped up on an elbow and asked Quig, "Who do you think killed Blithe McAdam?"

He mirrored my position. "The cops have a few suspects. I know you and Sage didn't do it."

Afternoon sunshine filtered through the curtains, giving his bedroom a golden hue. "How are you certain of our innocence?"

"Sage would've done something way over the top. She's never done anything in a small way. As for you, you're an innocent."

"I agree with your assessment of Sage, but not with your assessment of me."

The smile on his lips widened into a grin. "You're not innocent? You're a serial killer?'

"I've got mileage like everyone else, as well as moments when I haven't been kind. To misquote former president Jimmy Carter, I may have lusted in my heart for beautiful men."

"Long as you don't sleep with them, I have no problem. Beauty should be admired."

Oh. Was he changing our friends-with-benefits agreement? His comment might indicate a relationship shift. I needed to know. "To clarify, you want us to be exclusive?"

His eyes drilled into mine. "It's that way for me. I don't want to be with anyone but you. I've known that for a very long time. I take you very seriously, Tabby Winslow."

On the one hand his announcement thrilled me, but the parade of women through this place belied his earnest words. "Not buying that. I can name at least ten women you've dated in recent years."

"You noticed?"

"Of course I noticed. I live two doors down from you."

"Didn't think about our proximity that way, but those women meant nothing. Merely diversions until you were ready."

My hackles rose. "Really? How is now different from last month or last year?"

"My apologies. Poor word choice. I meant to say you're more receptive to spending time with me now. We're doing more things together. That sort of thing."

"We shared a bomb threat, a few lunches, and my cookies."

His voice roughened. "I especially love your cookies."

He loved my cookies? I glanced over, and he was doing his best not to burst out laughing. Another interpretation of cookies, one that was more risqué, came to mind. I pounded him with my pillow.

The pillow flew out of my hand, and he drew me close. "Exclusive, right?"

The tremor in his voice indicated how important this was to him. My heart quickened. I had to be honest with him. "Sure, but I reserve the right to change my mind."

His dark gaze sharpened. "Fair enough, but I intend to be very persuasive about being number one in your life."

* * *

"You done playing house with Quig?" Sage asked when I came home for a shower before returning to the shop.

"What do you have against him?" I asked, pausing outside my bedroom door.

"He's a playboy. I don't want you to get hurt."

I waved off her concern, needing my sister to understand I had this. "We talked about his dating history. That's all in the past. Quig wants us to be exclusive. I agreed but am now having second thoughts. Exclusive sounds permanent, as in set in stone like the Nathanael Greene monument in Johnson Square."

Sage gave a cautionary nod. "More like semipermanent. Brindle and I are exclusive as of last night, but the relationship doesn't necessarily have to end at the altar, for me or you."

"I'm taking it a day at a time. This is my first serious relationship. Everyone else lost interest right away."

"Probably because your good buddy Quig *talked* with them."

The implications shook me. Not only did Sage try to run my love life, but Quig too? It didn't jive with what I knew about him. "Why would you say that? Look, I appreciate your concern, but I'm a grown woman, same as you. Cut Quig some slack. He's really into me, and I enjoy his company."

Sage glared at me. "He's always been into you. He can't keep his eyes off you, and the rest of us cease to exist. It's creepy."

Was she jealous that I had a boyfriend? I wouldn't let her sabotage our relationship. "I have no misgivings about safety around Quig. I always feel safe around him. I don't know where you get *creepy*."

"Watch your step around him. He's not like us, and if you enter a long-term relationship with him, you can never tell him about our energy manipulation abilities."

"I know the rules. He is out of that need-to-know loop. Moving on to another topic, I'm grabbing a quick shower before I return to the shop to help Gerard."

"Suit yourself. I'm headed down to River Street to barhop."

As I bathed and dressed, I considered the powerful connection I shared with my twin. We didn't need to be touching to share energy, though it helped. What would it be like to share my life with Quig but always have to keep a big part of me hidden? I couldn't quite get there in my head. Now that I was focused on the present and the future, a stunning realization occurred: Sage and I shared a symbiosis, a need for each other's energy that necessitated nearness.

Even if we paired off with romantic partners, would that someone want to share a household with the other sibling or another couple? Was that why Mom and Auntie O had lived together? Was that why our aunt had drifted away after Mom died? She'd had no anchor in Savannah?

For that matter, if one energetic was an anchor, was Sage the anchor or was I? She drew from my energy at times, but I also drew from hers. As a family we'd never talked about the mechanics of our talents, but I would like to understand this better.

Back downstairs, Gerard was thrilled to see me. "Been busy since you left with the cops. People want to see what all the buzz is about here, and then I use my sales superpower to sell them candles, books about Savannah, and lotions. I sold four copies of Mary Kay Andrews's *Savannah Blues* today. If they're hesitant about the candle purchase, I hit them with a second round of logic that the candles are safety items and should be kept on hand for power outages and hurricanes."

Car traffic on Bristol Street had slowed to the rush-hour crawl. I set my phone and keys by the register. "Good selling point about the safety feature. I'll start using that when I cover the shop alone."

"I'm really glad to see you. I need to use the facilities and run across to Southern Tea for caffeine and a treat. My lunch sandwich wore off hours ago. Haven't had a break in foot traffic all day. It's been great for our bottom line, but exhausting."

I used my extra senses to study Gerard. He looked worn out, as in way beyond tired. I hoped Sage hadn't been down here siphoning energy from him while I was gone. "Scoot on over there, and take your time. I've got this."

"Thanks. Looks like you've had a fine afternoon."

My cheeks always pinkened with exercise. Guess I was still flushed. "After being *invited* downtown with the detectives and stuck in interrogation, Quig helped lighten my mood once I broke free of the cops."

"Lucky dog." Gerard looked away fast and sported pink cheeks himself. "Not about the cop stuff, but the afterward part. Is Jurrell Dawson locked up?"

Hearing that man's name made my fingers curl into fists. "Don't know and don't care. I filed a restraining order against him. Call the cops if you so much as see him walking past our shop."

Gerard nodded. "Got it. I wish this whole murder case would go away. I lie awake at night wondering if I will survive in prison."

"You won't go to prison. Sage and I will find Blithe's killer. Meanwhile, recharge at Southern Tea. Sit down and rest for a spell. I'm sorry you got stuck holding the fort alone today. These are strange times, for sure."

We did a dosey-do maneuver to circle each other behind the counter. Once Gerard stood on the other side, he heaved a sigh of relief. "Sometimes I have the nagging sense I'm meant to be elsewhere, but other times I'm reminded of how much I love this place. Today, I realized I enjoy it more when you're here. Your personality fills the shop and gets me going. When you're not here, I tire easily."

"Thanks." I blinked at the odd compliment as he departed. Could Gerard subliminally be affected by my positive energy field? Even when I blocked the more powerful and potentially lethal outgoing currents, I radiated positive baseline currents to center myself, and it seemed, others benefited as well. Odd that my natural emanations had had no effect on Jurrell Dawson.

Shoppers passed through our doors, some buying, some looking. When I noticed our popular products needed restocking, I brought out more guidebooks, lotions, candles, and lip balms, humming silently as I worked.

Sage would make dinner tonight, so after work I could rest briefly before our sleuthing began. Gerard's freedom hinged on us finding hidden connections, and I couldn't truly relax until his name was cleared.

My cell phone pinged to announce an incoming text message, so I grabbed the empty product boxes and carted them to the back room. Then I checked the text message from Quig. The ride-share driver Blithe McAdam had gotten fired had caught a DUI in Columbus, Georgia, all the way across the state from Savannah. *Luis Chickillo, what are you doing in Columbus?* I thought.

Quig's next message asked, *Are you coming over tonight?*

I'd already spent two hours with Quig today, and the time had passed without any notice of seconds, minutes, or hours. I wasn't sure how that time warp had happened, and now time crawled at a caterpillar's pace. This afternoon I'd checked the time left until closing, at least six times already. Besides, Sage and I had plans tonight to visit the Moonlight Fishing Hole to learn more about our alderman suspect.

I responded with a simple phrase: *Sister night.*

"You're killing me," he replied. "I want to see you again."

Getting to be a greedy Gus? is what immediately came to mind. Instead, I quickly sent back, *I'll see you in my dreams.*

The reply box stayed empty for a long moment. Then his cryptic answer appeared: *That* can be arranged.

Setting down the phone and returning to the showroom, I noticed my customers were gathered at the storefront, gazing through the ferns across the street. Much to my dismay, two cop cars and an ambulance were parked in front of Southern Tea Shop.

Uh-oh. New trouble on Bristol Street.

Chapter Twenty-Six

I edged close behind my shoppers gazing through the storefront window. "What happened?"

A blue-haired SCAD student with a pink backpack gave me the scoop. "The cops arrived a few moments ago, no sirens or nothin', and then a few minutes later, the ambulance came. Nobody's come in or gone out since EMS arrived."

"Gerard's over there," I said to no one in particular. "I hope he's okay."

My instinct was to race across the street and check. With customers in the shop, I couldn't do that. Instead, I grabbed my phone and texted Gerard. He didn't reply.

A sense of doom closed in on me. Gerard was in trouble. He needed me. "Okay, everybody out. I need to check on my staff person across the street, and that means I have to lock the door."

"Not so fast." A young woman handed me the small shopping basket she held. "I'm not leaving without these."

A distinguished man held up his finds. "Me neither."

"Okay. New plan. I'll check out whoever is ready now, but I need to get over there right away. Everyone else please vacate the shop."

"I'll check on Gerard for you," Blue Hair said. "If they won't let me in, I can at least get a visual through the glass. I'll be right back."

Some of the tension eased in my chest. "Thank you."

I hurried through the checkout procedures. No chatting up the customers with how great their selections were. I wanted them out of here. After the female customer was on her way, I started scanning the male's items. His steady perusal made me anxious.

"You look familiar. Do I know you?" I asked.

"I'm a local." He handed me his credit card. "Nice place here."

"Thanks." I did a double-take on the name imprinted on the card. Barrett Brendon Cranford. Also known throughout Savannah as BB Cranford, the power partner of the law firm Cranford, Aldrich, and Platt. The senior partner of the firm I used.

Heat seared my cheeks. "Thought I recognized you, Mr. Cranford," I said. "You look just like your portrait in your firm's lobby."

His eyes twinkled. "They say a picture is worth a thousand words. I'm not one for putting my mug on billboards, but my ex-wife convinced me to sit for that portrait. She said it made a statement."

I returned his card with the receipt. "She's right. It's nice to put a face with a name."

"Indeed." He collected his bagged items and departed.

Finally, I had the place to myself.

Pocketing my cell phone and grabbing the keys, I trotted across the shop and flipped the sign to "Closed." I was locking the door when the blue-haired young woman and her friends joined me on the sidewalk.

"He's why the cops are there," the young woman said, her eyes round with fear. "The EMTs are bandaging his hand."

The keys slipped from my grip. "Oh, dear. That is bad news. Thank you for letting me know."

Blue Hair collected my keys and returned them. "Are you going over there?"

Determined, I nodded my intent, but part of me dreaded what I would find. The rest of me needed to dash across the street. Gerard and medical personnel were an oil and water combination.

"Mind if I come too? Gerard is a friend to everyone at our school, and he's helped me more times than I can count."

Gerard's generosity didn't surprise me. "Sure."

We jaywalked directly to the shop, not that traffic was moving on our street anyway. Detective Belfor guarded the door. When I tried to enter, she blocked me, saying, "We have to stop meeting like this."

"I'm here to check on my employee, Gerard Smith."

"Your clerk is refusing medical transport."

Glancing over her shoulder, I saw Gerard with two EMTs. He looked my way and nodded, his expression grim. Two patrol officers were talking to the handful of customers sitting at the tables. At the counter, Detective Nowry had a red-faced Tansie Fuller in cuffs, her hands behind her back. He was in her face, and his angry voice carried my way, full of threats about the penalty for assault with a weapon. Oh no. Sweet little Tansie?

What on earth? The solid concrete under my feet felt like shifting sand on a dune. I braced my knees and clung to the doorway. I reran what Belfor had said through my thoughts, thanking goodness for having a decent short-term memory: "If he refuses to go to the hospital, you can't make him."

Belfor flexed her fingers. "He needs a tetanus shot at a minimum. He should have X-rays or an MRI on that hand. No telling what got damaged when she stabbed him. Hands are tricky."

"I'll make sure that happens. He doesn't like hospitals or anyone in a white coat. Bad memories."

"Even so, he has to make a living. My brother let a hand injury go and waited too long for repairs. Men can be pigheaded about their health."

"At least it's his left hand. He's a righty. May I sit with him?"

The detective didn't budge. "He hasn't given his statement yet."

"He'll be more cooperative if he isn't nervous."

Her sharp gaze pinned me. "You stepping out on Quig?"

My turn to flush. Savannah was chock full of busybodies. I wasn't aware the detectives kept tabs on my extracurricular activities. However, I wanted something from her, so I had to give a little to get a little. "No way. Gerard is like a brother to me. Why are y'all here anyway? Shouldn't a patrol officer have caught this call?"

"We were in the area."

Blue Hair stirred at my shoulder. I had the distinct sense she intended to bolt inside the tea shop. I put a hand on her arm to make sure she didn't do that. Took me a moment to place the sound she made on contact—a soft growl. I shot her a quelling look before turning back to Sharmila Belfor.

"Look, I don't know what happened. I wasn't here, therefore I can't influence his story. He's been through a traumatic experience. What's the harm in letting me sit with him?"

She didn't react for the longest time. "Just you, and no talking. One word and you're out the door."

I nodded and released Blue Hair's arm. "Thanks." Before she changed her mind, I slipped past her and hurried to Gerard's side. His expression brightened. While I had his attention, I made a motion like I was zipping my lips. He nodded his understanding as I sat with him. When I reached for his good hand, he clung to me.

The bandage around his left hand resembled a miniature hornet's nest. He rested the hand on a completely cleared café table, bloodstains marring the tablecloth. There were no obvious explanations as to what had happened in the tea shop.

With the café lights on at a hundred percent, the brightly colored décor seemed garish. The eclectic vibe had been replaced with an edgy silence and a burnt odor.

Tansie's face looked ghostly white as she yelled at me, "Stop asking questions, Tabby Winslow. You're stirring everything up. My boyfriend won't like it."

If I responded, likely I would be asked to leave. It wasn't easy, but I held my peace as promised.

My silence must've irritated Tansie, because she kicked a chair with all her might. It clattered to the floor. She cried out in frustration and then began screaming. The cops hustled her out of there, and I could hear myself think again.

Tansie had issues, especially if she was back with Macon, but no one else was stabbing people with a fork. I had little sympathy for her arrest. She'd injured my friend. I didn't take kindly to that. Once he recovered from her attack, I'd see about upending her little red wagon.

Slipping into my other-vision, Gerard's energy looked thinner and paler than usual, though his steady-eddy core remined rock solid. Compassion hummed in my veins. I wanted to know every detail of what had happened, but I kept my promise of silence.

The EMTs and cops had forms for Gerard to complete, and they copied his driver's license. While Gerard wrote with his right hand, he moved his right leg so it touched mine to maintain contact. It felt nice to offer him moral and physical support. Being so close, our energy fields overlapped, so he reaped the added benefit of a quick recharge of his aural field.

Once Gerard finished the forms, everyone was herded outside. The detectives locked the door with Tansie's keys. At least they didn't wrap crime scene tape around everything. The shop owner would be able to open tomorrow without losing an entire day of income.

Blue Hair and her friends rushed up to hug Gerard. The ambulance and the cop cars rolled out, and we civilians were blessedly alone.

I turned to Gerard. "I want to know everything."

Chapter Twenty-Seven

"I've always felt comfortable in the tea shop," Gerard said in a drama-laden tone, "and I adore their coffee. But the vibe felt wrong as soon as I stepped through the doorway."

"What do you mean?" I asked as I shepherded our small group across the street and into The Book and Candle Shop. I'd hoped the students would go away, but they latched onto us. When Gerard felt better, I'd ask him about this hero worship.

"Our place always feels so chill, and that's why everyone loves coming here." He paused and glanced at the art students. They nodded in agreement. "Other places are less chill, but not bad, if you know what I mean. The tea shop felt like a choppy ocean when I entered today. I almost turned around and left, but I really needed a break from working, so I approached the counter."

When he stopped speaking, I nearly tipped forward into the air space between us. "And?" I prompted.

A gotcha look came and went in Gerard's eyes. "Before I could order, Tansie told me we had to stop asking questions about Blithe. She blamed us for the cops coming to her place and upsetting her boyfriend. I swear on my life that she was red in the face and crying. Her raw emotion felt surreal because that woman is usually unflappable."

Another theatrical pause. This time I didn't bite.

"You can't stop there," Blue Hair said. "What happened next?"

He looked more cheerful, and appreciative of his audience. "I said I wasn't asking questions, yadda-yadda. She said Tabby was, and that was the same thing. I said no, it wasn't. Then I ordered an entire box of sweet rolls and coffee. I paid and carried my order over to the table I like in the corner. I wasn't there five minutes before she ran over with a big bacon-turning fork and stabbed my hand. She told me to stay away. I tried to leave, but she'd pinned my hand to the table. It really hurt. Someone called the cops, and one of the cooks from the kitchen came out and drew Tansie away."

Tansie's action was so out of character. "A fork? She stuck a fork through your hand?"

He raised his bandaged hand. "Here's the proof. Pretty sure my stabbed hand is making the rounds on social media."

I rubbed my temples, willing the gathering tension to ebb away like the tide. "I'm stunned."

"I'll fork her hand if you want me to." Blue Hair glanced at her friends. "We all would, and it would serve her right."

Gerard started to speak, and I shook my head and said, "Wait. Nobody should *fork* anyone. That's a criminal offense. You do not want a criminal record." I rewound that in my head and groaned at the way I'd phrased that request. "What I meant to say is young adults like yourselves have bright futures. Don't do something impulsive that impacts your chance at freedom and happiness."

"He's our friend," Blue Hair pointed out. "We look out for our friends."

"Tansie now has a criminal record to match her boyfriend's, and we don't know what she damaged inside Gerard's hand. That incident will impact the rest of her life and his. Her action was ugly and outright mean. Consequently, she was arrested, and she will be punished for it. The cops will handle this. Whatever she hoped to gain, the reverse is happening. A whole pile of bad karma will rain down on her. You don't want that for yourselves."

Blue Hair pursed her lips as if she expected bad news. "Who's Blithe?"

"The woman from my viral video," Gerard said.

"The witch you expelled from here?"

Gerard nodded, then caught my negative head waggle. He sighed. "The customer who took advantage of Tabby and Sage's big hearts. She was murdered. The cops think I did it because of that video, so my advice is to not do anything dumb in real life or on film because it hurt more to sit in that interview room for hours than it did for my hand to get stabbed."

The students looked anxiously at his bandaged hand. "Can I see it?" Blue Hair asked.

I shook my head. "No. The wound was cleaned and bandaged by a health professional. Now, everyone knows what happened. Gerard is clearly well enough to walk across the street, so he will recover. You guys have a few minutes alone with him while I see if my sister is upstairs. I need her to watch the shop while I take Gerard for a tetanus shot."

"We can watch the shop," Blue Hair said.

"Thank you, but no. You aren't on our payroll or insurance policy." Gerard, for all his bluster earlier, looked a little green around the gills. I'd grab a soda upstairs to increase his blood sugar. "Sit. I'll be right back."

.

I rushed upstairs, hoping against hope Sage would be there. No such luck. I called her phone. No answer. I left her a voicemail message about the emergency and my need to take Gerard to see a doctor. And I closed with "Sorry, I can't do the bar thing tonight as I don't know how long it will take for Gerard to get the medical attention he needs. Let's do a raincheck for the Moonlight Fishing Hole."

The cats followed me back downstairs, Harley leaping on the counter and Luna seeking a cozy chair in the sun. I called for a ride, and one popped up immediately. "Everyone out," I said to the students, and they left. When I offered Gerard the soda, he refused it. I said, "Did the EMTs give you anything for pain?"

"No. I refused meds because it didn't hurt. Starting to throb now."

"We're going to the nearest clinic." A small blue sedan pulled up in front of the store, and a text message appeared on my phone. "That's our ride."

After a ten-minute ride across town, we arrived at a walk-in clinic. Five people were already waiting. "Just great," Gerard muttered as we entered the lobby. "There goes the rest of my day."

I signed him in and followed him to a seat. "We're making sure it doesn't ruin the rest of your life. It's a matter of perspective."

"I don't like shots," Gerard said.

"Who does? Far as I'm concerned, injections rank right up there with the most embarrassing aspects of a yearly physical. We're being adults about this."

"Easy for you to say. You weren't stabbed."

"Give it a rest. I know it hurts, but at least you won't take a big financial hit. This medical appointment will cost less than an ER visit."

"No more sympathy?"

"I'm sorry you got stabbed, but there's a silver lining. This shows we're on the right track with our questioning. Now we know the cops are checking other suspects. Tansie has something to hide. My guess is it's about her boyfriend. If the police haven't found it, I will."

Chapter Twenty-Eight

The next day dawned dark and edgy, with lightning pops and jarring thunder. People who lived near water knew the sound of thunder carried a long way over open spaces, but the frequent bursts of lightning, as well as the cats huddling together, told me the storm hovered on top of us.

We were overdue for rain, so I shouldn't complain, but the turbulent weather brought barometric pressure changes and ignited the mother of all headaches. Sage swore I got headaches because I went around with my extra senses blocked. It was an unnatural state of mind for energetics. She, of course, had no such issue with the barometer and danced around the apartment, though, out of respect for my pounding head, she didn't blast her music today.

I wanted to rail against the fates that brought headaches to my world, but I took a pragmatic approach and downed over-the-counter meds. My doctor had offered a prescription medicine to stop headaches instead of treating the symptoms, but I'd declined. Besides, we were watching expenses right now, and specialty medicine was pricey. The cost of the over-the-counter meds fit my budget better.

Sage still worked one weekday at the nursery, to supplement her income and keep her car. I'd sold my car and now used a ride-share app for my errands. So far, I'd netted over three hundred dollars a month of money I would've ordinarily shelled out in car payments, plus I no longer needed gasoline, car insurance, car maintenance, or license plates.

It was a nuisance having to call a ride whenever I needed to go places, but I hated living with only pennies in my bank account a lot more. I'd saved the overage each month in a rainy-day fund.

Given the pounding rain, I hoped I wouldn't need that money today.

"What are you so jazzed about this morning?" I asked my twin over morning coffee in the kitchen. "You've got the shop today."

"No, I don't. Remember? We scheduled this swap weeks ago. I'm the acting manager at the nursery today. The boss is away, and I get to do everything I love in the place I love."

Her words caught me by surprise. I suddenly felt as low as a snake for needing to keep the shop going. "You don't love working in The Book and Candle Shop?" I managed to say.

She shrugged. "Not my first choice, or even my second. I do it because the shop would fail without both of us, and then we'd lose our home too. I love living here. These walls have good energy. For energetics like us, home is more than where the heart is. Home is where the latent currents don't give you fits. Something isn't quite right energy-wise over at Brindle's place, but there really isn't enough privacy here for either one of us to bring our boyfriends home for the night."

Her words made me reel. I knew she loved working with plants and that growing things satisfied her. To hear the shop didn't rank high in her priorities concerned me. Was I trapping her here with my desire to keep the family business afloat? We needed to discuss our dreams and goals. I could live and work in this space for the rest of my life and be as happy as a clam in soft mud.

I was so busy thinking about being a clam, I nearly missed what she said about bringing our boyfriends home for overnights. That thought sputtered in my head and died like a spent candle. I needed to respond, but what could I say?

The truth. "I never considered bringing Quig here, but if you invite Brindle for sleepovers, that's fine with me."

"No, it won't work with you here. Not enough privacy. I've thought about this a great deal and have been waiting for the right moment to bring it up. Even though I doubted Quig's motivations about dating you, I now believe he's good for you. With that said, the best thing to upgrade our personal space is for you to move in with him."

Her sudden reversal on Quig perversely made me dig in my heels. "Think again. Quig would smother me with orders. Plus, my cat lives here."

"Details that can be ironed out." Sage waved off my excuses and chugged her coffee. "You have no energy issues at his place, right?"

"That's right." Answering her question felt like I'd stepped into an alligator's mouth. I didn't like where this conversation was headed.

"Then that's what needs to happen long term. I can tolerate Brindle's place for a few hours. I need to live here to feel my best. The apartment I moved to for college wasn't good. I smudged my place and thought positively. I burned our aromatherapy candles. Nothing helped fix that space. I'm not moving out of here again. At first I thought it was Mom's good energy that made this place hum, but now I'm not so sure. Something about this apartment—"

"And Quig's place," I interrupted.

"About both places being right for energetics."

"Could be the building materials," I offered.

"Maybe these old bricks reinforce good energy, but most likely the source is underneath the building. Regardless, if we lose the business, they'll have to pry me out of here with a crowbar. I must live here. It nurtures everything that is right in me. That's why it makes perfect sense for you to move in with Quig. His place shares the same geography and natural energy field."

"Quig is fun, sexy, and kind, but I'm not head over heels in love with him. I'm not voluntarily leaving either. I didn't sleep well in the college dorm, and I was relieved to come home and get a decent night's sleep again. On the meager salary we pay ourselves, I can't afford to move out, and unlike you, I can't manage a second job with the load I have in the shop. Bring Brindle over for the night. Doesn't bother me as long as you keep the sex in your room."

Sage scowled. "It's not my preference, but it's better than nothing. I don't want you to be smothered by Quig. I would hate that for anyone."

"Sounds like a temporary work-around. We'll figure it out. Meanwhile, I'd forgotten about taking your day at the shop, but I don't have other plans—other than figuring out who killed Blithe. So I can do it."

"Good. You create amazing candles and soaps for the shop today. I'll reign supreme over at All Good Things Nursery and Landscaping. We'll recharge our creative sides. Never fear, we'll address our housing issue another day. And look—the sky is clearing."

With that Sage bopped off, happy as a songbird. It was nice to hear the smile in her voice again. I needed to face facts. The shop was right for me, but not for Sage. She needed to work with plants. If we didn't employ Gerard, we could draw higher salaries from the shop. Bad idea. Without Gerard, the shop income would plummet, and I'd work every day. Worse, neither Sage nor I had Gerard's keen talent for sales.

Being around Gerard centered me in some way. Odd that I'd never realized that before. I sat at the table, lost in thought.

How was it possible to have synergy with people like Gerard and Quig who weren't energetics? The longer Sage and I ran the business, the more I believed Mom and Aunt Oralee had purposefully withheld additional information from us.

For starters, the shop's physical inventory remained in line with what they'd stocked, but I couldn't remember my mom or aunt ever worrying about money. That led me to infer they'd had a hidden income stream.

I needed to call Auntie O again.

Chapter
Twenty-Nine

When Gerard arrived for work, dripping rain from his coat and ball cap, I was already in the stillroom, working on a website order of bridesmaid candle favors. He gawked and then grinned at me. "Thought Sage worked today."

I cut the heat to my wax melting pan and gave him my full attention. "This is her day, but she is the crew boss over at the nursery today. Plants are truly her passion."

Gerard chewed his thoughts for a long moment. "Is she quitting the shop?"

"Not if she wants this roof over her head, and I heard her say as recently as this morning that she never planned to move from our apartment."

"Never is a long time."

I couldn't read his expression, but his pinched tone troubled me. "Is something wrong, Gerard? Would you rather Sage be here today?"

"No, uh, don't tell your sister, but I prefer working with you. For some reason, I physically feel better when you're around. Sage and I get along fine, but I'm exhausted after a Sage day.

I'm relieved to see you. It means I won't have to fight supersonic fatigue tonight."

I understood better than he knew. Sage's icer vibe drained him throughout the day. I'd speak to Sage about her blatant thievery. Gerard had suffered enough for his transgressions against her. "I'm glad you enjoy my company, because I have the same companionship vibe when I work with you."

His eyes flared with hope. "You feel the sympatico too?"

"I do, and I'm glad we're friends."

The light dimmed in his eyes. "Only friends?"

Being firm about our platonic friendship always made me feel like I'd kicked a puppy. Even so, I wanted him to view our friendship as a bonus in the workplace. "Yes. We work well together. Time flies when you're here."

"Me too. I mean, I feel that way too. I've never experienced that at any other job."

My curiosity pinged. We'd inherited Gerard from my mom and aunt. However, by then we knew about his talent for salesmanship, so we kept him on staff. "We never talked about jobs you did before you came to The Book and Candle Shop. What kind of work did you do?"

"Didn't like college. Pizza delivery was my first job, but that lasted a summer. Then I worked in a big box hardware store for a while, but selling tools wasn't for me. I traveled overseas and did pickup work over there and in the U.S. when I returned. My job at the organic food market is where I met your aunt. She suggested I visit this shop. I didn't know anything about candles, soaps, and lotions, but the moment I walked in here, I felt like I'd come home. Your aunt hired me on the spot. I took the job and never looked back."

"I'm glad you accepted the post. You have a flair for welcoming customers, encouraging them to browse, and making the right suggestions."

He gazed out the rain-soaked window. "Sometimes I feel like I'm meant to walk another path, but I love being here. These customers respond to me. They see me."

"We hope you don't leave us for another job."

"I'm not leaving—not unless I go to prison for a murder I didn't commit."

I wished I had answers for him. "We'll figure out who killed Blithe McAdam. Don't worry about that." It was appalling to realize how little I knew about his family. "What did your parents say about your meandering work history? My mom would've jumped all over me if I'd done that."

"My dad's never been in the picture. My mom died when I was eight, then my grandmother raised me." He glanced away for a moment, sighed, then looked my way again, barely meeting my gaze. "I should've mentioned this before. Your aunt and my grandmother are friends. They've known each other for years."

I backed into the counter. "She knew you before you worked here?"

"She knew MawMaw took me in. By the time I lived with my grandmother, she had retired from working for the McAdam family. She told me some things that went on there. Because of that information, I made allowances for Blithe's ugly ways until her rudeness overwhelmed my compassion. That last time she came in, I lost it. I still felt sorry for her damaged inner child, but she'd had years to get her act together. The world didn't owe her a thing. MawMaw says everybody's got to make their own way in this life, but Blithe wallowed in a mudhole of her own making."

An idea surfaced, and I seized it. "I would love to meet Maw-Maw. She might know Blithe's enemies. Her insight could help us figure out who killed Blithe."

Gerard took his time answering. "We live together, but don't get your hopes up. My grandmother's memory is failing. Time is fluid for her, and often she lives in the past. When the cops took me, and you came over to check where I was, I'd already called my cousin to get MawMaw. That's why you didn't meet her then."

My jaw dropped at the load he carried. I moved closer and placed my hand on his arm. "I had no idea you were dealing with eldercare. Why didn't you tell us?"

"I don't want to lose my job. The money's good here, and a cousin brings MawMaw lunch every day. People in my family have trouble keeping jobs, and our couch stays full of relatives. It works out. So far, MawMaw hasn't wandered off or had personality changes. We take each day as it comes."

A sound philosophy. Guilt assailed me because I'd given him so much responsibility at the shop. Then reality clanged in my ear. Gerard chose to work here. This wasn't hard manual labor per se, especially for someone with his superpower for sales.

Even so, the man was always on duty. On his weekends off, he was a caregiver 24/7. "Who stayed with your grandmother when you spent the night in jail?"

"I called my cousin Promise to take MawMaw to her house that night."

"What about the night you stayed here?"

"My cousin John Paul was couch-surfing with us. He cared for MawMaw." His sigh carried the weight of the world. "Don't judge, okay? I needed someone to take care of me for a change. The vibe upstairs is great. *You're* great."

"Not judging. We all need to feel cared for and loved."

"Thanks. I appreciate that. Sometimes I get overwhelmed and feel lost, you know?"

"Yes. I've had those feelings." Just about every day. What did that say about me? Did I need to get out more? I shook my head to clear it. "What afternoon is best to visit MawMaw?"

"None. If you want to see her, come over before work one day. Give me a heads-up so we're dressed to receive company."

"Let's plan for nine tomorrow, if that's convenient. It always helps to have more information."

"Will do." A knock sounded at the front door, and Gerard's face lit up. "We have customers!" He trotted to the door and welcomed the ladies by name. I didn't have a clue who they were and liked it that way.

To each his own, I thought as I infused candles with good intentions while Sage immersed herself in plants at the nursery, and Gerard cooed over his customers. He kept a steady stream of conversation going all morning, and the front door kept opening and closing despite the morning rain.

I'd shelved the candle wax and scents and cleaned the workspace when a sharp rap sounded at the back door. Just as I reached the door, a key turned in the lock, and the door opened.

Auntie O had returned.

Chapter Thirty

"Land sakes, Orlando traffic is terrible," Auntie O said as she swept me in her arms. "Thought my bus would never get out of there."

I grinned at her wrinkled clothes, askew hat, and untied sneaker. Auntie O had never been one for making a fashion statement. She was in her sixties, petite, and slender. More than once she'd been mistaken as our mom. "It's great to see you. Is everything okay?"

She released me from the hug and cast a curious eye about the stillroom, her eyes settling on the candles I'd made. She sniffed in the scented air of the robin's egg–blue room, and the tension in her shoulders visibly eased. "Yes, I'm fine. I needed to come home and get my bearings for a bit. You kids keeping the bills paid?"

"So far, so good." I glanced outside, grabbed her stacked suitcases, and shut the door. "Gerard is worth his weight in gold. We move three times more product during the weekdays when he's here compared to the weekends when we have higher tourist foot traffic."

"I knew he'd be a gem from the moment I saw him. Glad he's working out for you. I was somewhat worried when he was so taken with you girls. Thought your sister would run him off, for sure."

"He's part of our team. Let's get your bags upstairs. You can have my room, and I'll take the sofa."

She gazed around the stillroom as if storing the sight up for years to come. "Nonsense. Keep your room. That apartment belongs to you girls now, and you need privacy. I'll bunk in here."

Her comment puzzled me. There was nothing soft in this room of business. "How?"

"Lock that door, will you?" Auntie O said, pointing to the shop threshold.

Intrigued, I did as she asked. In a room chock full of shelves and cabinets, one wall was blank. I'd never given that a single thought until Auntie O touched a panel on the solid wall. A slender cedar-lined empty closet opened in the space between our shop and the next. A stack of linens and pillows filled the top shelf.

I couldn't have been more surprised if a shark swam into the room and chomped on my leg. "Has that always been there?"

"Sure." Auntie O laughed. Then, seeing my face, her voice tightened. "Did you think I conjured it up?"

Knowing our family had been called witches in the past and how that label offended us, I hastened to explain. "Quite the contrary—I'm blown away. I never knew this was here."

"Brace yourself. There's more." She touched a higher place on the wall beside the closet. A Murphy bed folded down with creaks and squeaks.

"Wow. This was here all along too?"

She lowered herself on the mattress and cooed with pleasure. "Yep. We replaced the mattress a few years back, but this room was always good for overflows." She glanced at me sheepishly. "I'm the overflow now. Sorry for catching you off guard like this. Thought I'd manage well enough in Florida, but now I'm second-guessing my decision to relocate."

Worst-case scenarios ran rampant in my mind. Did she have cancer? "Is something wrong?"

"I'm wrong in Florida. This murder of Blithe McAdam is wrong. You kids need help."

Boy, did we ever. "We don't know who killed her. However, I just learned Gerard's grandmother worked for Blithe's family. I plan to visit her tomorrow morning."

Auntie O nodded. "Give Mary Maureen my regards."

"You two are close friends?"

"Something like that."

"Do you know things about the McAdam family?"

"More than I realize, I'm sure, but not nearly enough." She wiggled back some more on the bed and put her feet up. "I need a nap after all that road vibration. Would you be a dear and help me with those pillows and linens? I'll come upstairs in time to make dinner."

As we made the bed, I said, "Thanks for offering to cook, but we have a system for meals."

"Nonsense, I love to cook." She yawned and patted her pillow. "It's the least I can do. I should've come home sooner. Go on now, let an old lady rest her bones."

"All right." I gave her another hug. Thoughts of hidden spaces churned in my head. What else was hidden inside this building?

I wanted to tap every wall and see what popped out, but the customers in the shop and Gerard might think I was nuts.

Gerard was all eyes as I entered the shop. "I heard voices. Everything alright?"

I beamed at him. "More than okay. Auntie O is home for a visit, and she's resting from the trip."

"I've missed Oralee."

"She missed us too. We talked a bit about the case."

Before he turned back to me, he greeted a young lady who headed straight for our collection of books on Savannah. "I've never admitted this before, but sometimes I get the strangest sense we're—"

"We're what?"

"It feels strange to voice this feeling." He leaned closer and whispered, "That we're walking the same path as our ancestors."

"Huh." It was an unexpected and yet profound remark. I leaned close to his ear. "You think the McAdams, the Smiths, and the Winslows share a tangled history?"

"It's a definite maybe."

An older Asian woman wearing Key West colored knits and a sunset-inspired scarf hefted a basket of items onto the sales counter. "You two swapping secrets?"

"Always." Gerard laughed easily and reached for her basket. "Did you find everything you needed, Ms. Liu?"

"Yes. I came to shop for a niece's birthday and ended up with a basketful, as you can see."

Gerard cooed over her selections as he rang them up. I felt like a third wheel until the customer was out the door.

"Awesome job," I said. "And your memory for names is impressive."

Darkness stole across his face momentarily. "Usually. There are times I struggle for names. I always recognize faces, but lately I've wondered if my lapses are more than a long day. Maybe this is how MawMaw began forgetting."

"Everybody has forgetful moments. It goes with the aging territory." This twenty-something guy's memory lapses were normal, but I knew what it was like to get stuck on something in my thoughts. "I spent half an hour looking for my sunglasses the other day, only to find them atop my head."

He nodded. "I've done that before."

Now I worried about my memory. We needed a new topic. "I feel good about Auntie O's arrival. Perhaps she and MawMaw will kick this investigation into high gear."

"No telling what those two will do, but we need help. I need my life back." Gerard shuddered. "Keep Tansie Fuller away from me."

"Will do, though her violent streak surprised me. How's your hand today?"

He glanced at the bandaged hand. "Still tender, but she stabbed me with a meat fork."

"You take your antibiotics this morning?"

"Yes, Mom."

"Sorry." I waited until my cheeks cooled. "Solving a murder is challenging. Everyone has secrets. Blithe was rude and obnoxious, and I wish I'd truly found a way to help her."

"Don't go soft on me, Tabby. That woman used everyone. A long time ago she lied about something, and MawMaw got the blame."

"She was mean to MawMaw? Not cool. Any other thoughts about Blithe?"

"Maybe. Blithe 'saw' a young man once upon a time. She secretly met him at the square. Things did not go well for the boy."

"Who was he?"

Gerard sucked air through his teeth. "I never knew his name. But there's a chance MawMaw will."

"Let's hope so. We need a new lead to investigate."

Chapter Thirty-One

I stayed so busy with customers and the website order that I forgot to text Sage about Auntie O's return. When my sister came in the door of our apartment and saw the table set and pots on the stove, she glommed onto Auntie O like a sandspur.

"Oh, I have missed you," Sage said.

Auntie O's eyes twinkled. "It's good to be home."

Sage punched me in the shoulder. "Jerk. Why didn't you tell me? I would've left early."

"This was your big day of running the nursery," I said. "How'd that go?"

"Great." Her face brightened. "I potted seedlings. Everyone got along. Good energy hummed all day. Our sales soared after the rain stopped. Definitely a special day."

"So glad for you."

We spent the next half hour catching up and eating Auntie O's delicious veggies and cornbread. As we lingered over the empty dishes, my aunt said, "Tell me about Blithe McAdam."

Sage tipped her head toward me, so I shared what we knew with Auntie O, ending with "We don't know who killed Blithe.

We don't know how her murder weapon ended up in our still-room. It seems everyone on our suspect list has a motive, including Tansie Fuller, who stabbed Gerard with a fork, of all things."

"Stirring the pot makes the stew churn," Auntie O said cryptically as she finished her ginger tea. "We'll get Blithe sorted out. Now tell me about the boyfriends. Sage, you first."

Sage's mouth swung open, but words were slow to come. "Were you spying on us?"

"No need to spy with a blood connection."

"Explain," Sage demanded, leaning forward, urgency vibrating from her.

"If you insist, but I'm surprised you two don't do it. Marjoram and I got to where we communicated without words no matter how distant we were."

"What are you talking about?" I asked. "Are you a telepath?"

"Not exactly. This communication is an elemental connection. If something bad happened to either of you, I would know in the next heartbeat."

It took me a few moments to take in what she said. Auntie O and Mom shared an elemental link, which in turn connected Auntie O to our well-being. An *elemental* connection. I'd never heard of such a thing.

"I am reluctantly fascinated," Sage said. "While I don't want my privacy invaded, this sounds like a great skill set for safety reasons. How do we do it?"

"Land sakes, child. I can't teach you. It just *is*. Or isn't, as the case may be."

"I want to learn too," I chimed in. "What does it feel like?"

"Now you're asking the right question. It feels full. That's how I describe it. My energy has a certain signature I recognize, but I also recognize y'all's, too, because I shared that deep connection with my sister, your mother."

"Full?" Sage asked. "I have no idea what you mean."

Auntie O tsked. "I told Marjoram we should train you girls, but she said to let it be. No sense trying to force it if it wasn't there."

"Someone trained you?" I asked.

"Big Mama. She said the world was too harsh. She was right. But . . ."

"But what?" Sage insisted. "What aren't you telling us?"

Auntie O studied the shadowed window. "It changes you. Your mother, bless her heart, never wanted it forced on you. She never had a choice. Once I was in her head, I was never out, and vice versa. Our connection came at a high cost. Your father never understood, and he resented our closeness."

I thought about my precious moments with Quig. Sage must've had similar thoughts about intimacy, because our gaze flitted to each other, then away. "I need to think about this," I said. "I am used to having privacy."

Realization dawned. Auntie O, without my permission, had shared my feelings and emotions already. That's how she knew about our boyfriends.

Auntie O snickered. "You think I don't know what sex is? If you want sexual relations in a senior community, it's easy to find. I don't purposefully eavesdrop on your lives. However, I felt and responded to your troubled vibes, because of my preexisting connection with your mother."

The air felt ripe, swampy even. While I couldn't fathom the full power of elemental connections, I cared deeply for my aunt. "Wow. I'll respond by starting at the end. We will always need you. Never question that. Most days neither Sage nor I want to be an adult for another second. As for our private lives, we are dating. My relationship with Quig is casual."

Auntie O's expression darkened at Quig's name. "That boy has wanted you his whole life. Don't trifle with him. Commit or walk away. I expect more from a Winslow than a casual fling."

Her setdown wounded my pride. I wanted to seep through the floorboards and hide under the building for twenty years, because she made me stare into the mental fog I used to disguise my feelings for Quig. My fingernails dug into my palms. I nodded.

Auntie O confronted Sage next. "What's your story, young lady?"

Sage fiddled with her silverware. "I'm seeing Brindle Platt, our attorney. He asked me to move in with him. I can't, of course." Sage glared at Aunt Oralee. "We need answers to so many things. For instance, how does this residence make me feel whole?"

"Lots of secrets buried in this town. Some need to stay buried. Marjoram and I had the same observation about the healthful benefits of living here. I can't explain it. Somehow our family landed on Bristol Street, and it's perfect for us."

"What if the shop fails and we lose everything?" Sage asked.

"That's why I came home, to make sure that doesn't happen," Auntie O said. "I've had a long day and need a good night's sleep. Everyone has enough to consider tonight."

When our aunt left, Sage and I circled each other like trapped animals. "Screw this," Sage said. "I'm going to Brindle's place."

"Wait." I grabbed her arm. "You're stealing Gerard's energy every time you work together. It has to stop."

She wrenched free, her gaze fierce. "Why should I? He hurt me. This is payback."

"You are rude to him most of the time. Forgive him and move on."

"You don't get it. Only two types of people in this world. Predators and prey. I'm a predator. He took from me. That's unacceptable."

Her words chilled me. Good chance my twin would have no qualms about totally draining Gerard. How had we come to this bend in the road? "Get over yourself. It's been two years since y'all tried the couple dance. He knows working with you exhausts him. Did you forget we need him? His sales ability allows us to keep our home. Never forget how important that is. Did you know he's taking care of his live-in grandmother with memory problems? Your petty revenge will wreck two families. Top off your energy elsewhere, or we'll all be looking for homes and jobs."

My twin stuck out her tongue and darted to her room. I heard her in there briefly, then her room went silent. She must've escaped through the window again.

I flopped on my bed with thoughts churning. It would be a long night.

Chapter
Thirty-Two

When I dragged myself out of bed the next morning, Auntie O had coffee, tea, and fresh muffins made, and she was fully dressed in bright splashy colors, her shirt half tucked. In my gym shorts and old T-shirt, I felt woefully underdressed. I mumbled thanks as I caffeinated and ate.

"I'd ask if you slept good, but it's written all over your face that you didn't," Auntie O said. "Where's your twin? She needs to eat more. She's too thin."

I shrugged. "At Brindle's."

Auntie O smiled brightly. "Can't beat pheromones, that's for darned sure."

Pheromones. A biology class word. Hormonally based chemical attractants released into the air. "Hers or his?"

"Um."

Auntie O bustled around the kitchen, wiping everything down, and her energy bathed me in serenity. I fought the urge to dwell in that maternal space and stood. "It feels so nice when you're here, but you're a guest. Let me do that. Sage and I can manage meals."

She stood firm, her gaze narrowing. "Both of you are running on fumes, and you know it. I'm happy to cook meals and tend you girls for a spell. Once everyone is back to par, we'll reassess who does what."

I recognized *The Look* and knew it was important to her that she contributed. "Thanks for your help. I need a quick shower, then I'm headed over to meet Gerard's MawMaw."

"Yes," Auntie O said, draping the dishcloth over the sink divider. "I'm coming too. I'll wait for you downstairs."

Given that she was already dressed, I hurried and was downstairs in fifteen minutes. "Where's your car?" my aunt asked.

"Sold it. I get around town cheaper with a ride-hailing app. That eliminated car payments, repairs, and insurance."

"What a coincidence. I had the same blinding insight about my vehicle, hence the bus ride here."

"Sage has a car, and I'm sure she drove over to Brindle's last night. I'll call us a ride."

"Times are a-changin', aren't they?"

For some reason, her remark tickled my funny bone. "Not fast enough it seems. While we're waiting, I'll download a local ride-share app to your phone."

Auntie O followed me through the shop and out the front door while we awaited our ride on the sidewalk. In minutes we were underway. "Lordy, these familiar sights are welcome to my tired eyes," she said. "Riding around town feels special. Oh, how I've missed Savannah. Seems like I've been gone for years."

"Mm-hm." I said, not wanting to converse about anything meaningful in front of our driver. I glanced out the window with interest, hoping I'd never move from Savannah or Bristol Street. These streets and squares were encoded in my DNA, or so it seemed.

One day, I'd learn more family history from my aunt, but now wasn't the time. I hoped against hope Gerard's grandmother could help us.

Gerard and MawMaw lived in a house on the west side of town, I remembered. Everything looked comfortably suburban, with tidy yards and trimmed hedges. I'd worn khakis and a white blouse, the perfect bland foil to Auntie O's canary-hued plumage and cockeyed hat.

Unbeknownst to me, Auntie O had packed muffins in her tote and presented them to MawMaw who exclaimed over the muffins and her long-lost friend. Gerard ushered us inside with a huge grin on his face.

*   *   *

Soon we four sat around a cozy table in their sunny kitchen, the air redolent with coffee and laughter. After the elders swapped stories and wound down a bit, I cleared my throat. "Ms. Smith, I hope you don't mind if I ask you a few questions."

"Gracious gal, I love questions among friends, and call me MawMaw or Mary Maureen, like everyone else."

"Yes, ma'am." I took a deep breath. "As you know, the police found Blithe McAdam's murder weapon in our shop. None of us killed Blithe, but the cops zeroed in on Gerard. My sister and I are trying to clear his name. Do you remember anyone who hated Blithe enough to kill her?"

"Well, now, about time somebody asked what *I* thought," MawMaw said, stacking one palm atop the other on the table. "I don't hold no truck with people takin' advantage of others. Those McAdams did that. They took and took from everyone, and that's no secret."

I nodded in encouragement. "Gerard mentioned you worked for the family."

"That I did, for twenty-six years. They turned me off with no warnin'. Just one day I was shown the back door. I know a lot about that family, and I don't owe them two seconds' worth of loyalty for the way they dumped me. Livin' on one of the squares and descendin' from an Old Savannah family gave them airs. Nothin' they did seemed wrong to them. Not nothin'. I don't even remember all the people they got crossways with. But for sure, Blithe's dad and Harmon Dawson got into it."

"Jurrell's dad?" I asked. "Didn't think they ran in the same crowd."

"Harmon is his so-called father. He didn't like Junior sniffin' 'round his gal," MawMaw corrected. "And there wasn't no runnin' involved when it came to personal matters like this. Moxley McAdam Jr. had a way about him that won him certain *favors* all over town. Junior charmed all the young ladies, black and white."

"Wait a minute," I said, reeling a bit at the news. "I've heard the rumors about Jurrell being of mixed race, but how do you know for sure, MawMaw?"

She beamed. "Lawsy, I just know. Trust me, the Dawson boy is a McAdam."

I believed her. Given her former employment in the McAdam household, she had a wealth of insider knowledge I needed to hear. "What else can you tell us about Blithe and her family?"

She exchanged a telling glance with Auntie O, and I groaned to myself. More secrets. This could take all day.

"People thought highly of them for years upon years, but reputations are like dandelion puffs. One good breeze and they're gone. See here, Moxley ran a shell game with his investment company, and it ruint him. Every dog in the fight jumped on the dogpile to bite him while he was down, once word got out."

"Anyone threaten him?" I held my breath as I waited for the answer.

"Plenty of folks, but those 'uns passed on. Some like our medical examiner are next generation, but Dr. Quigsly III never forgot Junior stole his thirty grand. If you want to find out who got that man fallin'-down drunk enough to fall off the pier and drown, turn your eye on the man's victims."

Quig's dad got taken? Didn't see that coming, nor did I suspect Moxley's accidental death was anything more than it seemed. How many people had he fleeced? "Is that widely known that he had help in getting dead?"

"Nope, and I will deny mentioning it if anyone asks. Not hard to do as my wits get scrambled every afternoon."

"I can help you with that," Auntie O said.

The women exchanged another meaningful glance. "Good to know," MawMaw said. "My, my, look at the time. I need to rest my eyes for a spell, and my grandson must go to work. Has two demandin' bosses, or so I hear."

"Gerard runs circles around us in the shop," I said, patting her hand. "We're glad he's with us."

"Expect he's glad to be there too. Now y'all move along so's I can rest and purge the McAdam ugliness from my head."

"One more thing. Earlier Gerard mentioned teenaged Blithe slipped out to meet a young man at Johnson Square. Who was he?"

MawMaw frowned. "A nobody according to her father. Moxley wouldn't let her date anyone with less than half a million in the bank. Blithe snuck out a few times anyway, but her father always caught her. The last time he threatened to turn her out on the street. Blithe caved."

"Thank you for sharing that." While it was disappointing to have a lead go belly up, I learned Blithe had feared her father. I dug my phone out of my purse. "I'll hail a ride now. Sorry if we stayed too long. It was a pleasure to meet you."

"You don't need a ride service. Gerard will take you." Maw-Maw turned to my aunt. "Oralee, I know you want to rest your eyes too."

My aunt covered her surprise with a fake yawn. "I sorely do."

Bottom line, Gerard and I were sent packing, and MawMaw and Oralee were up to their old tricks. In any event, we had a shop to open, and they were of an age to do whatever the heck they wanted.

"She'll take good care of MawMaw," I said after we got underway in his white Cabriolet.

"She'd better," Gerard said, accelerating onto the interstate ramp. "That woman means everything to me."

The sharp edge to his voice commanded my attention. Gerard's pleasant nature every day in the shop served as his personal shield. At-home Gerard showed his vulnerability. I respected his willing nature at work, and now I respected him even more for his depth of feeling for his grandmother.

Chapter
Thirty-Three

After we opened for the day, I checked upstairs, and Sage wasn't home yet for her shift in the shop. I puttered around the store with a duster, making sure The Book and Candle Shop looked its best for the day, while Gerard dealt with our early-bird customers. My thoughts shifted to linking the information I had learned to what I already knew about the McAdam family.

MawMaw said Blithe's dad, Moxley McAdam Jr., was a tomcat.

Jurrell Dawson was Moxley's son, and over the years there'd been rumors our city alderman, Rashad Vernon, might've had a different father. Since his mother had worked for Moxley's business, it seemed quite likely he fathered her child.

My musings kept getting interrupted as people streamed in the shop, chatting with Gerard, delighting over our tester samples. I headed to our book section and began wiping the books down. *"Dust is not our friend."* Funny, I could hear Mom saying those very words as she taught us to tend our wares. I missed her.

From early on, she'd coached us to be strong. As someone who was shunned by most kids and bullied by the rest, I'd decided long ago that if you weren't my family or Quig, I didn't trust you. Having that guideline made it easy for me to navigate the world.

Now, at thirty, I held a different perspective of the nature versus nurture discussion about someone's behavior. Regardless of family income level, most kids with caring parents turned out okay, while some kids with advantages went bad for no reason. Kids with poor to no parenting could go either way. Applying this to the certainty of Rashad Vernon's heritage, he'd navigated life fine with imperfect parenting.

On the other hand, Moxley Jr. helped himself to what he wanted, whenever he wanted. For two decades, his family's firm, McAdam Investments, had been a huge deal. After Moxley Jr. took the helm from the Old Man, he stole people's money all day, partied all night, and committed serial adultery whenever the itch struck. Then his pyramid schemes collapsed, and his clients raised sand at his thievery. A few days later, a drunken Moxley fell off the pier and drowned.

I finished dusting the books and moved on to the soaps, lotions, lip balms, and cleansers, stopping to fetch a shopping basket for a grateful customer with an armful of treasures. Gerard had chamber music playing softly in the background, and it focused my thoughts. Which in turn, fueled my need to understand the mysteries surrounding the McAdam descendants.

With Blithe's mother already dead and then Moxley's drowning, Blithe had no family left. In the end, her lawyer, Barrett Cranford, found the orphaned daughter a new condo on East Starling.

Blithe was even more alone after that. Thank goodness she had little Boo Boo to keep her company. In the span of a month, Blithe lost her home, her family, and her prestige. No wonder she suffered from debilitating headaches.

If Sage and I lost our home, we'd be devastated, in more ways than one. We'd inherited family traits from our parents, and we'd turned out to be talented energetics like them. By all accounts, Sage's math skills came from Dad, while her green thumb and cooking ease were from Mom. I'd gotten Dad's knack for sizing people up, his sense that everything had a place, and his chameleon-like ability to hide in plain sight. From Mom I'd inherited a stronger energy manipulation talent than I could handle, which, combined with Dad's contribution, landed me atop the energetic spectrum.

Nature and nurture determined who we Winslow twins became. What about Moxley McAdam's children? Who inherited his ruthless streak? Not Blithe. She'd been a hot mess of attitude and superiority. When her world fell apart, her days were numbered.

Moving on, her half brother Jurrell had no steady job and spent his days berating small businesses on his podcast. So, he'd either monetized his podcast or had a secret income stream. His blitz attacks were ruthless.

Eileen Hutson, Blithe's next door neighbor, claimed Jurrell and the alderman visited Blithe's condo often. That observation had initially led me to assume Rashad was Blithe's boyfriend, despite their divergent lifestyles. Now it was likely Rashad was her half brother. Given his accomplishments, he could be ruthless too.

Maybe Eileen heard more through her condo walls than she'd shared. I needed to talk to her again.

Sage entered the shop from the stillroom, fully dressed for the day in all black, her dark mood apparent in her body language and flashing aura. I walked over to her. "Morning," I said. "Are you all right?"

"I will be. Brindle and I had an argument," Sage said. "He is not a nice person."

"His career immerses him in dark energy. He doesn't always get to represent nice people like us, so it's natural for him to detox after work."

"He shouldn't do it on the nights I come over. It ruins our fun."

"Look, I'd made plans to do more investigating to clear Gerard today, but I can swap shifts with you if you need the day off."

"I'm sorely tempted, but I can work. I'll do our monthly inventory today. Any new information about what went down at Southern Tea Shop?"

"No, and it isn't safe to go over there." I stashed the duster and faced my twin. "Tansie blames us for keeping the investigation active. She was arrested and will be out on bail soon, if she isn't already."

"Aren't you curious why the waitress stabbed Gerard?"

My sister hadn't been interested in Gerard's troubles lately. Her renewed interest in one of our suspects made me cautious. "Not as much as you, apparently. What gives?"

"Tansie wouldn't hurt a fly. Someone riled her feathers to make her act out in such a way. My guess is her boyfriend. I hoped to ask Auntie O to fill in for me this afternoon while I investigated Tansie's home life, only Auntie O isn't here. Do you know where she is?"

I shot her a calculating look. "She's visiting an old friend, but I want to hear your plans."

With an eye to customers in the shop, I drew my sister to the stillroom, so we didn't have to whisper. "I'm questioning Blithe's neighbor again. I have new information to run past her."

"Be careful. Last night I had a revelation we needed to stay close. That you were inviting danger with this investigation."

"I can take care of myself."

"You could if you stopped blocking your energy talent. Until then, I'm very concerned. You're the only sibling I have, and there must be two Winslows for the shop to thrive. Accept who and what you are. Don't screw this up for us."

Her selfish line of reasoning whirled through me like a tornado. "I promised to find out who killed Blithe," I said through clenched teeth, "and I stand by my word."

"Brindle says they have a strong case against Gerard. He's going down. Why waste your time?"

I froze and then fury blazed through my body. "Gerard is not merely an employee, and you know it. I can't believe you'd turn your back on him after all you've done to him."

She looked at me through slitted eyes. "I just did."

"Forget it." I pushed away from her and stalked up the apartment steps, driven by indignation. Why couldn't Sage show some compassion? Was she hell-bent on warping me to be as unhappy as she was?

Chapter
Thirty-Four

Eileen Hutson answered her door with a puzzled expression.
"Yes?"

The deep raspy voice of Blithe's former neighbor again caught me by surprise. She sounded like she'd smoked two packs of cigarettes every day of her thirty-something years on the planet. The yummy scent of peaches and crème wafting out her doorway made my stomach rumble.

"I'm Tabby Winslow. I was here a few days ago, seeking information about your neighbor's dog. I brought a thank-you gift for your kindness." I gave her the handled bag of soaps and a small candle. "I hoped to ask a few more questions, if you have time."

"Thanks. I have a few minutes." The door closed, a chain jangled, and the door opened again. Eileen glanced at the cloudy sky with trepidation before stepping outside on the small slab stoop and closing the door behind her. She vibrated with tension as she tucked her hands under her barred arms. "What do you want to know?"

As tense as she was, I'd better start with something easy, or I'd be the only one standing on the cobblestone sidewalk. "Any word on what happens to Blithe's condo unit?"

"I assume it will be sold." Her fierce gaze relaxed. "The association is seeking her lawyer or next of kin. Last I heard no one knows if she even had a will."

"I believe she does as I heard her will donated everything to charity." Her next of kin was most likely her half brother, Jurrell Dawson, and possibly Rashad Vernon. There was a scritch-scritch-scritch sound coming from Eileen's condo. "Y'all might try BB Cranford for her lawyer. He was her father's business associate for many years."

"I'll pass that along. Thanks." She paused as a large truck rumbled past on East Starling Street. "Blithe's death caught us off guard. She was in her thirties, for Pete's sake." She met my gaze and then glanced away. "Rumor has it that two people were sneaking around the complex a few nights ago."

Couldn't have been us. Sage and I were so careful to avoid being seen. When Eileen didn't accuse me outright, I hurried to fill in the void of silence. "Gracious. That must be frightening. Is there a history of criminal activity in this neighborhood?"

"My next-door neighbor got murdered. That's a major crime."

"Point taken." She had me there. I nodded. "Moving on, last time we spoke, you mentioned that Jurrell Dawson and Alderman Rashad Vernon visited her and that Rashad argued with her loudly about money. Did you hear them talking about anything else?"

She sagged against the closed door. "He wanted her to donate to his campaign fund."

The scratching sound stopped. "He just got reelected. Was he scamming her?"

"She asked the same question. He said he sought financial backers all the time to have sufficient funding for the next election."

Sounded like a scam to me, but maybe that was how politicians rolled. I decided to come right out with what I really wanted to ask. "Did the alderman ever mention his father?"

"I don't recall. No, . . . that's not right. One time he said, 'The old man screwed me, and you have to make it right.'"

"How strange. Did Blithe respond?"

"She changed the subject to her favorite topic—her headaches." Eileen rubbed the back of her neck. "He didn't make much sense that night."

"How so?"

"Something about pictures. He'd be shouting, and then his voice would fade too soft to hear. It seemed strange to me that he talked to Blithe about his father. He's a grown man, an elected official. Why would he ask a woman in chronic pain for anything?"

If he and Blithe shared a dad, his mention of his father to Blithe made perfect sense. Her comment about pictures intrigued me. "Were the pictures incriminating? I could imagine a scenario where a politician did the wrong thing and paid blackmail to hush things up."

"Who knows? His speech kept slurring, like someone who's had too much to drink. It was hard to make out most of what he was saying. Clearly, he thought Blithe could fix his problem, but she couldn't even fix herself."

"I wish I knew what his issue was. It might be relevant to her murder."

"Murder." Eileen shuddered. "I am so screwed. Who's going to buy a murder condo? Only a whack job or a hit man would relish such bad mojo, and that will ruin our property values. Two neighbors are already talking to real estate agents."

I glanced at the unit beside Eileen's end condo. Blithe's place could be smudged to restore it. Cleansing with sage was a Native American ritual adopted by feng shui believers, New Agers, and others. We didn't sell sage at our shop, but it was available in Savannah. On the other hand, the stain of death was hard to remove from a place, no matter how hard you cleaned or prayed.

"Sorry about that, truly I am. I couldn't imagine moving from my home." A burst of yapping erupted inside Eileen's place, igniting a new question. "Did you get a dog?"

"Helping out a book club friend for a few days." Eileen placed one hand on the doorknob, her palm more than covering the knob. "I should go before he destroys my house. He ate one of my sneakers for breakfast. He's such a handful."

Nothing about her hand looked dainty. It looked sturdy, as if she could pound nails all day. "Thank you for your time, and if your book club ever needs a place to meet, I hope you'll consider The Book and Candle Shop."

"We will. Thanks for the gift and the conversation. It's nice to have someone to talk to. Not many people visit."

"You're not from here?"

"I needed a fresh start, and Savannah is where I landed." Her watch sounded an alarm. "Thanks again, and please excuse me. It's time for my medication."

After she closed the door, I heard her speaking in the soft voice people reserved for kids and puppies. She might be pet sitting for a friend, but she didn't sound upset with the dog who ate her shoe. Eileen seemed lonely, so I was glad she had the company of her friend's pet. I walked home, this time focusing on Eileen Hutson's past. People who needed a fresh start were running from something. I should search her history online.

* * *

I returned home at close of business to find my twin in a rage in the apartment.

"You have some nerve," she said. "This is all your fault."

"I have no idea what you're talking about."

"You knew I was upset, and you left me here anyway. With him."

That stopped me. Icy shards chilled my bones. "What happened to Gerard?"

"He kept annoying me that's what. I couldn't take it."

"What did you do, Sage?"

My twin glared at me, sending the intangible demand for energy. Her stormy mood and flaring emotions had me sealing my energy from her. "What did you do, Sage?" I repeated.

"I drained him, that's what." Her dark eyes flashed with challenge. "He started telling me what was best for the shop, and it isn't even his shop. It's ours. I had to put him in his place."

"Oh no. Did he drive home like that?"

"No. I left him on the floor down there like the rotten scum he is."

"You went too far." I hurried to the door, but an icy barrier stopped me from taking another step.

"You're going to help *him*, when I'm your flesh and blood, and *I* need your help?"

I whirled and glowered at her. "Grow up, Sage. You can't act like this. What you did is a crime. Gerard may be dead down there for all I know. Did you kill him?"

Sage blinked a few times. "I don't know. I don't care. I shouldn't have to put up with him."

My energy roiled so hard I felt like I would throw up. I was furious with my twin. So furious I wanted to blast that smile off her face, but first I had to check on our employee. "Remove the barrier, Sage, or I'll hit you with everything I've got."

"You wouldn't dare."

I hadn't been this aggravated in years, but I would've remembered having this much energy. My aural field pulsed and snapped with fury. "I would, and we'd both go to prison for killing someone. Everything we've worked for, our family worked for, will cease to exist. Stop what you're doing right now. It's self-centered and wrong."

The icy barrier flared, pushing into my personal space, then winked out of existence. I turned the lights on in the stairway and raced down to the shop. Gerard lay sprawled on the floor. I couldn't find his heartbeat at first. It was so faint. I focused good energy on his heart, willing it to beat with regularity and strength. I held Gerard's hand tightly and used my other hand to dash tears from my face.

"Come back to us, Gerard," I urged. "It's too soon for you to go. Wake up. You can do it. Forge a way through the fatigue."

"Why didn't he slink out of here with his tail between his legs?" Sage asked from the doorway.

"You went too far. Isn't it enough that you're messing with his head so often? Do you have to destroy his body too?"

"He's a cheater."

"Other boyfriends have been unfaithful to you. I don't see you attacking them. You move on. Your anger at him is way out of proportion."

"Those other guys weren't worth my time. He hurt me."

She quested for my energy again. I shook my head adamantly. "You can't have my energy. This innocent man needs every bit I can spare, and then some. If you were a decent person, you'd help me bring him back."

"Screw you both." Sage stormed up the stairs.

"You're a monster," I shouted at her.

Gerard's eyelids fluttered. I drew my attention back to him. "Keep coming, buddy. Come back to the living." I'd used up all my reserves. Cautiously, I kept a slow trickle charge going into him, knowing I would pay later for over-draining myself.

My neck ached with tension. My hands burned with spent energy. My knees throbbed from kneeling so long, but I kept the steady patter of soothing talk going, using every tool I had to revive him. Finally, he opened his eyes and stared at me with rapt fascination. "I love you, Tabby."

I was so relieved to hear his voice, I didn't snap at his false puppy love for me. "I like you, Gerard, but not as a boyfriend. As a very good friend. Welcome back."

"Rats. I can't tell you how many times I've longed to wake up holding your hand."

"How're you feeling?"

"Like a semitruck ran me over, but what else is new?"

"We need to get you home."

He frowned. "Not sure I can stand. I'm so tired. How'd I get on the floor anyway?"

Loyalty wouldn't let me reveal my twin's evil deed. "Sage said you collapsed. I came as soon as I could. If you're feeling that bad, I'll call 911."

"No need for that expense. If I can get up, I can get home."

"Tell you what. If you can get up, I'll drive you home."

"Deal."

Chapter
Thirty-Five

Auntie O was at Gerard's place when Gerard and I arrived. Turned out she'd cooked dinner for his family tonight. Once Gerard had a bite to eat, his color looked better, and he steadied on his feet. We got him and MawMaw settled for the night and took our leave in a rideshare car, keeping quiet until we reached our apartment. I nodded off on the way home.

"I want to hear everything," Auntie O said, fixing a pot of tea and setting out a plate of cookies.

A door opened and Sage joined us, her lower lip jutting out, her arms crossed, and her eyes still blazing fury. "What lies did you tell her, Tabby? Trying to win her over to your side same as you do everyone else? Aren't you tired of being Saint Tabby?"

I bit into a cookie. "I told her Gerard fainted at work. That's all. You have no reason to be mad at me. I spent the last two hours mopping up your mess. You know better than that. There's no excuse for what you did."

Sage crumbled and cried. And cried. I wouldn't go to her. Not yet. Auntie O gave me a disgusted cluck and drew Sage in her arms. "Now, now, dearie. It can't be that bad."

The story tumbled out of Sage. To hear her tell it, the entire world was conspiring against her. Then it was my turn, and I stated the cold hard facts of my sister draining our clerk to within an inch of his life. Auntie O kept glancing from one of us to the other.

"She called me a monster," Sage accused, coming away from Auntie O and leveling her finger at me.

I glared at her. "She nearly killed Gerard. Because he *annoyed* her."

"He wasn't that far gone. You woke him up."

"I used my reserves and more to save him. I could've died too."

Sage's lower lip trembled again, and she slouched and vamped around the room as if it were a staged death scene. "I am a monster." She railed a bit more before subsiding in a chair, cradling her head in her hands. "I'm so exhausted I can hardly think, but I'm sorry. I'm so sorry. I was selfish, but I couldn't stop myself. I don't know what came over me."

Auntie O took a chair and groaned from the effort of sitting. "Lawsy, this has been a long day. Sit down, Tabby. Eat cookies and drink tea. You need the boost."

"I don't have time for her drama," I said.

"You will sit down, Tabby Winslow. Right now. Trouble is coming after us. It's insidious, and we can't avoid it. We can only succeed with a united front. We have to be strong."

Hurtful retorts sprang to my tongue, but I swallowed them and sat. Sage hadn't touched her cookies or tea. She stared ahead at nothing. I'd saved her twice tonight, and this was the thanks I got?

"Let's review the basics. Family sticks together. That's the most important thing. Our family has always been mindful of their power. We don't wield it indiscriminately. It is to be used full force only in matters of life and death. There's no excuse for what happened today, Sage. You know better. Tabby, you're not off the hook either. You burned too much energy rousing Gerard. We are the last of our line. We must preserve the legacy."

I didn't need a guilt trip. All I wanted was to lie down in bed and sleep. I stared at my hands, seeing how they trembled. Somehow Sage also held her peace during Auntie O's lecture.

"On a positive note, no one died. Tabby made sure of that. On the negative side, we fell apart. Communication is key. Sage, why did you go to work so tired and out of sorts?"

"I thought I could do it, but I burned a lot of energy at Brindle's place without the normal in-my-sleep recharge that occurs here. It's easy for the rest of you to accept Gerard, but every time I see him I'm reminded of how he cheated on me with those men in Europe."

"Would you have felt the same way if it was women?"

"I'd have killed him on the spot," Sage said. "Kidding." She sighed. "It wouldn't have mattered. I didn't know he was bisexual at the time. That threw me off my stride, and I can't get past that."

"Gerard has dated men and women since," I said, "but he never does it at the same time. Is there even a remote possibility he sabotaged your relationship because he didn't know how else to break up with you?"

"I see where you're going with this," Auntie O said with a kind nod. "Gerard acted out of character when he was with you and that's what bothers you, that he didn't want to be with you."

Sage shook her head. Nervous little shakes that barely moved her long dark hair. "No. I fogged his memory of our relationship because he still wants me and all the others."

"Are you sure?" Auntie O asked.

"I'm not sure of anything tonight. I want to go to bed and sleep for three days."

"That can't happen," our aunt stated firmly. "Both of you must spend the weekend investigating Blithe's murder. We will help Gerard because he deserves our help."

"I don't want him in my life," Sage said. "I know I agreed that he could stay, but he's making me nuts. I can't take it anymore."

"We need him." I sipped my tea. "The three of us in this room combined can't sell what he sells in a day. You have to accept that fact, Sis."

Sage sighed again. "I accept it, but I don't have to like it."

"Okay, family meeting over," Auntie O said. "You girls hug and make up. Don't ever go to bed this upset at each other. It hurts your soul."

We stood there as awkward as young teens at their first dance. Then I opened my arms and Sage mugged me. Her energy lapped at me, but I couldn't even push the dark stuff away. Sage's eyes clouded with concern as she quickly pushed energy my way. "You're going to bed."

* * *

Usually in perpetual motion, Gerard spent the next day parked on a stool, his shoulders rounded with tension, his stabbed hand resting on the counter. He perked up when customers entered, but as soon as the shop emptied, he sighed out the weight of the world. I was counting the minutes until closing time and wondering what my wayward sister was doing.

He wasn't himself, and his wrist must have hurt terribly. "Go home," I urged for the third time. "I can manage the shop for the rest of the afternoon."

"No can do. I need to pay my lawyer bill. Besides, the hand doesn't hurt as much today as I expected. Despite my fainting spell yesterday, I feel strong in body. If only I could shake this murder rap."

"Let me ease your mind a little about the lawyer bill. Brindle's office will work out a payment plan with you. You don't owe the money all at once."

"Good to know."

A group of college students came in, and Gerard beamed, even moved off the stool to greet them. I heard him giving advice on how to navigate to different Savannah destinations. The kids hung on his every word. The change in him after they exited with bags of our goods was like night and day. He looked even more morose.

"Will you visit me in prison?" Gerard asked.

My heart panged for him. We'd been trying to clear him for days now, and the right answer was slow to come. "You're not going to prison. We'll figure this out. Auntie O is helping us now, so we will identify the real killer soon."

"Those detectives have been nosing around at my fave night club, Salty Pecs. Guys tell me the cops are asking about mistakes I've made in my life. About how angry I can get."

"You're a good person, Gerard. I can't imagine you did anything to Blithe."

"Thank for that, but having a few memory gaps concerns me. What if I'm a twenty-first-century Jack the Ripper, and the memories are so horrific I banished them? I'd fight harder for my freedom if I didn't have empty spaces in my memories."

My new theory of him doing the wrong thing to make Sage break up with him seemed more likely by the minute.

"Stuff happens, and we have to deal with it," I said, turning to Gerard. "Say, how was MawMaw this morning?"

"She seemed better for Oralee's visit. This morning, she rose before I did and cooked breakfast. It was like ten years rolled away from her life. I hope your aunt stays in Savannah and visits her regularly."

"Me too. By the way, she said something about visiting your grandmother again later today."

Even as I replied, I began thinking about the addled wits and paranoia that often occurred in Alzheimer's patients in late afternoon. Auntie O probably amped MawMaw's energy field to rev her engines. Too bad those energy tune ups were fleeting, and their usefulness was limited.

People with this challenge lost ground even with optimized energy. When the "fix" wore off, it prompted a huge spiral into the disease. Mom tried to stave off the inevitable for a similarly afflicted friend for months, to no avail.

The process drained Mom to exhaustion, leading to her fatal heart attack. Her friend's family reacted badly to the abrupt mental decline, dumped Veronica in a cheap nursing home, and waited months for her to die. All the while, Veronica lived in terror because she didn't know where she was. I didn't want that for MawMaw.

"I hope Auntie O moves home permanently," I said. "She misses us, and we miss her."

Gerard's face fell. "Except there's no room for me to sleep on your couch again."

"You don't need to crash with us. You've got your grandmother for moral support. She's a gem."

He chewed his thoughts for a moment. "Enough about my family. What do you see in Quig? He's nothing like you."

"I'm comfortable with Quig in many ways. We're good together."

"When's that fancy shindig you're going to with him?"

"Tonight. Thanks again for helping me find the right outfit. I will make a statement in that gown."

Gerard groaned. "You'll look like a goddess for him."

"I'll look like me in a fancy dress."

"Goddess."

"Me."

Chapter
Thirty-Six

Quig took one look at me in the black gown and whistled. "Ten minutes at the gala. We'll breeze through the crowd, duck out the back door, and spend the rest of the night at my place."

I hoped it wouldn't take ten minutes for me to get into his Hummer. The Godet panels on the formal gown allowed me to walk in an abbreviated stride, but this dress wasn't meant for ascending into such a lofty ride. I gazed over my shoulder at him. "A little help?"

He lifted me in his arms and set me on the seat. "At your service, my lady."

I gave him a sultry glance. "Gerard said I looked like a goddess, but I thought he was kidding."

"Definitely a goddess." He shut the door and climbed in the driver's seat, but he didn't start the motor. Beads of sweat dotted his forehead. I'd never seen him at such a loss. He mumbled something.

I leaned close. "What?"

"It's too soon," he said.

"I don't know about that, but we'll be late if we sit here much longer."

He gazed at me again and came to a decision. "The gala can wait. Out."

I laughed as he carried me off into the evening.

* * *

Much later we made an appearance at the gala. My hair and makeup weren't what they had been, but what the hey. Goddesses could style their hair any way they liked. We danced and noshed and made small talk.

When Quig was drawn into conversations, I retreated if it was county business, but he kept a firm grip on my hand, regardless.

A lanky senior with a golden-haired comb-over and a natty tuxedo, BB Cranford III, oiled over to pump Quig's hand. "You're doing a fine job in the morgue, Doc. Glad to have an ME at the helm down there for a change."

"Thank you, sir."

He turned to me with amusement in his eyes. "Ms. Winslow."

"Good to see you again. Hope you're enjoying the candles from our shop, Mr. Cranford."

"I am. Our law firm thanks you for your family's patronage over the years. Young Platt still doing a good job for you ladies?"

"He is," I answered, feeling like his gaze was a little too sharp, his tone too stern for some reason. I waited for his next parry, readying myself to go on the offensive, if needed.

Cranford scowled. "Brindle is keeping company with your sister."

"That's true," I answered, my energy revving. *Keeping company* was old school for "dating." Odd of him to mention that.

Winslows were old Savannah, but not highfliers. Cranfords had long been in the camp of the haves regarding wealth. We were have-nots. I silently dared him to say anything negative about my family.

"Good, good," he said absently as he gazed at a clump of people across the room. "If you will excuse me, I see someone I need to catch. There's always something going on in the City of the Dead."

Ah, I hadn't heard that reference in a while. Early in the city's history, yellow fever had killed untold numbers of people. They were buried outside Savannah's city limit of the time. As decades passed, graveyards were leveled in the name of progress and built upon, giving rise to the various ghost tales around Savannah.

We murmured goodbyes. Quig grinned down at me. "I thought for a minute you might slug him."

"His family has a long history of looking down their noses at mine. I don't know why Brindle works for that stodgy firm. He should go out on his own."

"No way he could rake in the same salary he draws as a partner at Cranford, Aldrich, and Platt. Being a partner is a big deal in the world of attorneys."

"Brindle is a decent lawyer. I don't care for Cranford's personality, even if he is a hotshot in Savannah."

"I would have a small social circle of acquaintances if I only dealt with people I liked. Power brokers like Cranford can make or break me. Rumor is Cranford and a buddy of his from another firm drove the previous coroner to drink. You may think this gala is only an occasion to dress up, but I'm here to make sure I keep my job."

I'd never thought about the networking aspect of his work. "Gotcha. I'll try not to make any enemies for you here tonight."

"Good. I enjoy my work."

Later when a county commissioner asked me about our aromatherapy candles, Quig wrapped his arm around my waist until the man moved on. Our privacy was short-lived.

Detective Chase Nowry strolled into view, drink in hand. "Ms. Winslow, Dr. Quigly."

We responded politely, but I immediately felt uncomfortable, as if he might arrest me for my form-fitting gown. "I'm surprised to see you," I said. "Wouldn't think you'd be interested in a charity gala, detective."

"My wife was on this board. After she passed, they asked me to step in, so here I am. My partner and I haven't seen you in a few days, Ms. Winslow, but let me reiterate that crime investigation is no amateur matter."

I stiffened. "I have no choice, sir, since you are set on my clerk as the prime suspect. All the people close to Blithe are cloaked in secrets." I ran through my findings, sure that my amateur prowess would floor him.

Instead, his face flushed tomato red. "Miss Winslow, you're playing with fire. People with secrets are dangerous. Don't stick your nose where it doesn't belong."

I found his comment offensive. "You were aware of the secrets I discovered?"

"What I know is none of your business." He turned to Quig before he wandered off. "Talk some sense into her."

"He means well, and he's a good cop," Quig said after the man hurried away.

"Whatever comes out of his mouth, I always have the sense he's marking his territory. If it wasn't socially inappropriate, he probably would've peed on his suspects to mark them as off-limits."

Quig gave a belly laugh. "Now that's an image I don't want in my head. Care to dance?"

A smile beamed through my entire body. "Yes, I'd love to."

Quig led me out on the floor for a slow dance. His breath feathered my neck. "I wish we were back at my place already. Networking is hard to do when you're at my side. The world fades, and all I see, all I want, is you."

I missed a step, and he stopped too. "That is the nicest thing anyone has ever said to me."

"I meant every word." Quig's forehead touched mine, and we eased into dance again.

He hummed along with the music, and while I thoroughly enjoyed the moment, little nigglings slipped into my head. This was the first time we'd ever been to a fancy event together. Was he in love with me? For that matter, was I in love with Quig? If so, his friends-with-benefits offer had been an excellent lure to catch me.

We stopped for drinks at the open bar and retreated to the far side of the room to hear ourselves think. Before I could mention the case, we overheard a heated phone conversation beyond a nearby cluster of potted ficus trees.

"I'll get you your money, BB," the man said.

In the edgy silence that followed, my heart raced. He must owe a lot or owe the wrong person.

"I need more time," the man said. Then after a moment, he swore aloud.

The man walked around the trees and slammed to a halt when he saw us. Moisture dotted his tanned brow. "Dr. Quigsly and Ms. Winslow."

"Alderman Vernon," Quig said, and I managed a strangled hello.

We waited for him to speak. No one else was nearby, and there wasn't any graceful way he could move on knowing we had heard his phone call.

Rashad flashed a wry smile. "My apologies for disturbing you. I have a prickly family situation right now. Nerves are strained, and people are upset."

"Families are challenging," I offered.

"That's the truth. You're damned if you do and if you don't, and heaven forbid if you take sides in a family quarrel. The rift grows wider."

"Especially if there's money involved," I added.

He stilled for a few moments and then waved it off. "This is a party. Where are my manners? You lovebirds sought privacy over here, so I'll move along."

He left, and Quig and I gazed at each other. I couldn't address the lovebird comment, so I tried something else. "Looks like our alderman is in financial hot water," I said in a quiet voice.

"Money troubles are a good motive for murder."

"I went there too. Why would BB Cranford loan him money?"

Quig shook his head. "Don't know, but Rashad might've borrowed if he thought he'd come into an inheritance. Perhaps Blithe lied to her alleged half brothers about her trust fund. If so, they must've been stunned when she died penniless."

"Maybe, but those two men visited her condo often. One look and they could see Blithe wasn't rolling in dough." I thought about it some more. "It's likely she told them she had an inheritance. Some hoarders also hoard money too. So, if she told them her money was in the bank, then it's possible the alderman, who by his own admission always needs campaign money, killed her in a fit of rage when it didn't work out. That deadly blow could be a crime of passion."

Quig seemed to mull that over. At last, he spoke. "If she kept a bat handy for security reasons, he could've grabbed the bat and struck her. That fits with a crime of passion."

"He's more high-profile than our other suspects. He has the most to lose. Perhaps he tried to sweeten the pot."

"You're implying he promised people money for votes?"

I thought more about that. "In the money-for-votes world, money pays out closer to election time. Now if someone bank-rolled him, who's to say he wouldn't grease the wheels for projects in his district in non-election years. Wonder if cops monitor his calls."

"Anything is possible." Quig drew me close for a kiss. "But we're supposed to be having fun tonight."

His gaze swept my length, and everything in me danced to his tune. "Perhaps we should forget the case tonight."

"Absolutely."

Chapter
Thirty-Seven

As I tucked into my eggs and bacon at breakfast the next morning, Sage and Auntie O asked about the gala. "Lots of glittering lights, dress-up clothes, and libations. That was about it."

"We want details," Sage said. "Did Quig like the dress?"

The hunger in his eyes when he'd seen the dress was priceless. I would treasure it forever. "I believe so."

"You're grinning. You never grin before you're fully caffeinated."

"Can't help it. I'm happy."

"Because of the dress?"

This strong emotion I had for him felt too shiny and bright to share. Except happiness bubbled out of me. He'd done that, spent hours making me happy. It must be love. "Because of Quig. You were right earlier, Sage. He wants me to move in with him."

"Don't move on my account," Auntie O said. "I'm fine in the stillroom."

"I'm not going anywhere yet, but I may try a few overnights to see how it feels. This deepening connection with him is new and fragile, and I don't want to mess it up. What if he hates my morning breath?"

"Then I'll clock him but good," Sage said loyally.

"Thanks for having my back," I said, meaning it.

"Always."

"What about your budding romance?" I asked. "Is Brindle everything you hoped for?"

She hesitated before speaking. "At times Brindle gets on his high horse and rants about whatever has his goat. I'm less fond of him then, but he's solid, you know, and very huggable."

I'd privately thought for some time that Brindle could be a warrior poet. A man who lived and died by the sword of his words. While oration and debate were great traits in a lawyer, I wasn't sure they translated into boyfriend material. "Does he make you happy?"

"Yes."

No hesitation there. I beamed. "Good. Now we need to find someone for Auntie O, and we'll all have romantic relationships."

"Don't get too full of yourselves, ladies," Auntie O said. "I had my pick of companions in Orlando, but none competed with the lure of home. I'm needed here."

Her hands-off message rang through loud and clear. "Moving right along, here's what Quig and I overheard last night." I gave them the short version of the alderman's call to someone named BB and subsequent excuses for debt nonpayment to a family member. "Could be nothing, but it might be related to the case."

Auntie O's gaze narrowed. "Interesting. His wife and kids already have a direct pipeline into his bank account, so probably not them. His parents died several years ago, and he was an only child. This intrigues me. Gotta be BB Cranford, and he's not the alderman's family. Why lie about that?"

"People lie all the time. The alderman expected money from Blithe before she died, claiming it was for the next election. According to the neighbor, Blithe had no money to spare."

"His parents gave him everything and then some," Auntie O mused. "That guy always has his hand out. People like him believe what's mine is mine and what's yours is mine too. MawMaw said Rashad won his seat by going along to get along."

"What I don't get," Sage began slowly, "is *why* he asked Blithe for money. According to the neighbor, Rashad visited there, so he saw how she lived. Even if she left him everything she owned, that wouldn't amount to anything. His close association with her makes no sense."

"Unless he's a McAdam," I added. "Then he might've felt cheated. From his perspective, Blithe had a fairy-tale childhood. Is it possible he and Jurrell Dawson conspired to kill their alleged half sister and divide her money?"

"What if Rashad killed her, and Jurrell is blackmailing him?" Sage asked. "You might've witnessed a falling out among thieves, and the alderman could've told the truth about a family crisis."

"If so," Auntie O said, "Jurrell Dawson is on borrowed time. The alderman would remove Dawson from the picture."

"Another death?" I asked.

"Most definitely," Sage said. "Jurrell Dawson is volatile. What if his half brother set him up to take the fall?"

"Speculating is pointless. We need facts," Auntie O said. "You girls spend the day figuring this out. I'll help Gerard in the shop. We'll sell the heck out of merchandise. Gerard and I had a system back in the day, and I'm confident he'll outdo himself today."

"Thanks for taking my shift today," I said. "I appreciate the chance to visit our suspects. Speaking of which, what did you learn yesterday, Sage?"

Sage ducked her heard. "I couldn't find Tansie, then a friend from the nursery talked me into a massage and a movie. I needed to get my head back together, so I played hooky. I'm ready to go today. I've had my issues with Gerard in the past, but he doesn't belong in prison. I will stay on task from now on."

"Good because I need your help." I turned to my aunt. "And you, Auntie O? Did you and MawMaw come up with anything new?"

"It wasn't a good day for MawMaw. Soon as I asked her about the McAdam family, she became agitated. I spent my time there calming her down and calling people I used to know. All the jibber-jabber wore me out. I'll leave the sleuthing to you young-sters from now on."

Her conclusion relieved my fear she might inadvertently land in trouble. "Having another set of hands in the shop right now is a godsend. That gives us twins opportunities to investigate sepa-rately and together. We've got to be getting close."

"All right. We have a plan." Auntie O rose. "I cooked, so you girls catch the dishes. I'll be in the stillroom until it's time to open the shop." She clapped her hands three times, and both cats went on high alert. "Come along, Luna and Harley. We have a busy day ahead of us."

"What was that?" I asked after Auntie O and our cats marched out in single file.

"Mischief is afoot." Sage grinned, stacking our empty plates along her arm. "The sooner we clear Gerard, the sooner we get our lives back. Let's knock this out."

"Two heads are better than one. Deal."

Chapter Thirty-Eight

Since Tansie Fuller was closest, we started with her, only she wasn't at work across the street. The owner of Southern Tea Shop, a gruff woman named Barbara who looked like she'd rather pull out her toenails than wait tables, told us she'd fired Tansie. Then she asked if we were applying for the waitress opening.

"No, we own The Book and Candle Shop across the street," I said.

"You're Marjoram's twins?" she asked.

"Yes, ma'am," Sage said.

She gave a curt nod. "Well, that's all right."

The woman bustled away, and we walked out into blazing sunlight. I fumbled for my sunglasses. "That was a waste of time."

"Doesn't matter," Sage said. "I know where Tansie lives."

Sage drove us to the west side of town. "How do you know that?" I asked.

"Simple. Brindle has resources at Cranford, Aldrich, and Platt. Once we made our list of suspects, I noted everyone's home address, even that rideshare guy."

Reading between the lines, she'd likely snooped through Brindle's stuff to get those addresses. "Find anything else in his computer?"

"Like what?"

"Like arrest reports or an indication one of them is a stone-cold killer?"

"No. That's what I have you for."

Hmm. I didn't like the sound of that.

Sage cleared her throat. "I know why you did it."

"You lost me."

"Why you shut down your energy talent. Being out of control is super scary. I nearly killed someone because I was in a wretched mood. I don't ever want to do that again."

"You shutting down your icer talent?"

"No way. I need it, and I have to be more when you are less."

"Interesting perspective."

She grunted, and I spent the rest of the ride considering how my decision had thrust added responsibility on my twin. Not once had she complained about doing more than her fair share.

Energy talent mirrored in each of us, half-light and half-dark. Every day we stood on the edge of shadow, and at each crossroads we dwelt in light or darkness. Our choice. Or was it?

* * *

Tansie opened her door but didn't unlatch the screen. She planted fists on her hips and glared at us. "What do you want?"

"We want to talk to you," I began.

"I have nothing to say to you. Y'all put me out of work and made everything worse."

"That's not true," Sage said. "Everyone is accountable for their actions. No one made you stab Gerard with a meat fork."

"You don't understand," Tansie said. "My life is a house of cards. The slightest breeze and it'll fall apart."

Her anger appeared to be fueled by fear. I could work with that. "We want to understand, Tansie. What's going on with you?"

"Preggers, for one, and no job. My boyfriend doesn't know about either issue—he thinks I'm home for that time of the month. He can't handle stress, cops, or even Winslow sisters, for that matter. He's upset all the time."

"Your boyfriend is Charlie Rowe?" I asked, unsure because she didn't stay with a guy very long.

"That's been over for months. I'm back with Macon Bigsby."

"Oh, Tansie." My heart went out to her. Macon had a revolving door pass in and out of prison because of his belligerent nature. I went cold thinking of his meaty fists pounding into Tansie's slim frame. "Does he hit you?"

"He doesn't mean it. When he's upset, he can't control his feelings."

"Or his fists," I added. Macon had a reputation for starting bar fights in Savannah. "Even if you don't mind getting beat up, consider the baby."

"Why stay with him?" Sage asked.

"We're in love," Tansie said.

"Getting beat up is not love," Sage said. "You need help."

Tansie's chin went up. "I don't want help. I want Macon. He understands me better than anyone. Better than my mom who left me to fend for myself, better than my dad who pimped me out for cigarette money when I was twelve."

I wanted to draw her in my arms and shower her with good energy. "Parents are supposed to look out for their kids." I paused for a deep breath. "While Macon may look like a rescuer by comparison, I'm worried for your safety. His temper is legendary."

"He got my dad off my back and out of my life. For that I'll be forever grateful."

"He's a loser," Sage reiterated. "If he punches your belly, he'll hurt the baby."

"Macon will kill you for saying that." Tansie's eyes rounded, then narrowed to fierce slits. "Look, I hated Blithe, but I didn't kill her. You gals take your perfect looks and your perfect family and get the hell off my property," Tansie shrieked as she slammed the door in our faces.

"I'm sorry," I said to the closed door. "Sage shouldn't have been so blunt."

Sage mouthed to me, "I meant every word."

I quelled her with a glance worthy of Mom. The silence outside Tansie's door felt prickly. "Let's go," I whispered.

Sage and I trooped back to her car. "That went well," I said.

"Not," Sage said. "Since when does anyone say the Winslows are a perfect family?"

I compared Tansie's place to the others on the street. Hers had a tidy yard and zero cars mounted on concrete blocks in various stages of disrepair. "Since Tansie said so. I can't imagine growing up the way she did. Mom and Auntie O were always there for us. We had each other too."

"Still do." Sage cranked the car and pulled away. "Guess that makes us look normal, but we'll never meet that expectation."

"It's a matter of perspective. We had consistent, loving parenting; a roof over our heads; and no worries about where our next meal was coming from."

Sage made a few turns before she answered. "Why are there labels for normal and abnormal anyway? Every family has a degree of dysfunction."

"Good point. Even if we didn't learn more about Blithe's murder, we succeeded in stirring the pot. Who's next?"

"You got the address for that rideshare guy handy?"

"I do. Luis Chickillo lives in Garden City." I shared the street address from Sage's purloined list, and she began making turns to get from state road 25 to state road 20. "This could be a wasted trip. I don't know if he's still in jail from that DUI over in Columbus."

"Brindle said he'd been released for his first-time offense after paying a $300 fine. He's looking at a year of probation."

"I bet he wishes he could take back his decision to drink and drive."

The houses got smaller as the roads got faster. I'd lived in Savannah all my life and I'd never been to Garden City. Judging by appearances, it seemed farther away from historic Savannah than the miles suggested.

Though I was still thinking about Tansie's situation, I was watching the house numbers on mailboxes. "You missed it," I said.

"Yep. Wanted to get the lay of the land first. One vehicle on the property."

"Huh. There's a brick framework for a carport attached to his trailer, but there's no roof to protect the car. His place needs power washing."

"Hurricane could've taken the roof. Or the property owner could've run out of money."

"No toys or bikes in the yard, so no kids live here."

Sage made a three-point turn in a neighbor's driveway, and we crept toward Chickillo's place. She parked on the street, with the car's grill headed east.

"I'll do the talking this time," I said, unbuckling my seat belt and opening the car door. "We need information instead of doors slammed in our faces."

Sage shook her head. "Talk all you want, but I get my say too. That's only fair."

My twin meant well, but maybe I could spin what she said so it sounded less caustic. Or maybe I should talk so much she couldn't get a word in edgewise.

We walked side by side up the sandy driveway. Despite the dirty exterior of the mobile home, the grass was neatly trimmed, the yard spotless. A bright blue SUV slumbered in the unroofed carport. Trees added shade and zebra stripes of shadow to the sunny yard. A neighbor's dog yapped in the distance.

"So much for sneaking up on anyone," I said. "That dog is noisy."

We hadn't gone ten steps into the yard before his front door opened, and we heard the unmistakable racking of a gun. "Down," I shouted to Sage as I flopped on the ground.

Chapter
Thirty-Nine

"I am not getting my white shirt dirty," Sage snapped at me. "I can't see his weapon, and he hasn't fired yet, so he's counting on the scary sound to run us off. Get up."

I stood, wiped the sand off my jeans, and tried to speak, though my pounding heart made it difficult. "Mr. Chickillo don't shoot. I'm Tabby Winslow, and this is my sister, Sage. We want to talk to you about Blithe McAdam."

"No," he shouted. "I spoke to the police already. Go away."

A welcome breeze sighed through the tall pines. "Please give us a chance. We're not the police. Our clerk at The Book and Candle Shop is a suspect in Blithe's murder. You knew her better than we did. Can you help us point the cops in the right direction?"

A dark-haired man peeked around the doorway. His classic Hispanic features were marred by a snarling expression. "No cops. They take me in because they no like Latinos."

My fingernails bit into my palms. "I'm sorry. I know how you feel."

He stepped outside onto the tiny platform atop three wooden steps, the gun nowhere in sight. "She mean lady. Use bad language no lady should hear. Never tip. *Su perro*, uh, her dog, *comer*, uh, eat, *mi auto*."

When he started to speak again, Sage raised a hand. "She took advantage of everyone, and you're right she was bitter and mean."

"She talk bad news to boss lady. I get chopped."

"Can't you apply to another rideshare place?" Sage asked.

Luis scowled. "Sand Gnat Express only rideshare company to hire me. I quick to learn city. *Bueno* driver. Now no company want me."

"Where'd you take Blithe?"

"Most times, she go to Bristol Street. Your shop, the wine store, the tea place. She meet him there."

"Him?" I stepped closer. "Please explain."

"Her brother. They visit there once a week. She tell me wait and take her home later. I lose *mucho dinero* doing that."

Even with my limited Spanish, I knew that phrase meant "much money." Sounded like Blithe had made this man's life a living hell. "What's her brother's name? Did he use your rideshare service?"

"No ride with me. His car, very fancy." Luis rubbed his thumb and fingers together. "*Muy caro*, uh, very big dollars. Mercedes."

No way a local podcaster like Jurrell Dawson could afford an expensive car. Had to be Blithe's other half brother, Rashad Vernon, the city official. "What did she say about him?"

"Plenty. No music and no open windows for her, so I hear. She *irritado* with him 'cause he begs her for money."

My mind linked his words with those of Blithe's neighbor, confirming that Rashad needed money from her. Blithe owed money all over town, so eating out made no sense. Unless—and it was a big unless—she thought she had money. Perhaps her father *had* provided for her. If so, either she couldn't access the money, or it had vanished. Who controlled her money?

As I pondered the possibility of Blithe inheriting money, Sage asked, "Would you recognize him in a photo?"

He shook his head. "He, how you say, connected. No *bueno* talk against him. I need work. I no mess up my chances."

I understood his hesitation only too well. If the alderman was the man Chickillo was talking about, then he could be very influential with area employers. "Did Blithe ever go anywhere beside Bristol Street?"

"She go to Nepal Street." He tapped the inside of his elbow. "She gift blood there. You know blood?"

"Yes," I said. "Her father chaired many blood drives. She must've gotten into the blood donation habit."

"More Daddy issues," Sage whispered to me. To Luis she asked, "What about church or restaurants?"

He shrugged and mimicked walking fingers on the back of his hand.

Given Blithe's chronic headaches, I doubted she walked anywhere. Maybe she used a delivery service. I'd figure that out later. "What kind of work are you seeking, Luis?"

"Maybe cook food. I adore food truck to sell Mexican food. But too much *dinero*."

This guy needed help, and I might be the gal to help him. "I know of an opening. The Southern Tea Room, across the street from us needs a waitperson. If you hurry, you might be the first to apply for the job."

His body stiffened board-straight. "I no, uh, smart with tea."

"Don't worry," I said, hoping he was talking about restaurant experience. "A waiter takes orders and serves food. Their regulars are decent tippers. Barbara, the owner of the tea shop, also owns a food truck. She might strike a deal with you if you work for her first."

"Why help me?"

"I shared an opportunity. That's all. It's up to you to get the job." I motioned for Sage to follow me. "Let's go."

We hadn't gone three steps before Luis called out, "*Gracias*. I go to tea place."

"You're welcome," we chimed in together.

We sat in Sage's car and faced each other. I shared my thoughts. "Blithe's inheritance bugs me. Since it makes no sense that a city official would beg an impoverished relative for money, I jumped down the rabbit hole of 'what if Blithe received an inheritance from her father?'"

"I see. Blithe came from money, so her father would've specified money for her in his estate. What we assumed to date is that her father was broke. Turning that assumption on its head, what if she inherited but someone stole Blithe's inheritance?"

I nodded. "It's a rabbit hole, but the logic of it follows."

"Except if someone took her money, why kill her?"

Why indeed? I thought about it some more and hit upon an answer. "Killing Blithe would halt inquiries about her father's estate and prevent her making a stink about her missing inheritance. From a thief's perspective, it would be brilliant."

"Let's keep going. Where to next?" Sage asked.

"Either half brother. Let's decide on the drive back to town."

Sage nodded and got us on the road. "Did you believe Luis? His energy kept flaring."

"He seemed nervous to me. That alone would flare his energy."

"Did you see it?"

I swallowed my automatic retort because I had used my energy to help Gerard recover. I just didn't whip out my energy talent today. "No. I didn't."

"Why?"

I studied the homes we passed, stalling. "You know why. It isn't what I do."

"It is too your thing. Quit hiding under that pitiful-me umbrella, and use your complete skill set. Gerard needs you at your full potential, and so do I. We wouldn't struggle financially if you were fully invested in the shop."

As yards melted into pine forests, my anger sizzled. "You blame me for our financial problems? That's not fair."

"I'm all in. You aren't."

"Your heart lies in gardening. I work more shop hours each week than you do."

"That's on you. It isn't about quantity, it's the energy you put into our business. That makes our shop thrive."

Before I could respond, my phone rang. Gerard. I answered quickly. "Hello."

"I've been arrested. They say I'm a flight risk because I have a passport, so no bail," Gerard said. "You're my phone call. Get my lawyer down here now. I can't remember his phone number.

I flashed cold, then hot as I listened.

Sage swerved. "Look out, Tabs. You're emitting lightning bolts of energy all over the car. I almost crashed when you surged."

I ended the call and stared at my sister. "Gerard's been arrested."

Chapter Forty

Sage pulled into the nearest parking lot and called Brindle Platt. She explained the situation, and the lawyer said he was leaving now to help Gerard.

When Sage ended the call, she stared at the grassy median and the cars zipping by on the busy street. "This just got real. Gerard has the morals of an alley cat, but he wouldn't murder anyone. We must figure out who killed Blithe today."

"Far as I'm concerned, our suspects all have strong motives and secrets. How can we cut through the static and solve the murder? What if we aren't even looking in the right place?"

"Gerard didn't do it," Sage said. "I'm certain of that."

"You believe in him now? What changed?"

"You changed my mind with your faith in him. We should let Auntie O run the shop solo today, and keep putting the pressure on our investigation."

"Agreed. Let's talk to Rashad next."

"All right." I glanced at the list of addresses she'd made. "His home or City Hall?"

"Let's buzz City Hall first. If Rashad's Mercedes isn't there, we'll check his home."

"Fine." I cleared my throat. "About what you said earlier. I *am* all-in on our shop. I've stopped shielding fully, which is why you felt the power surge when Gerard called. It's new territory for me, learning how to parse my talent into everyday thoughts and actions. Bound to be a few hiccups."

Sage perked up visibly. A wisp of a smile graced her lips. "You mean it?"

"Yeah. It's time. I'm not scared anymore."

"Your talent was always stronger than mine, so I understand your hesitation, especially after I lost control. If it weren't for you, I couldn't operate the shop, even with Gerard."

Odd how Sage thought I had greater power than she did. My talents were strong, but hers were turbocharged. "We're all part of the shop's success—you, me, and Gerard."

"Agreed. Let's track down our city alderman."

* * *

A Mercedes occupied Rashad Vernon's named slot. Sage parked in a nearby public lot, and we strolled toward City Hall. Sunshine warmed my face, and I couldn't help thinking, how long until Gerard felt sun on his skin again? I had to figure this out.

If Rashad Vernon seemed innocent, we'd try the other half brother, and then the neighbor again. Gerard wouldn't languish in jail if I could help it.

We sailed through building security. I was glad Sage didn't make a tacky comment about how she should have brought her gun. The old Sage would've said something snarky like that despite her not owning a gun.

The next barrier was the alderman's assistant, Kirk Flemming. He appeared a little older than me with graying temples and professional attire in three shades of charcoal gray. "He's in a meeting right now, but he'll be free soon," Kirk said smoothly. "Your names?"

"Sage and Tabby Winslow," I said. "We're constituents, and we want to discuss crime in our neighborhood."

"I see." The man made note of our names.

We sat and felt minutes of our lives swirl down the drain. Minutes that kept us from our self-appointed task of finding a killer. Finally, an elderly woman left the alderman's office, all smiles. Kirk buzzed the alderman and explained he had more visitors, and we were granted access.

"Come in, come in. How can I help you today, ladies?" Rashad Vernon invited us into his office, his face displaying interest. "My aide mentioned your concern about crime in the neighborhood. Y'all are on Bristol Street, right? The Book and Candle Shop?"

He knew our names and our shop—he'd been there and we'd argued—but he didn't mention the trouble we'd had recently? I smelled a rat.

"Yes. The city cops arrested the wrong killer for Blithe McAdam," Sage said, "Our shop clerk, Gerard Smith, is innocent."

He raised his hands. "That's out of my jurisdiction."

"As it happens," Sage continued in a barbed tone, "a witness placed you in Blithe's condo near the time of her death. She said you two were arguing loudly."

I held my breath, hoping this man wouldn't call security. Tension vibrated off Sage. Sometimes when she got this wound up, she came across like a bully.

I needed to smooth things over before she got too confrontational. "What she means to say, Mr. Vernon, is that we believe you have a close tie to Ms. McAdam."

His face remained in a polite congenial mask, but danger flashed in his eyes. "I'm not sure I take your meaning."

My sister started to speak. I nudged her foot and shook my head. In a kinder, gentler tone, I said, "Our sources indicate she's your half sister."

His honey-caramel-hued skin darkened. "Your sources are mistaken. I am an only child."

"That may or may not be the case," I continued, "but several facts lead me to believe you are a McAdam. First, campaigns cost money."

"That's true."

"You faced a fierce challenge last time, and your opponent swears she'll run again."

"Yes."

"Therefore you must plan ahead to keep your seat. That includes fundraising."

"I don't see your point."

"Donors require courting, and oftentimes politicians dip into family finances."

Alderman Vernon scowled.

I continued. "Blithe McAdam should've had deep pockets. Her wealthy family once lived on a famous square in town. If Blithe promised money but didn't deliver, you would be furious. Further, as a blood relation you must've felt she owed you."

"Hogwash." He studied me for a long moment. "You're bluffing."

Sage couldn't contain herself. "She's telling the truth. Another witness said Blithe confided her brother the alderman had begged her for money. That's two people close to her who say you're her brother, and now we know. That's not much of a secret."

Alderman Vernon rubbed the back of his neck. "As a public servant, I take my duties seriously. Parentage isn't relevant."

"The thing is," I said, jumping back in before Sage spoke again, "Blithe's alleged trust, your concurrent need of money, and your presence in her condo the night she died indicate you were close."

A haunted look filled his eyes. "I didn't kill her," he managed. "She promised to fund my campaign. Said she had scads of money in her trust. I counted on her. However, her bank account ran dry, and her credit cards stopped working."

"Why visit her then?" I asked.

"Once secrets spread, they're unstoppable. My half sister could be . . . persuasive. She had one emergency after another. Once she offered to finance my next campaign, I accommodated her for that reason in the beginning, paid some of her past-due bills."

His concession caught me off guard. "You admit the familial association?"

"Why not? She can't hurt me anymore. Tell you the truth, I felt sorry for her. She wanted people to notice her, but no one did. Look, I can't help who my parents are, any more than you can. I hid my connection with Blithe because she was rude and patronizing to people. I need every vote. Keeping her on the downlow was just good politics."

The more he spoke, the worse I felt for Blithe. Her parents had isolated and abandoned her. Her half brothers were ashamed of her. No one had loved her unconditionally. At least her little dog had provided some comfort.

"Did Jurrell kill Blithe?" Sage asked.

"How should I know? Jurrell is toxic. He spews dragon fire with every breath." Rashad cocked his head to the side. "His mission is to close Bristol Street businesses."

I stilled at this new information. "Why?"

Seconds ticked off the clock, each one weighted with increasing portent. "You didn't hear it from me," Rashad began as he leaned forward, "but developers will gut those old buildings to create new condos with shops at ground level."

That was the missing puzzle piece. Our homes were at risk. Our livelihoods too. Perhaps our lives if we lost Bristol Street. "Not happening on my watch. The charm of Savannah is the old buildings. If they rework old buildings, history vanishes. We'll be just another city."

Rashad slumped in his seat, raising a weak hand of protest. "Don't shoot the messenger. During a building's life span, quaint becomes run down, and urban blight follows. The residential high-rise surge at the riverfront will engulf the entire historic district."

"Zoning ordinances prevent that from happening," Sage said.

"Here's the thing about politics," the alderman said. "For every rule, there's an exception. Blighted properties are targeted for renewal first. The city aldermen will grant variances. It's the cycle of life."

"That stinks," I said. "Surely citizens fight back."

"Sometimes. Then residents flee to the suburbs until cities reinvent themselves." He looked me in the eye. "The machine of change takes no prisoners. The aldermen choose progress to keep Savannah viable."

"Bristol Street is productive," I countered. "There's no blight. Why target us?"

"Location matters. Your section of Bristol Street is near downtown. You can walk to restaurants and the Savannah River. You can hop on an interstate easily or bug out to the islands for a beach day. That's prime real estate. This isn't the first push to redo Bristol Street. These plans arise every few years."

"Doesn't matter," Sage said, "We're not selling."

"You'll be evicted if you can't make your mortgage payment. They'll buy the street shop by shop. You'll be squeezed out."

A chill snaked down my spine. Someone knew Gerard was the key to our sales and realized we anchored our block. Had they framed our clerk to gain our commercial real estate? It sure looked that way. I couldn't stop shivering.

"Bull," I said emphatically. "We'll fight this to the death."

Chapter
Forty-One

After meeting with Rashad Vernon, Sage and I strolled to the nearest park bench. "I'm blown away," I began slowly. "Am I understanding correctly? Blithe McAdam was collateral damage? She was killed to frame Gerard so our shop would fail?"

"Not just our shop, a big chunk of Bristol Street. There's a pattern of damage," Sage continued, picking up my conspiracy thread. "The teashop lost Tansie, their best waitress. That robbery at the wine store hurt their business. The bomb scare and Gerard's arrest happened at our shop. Bristol Street is under siege. Our enemy has deep pockets and is into strategy."

We fought a nameless, faceless threat. "Makes sense, except our suspects don't fit that profile. We missed someone."

Sage chewed her thumbnail. "Investigating Blithe's murder diverted our focus. Even if we save Gerard, this land-grab nightmare continues."

"We must alert our neighbors. Otherwise, the streets fall as the alderman foretold. I don't want that future."

Sage beamed. "A neighborhood meeting will help."

Cars zipped past on the street. People conversed as they strolled the sidewalk, but I made no move to leave. "Even better, if a similar-attack occurred before, we know someone who stopped it. Auntie O will know what to do."

"Good plan." Sage rose and gestured for me to join her. "Let's grab lunch and resume our suspect hunt afterward."

We headed home in Sage's car. "I wonder if Mom and Auntie O were as blindsided by this power play as we are," I said a block later.

Sage glanced repeatedly in her rearview mirror but said nothing.

"What?" I asked.

"The car behind me keeps coming too close."

I turned to look at the older model car, but the windshield glare obscured the driver's face. "Why's he doing that?"

"I have a bad feeling he might ram us on purpose."

"Traffic light ahead just turned red," I blurted out as I mirrored her fear. "Should we brace ourselves or jump out?"

"Brace yourself." Sage stopped behind a large SUV. "He's coming in fast."

I gripped the armrest, pressing my head into the headrest.

The vehicle struck, forcing us into the stopped SUV. Plastic crunched and broke, metal screeched. The change in momentum stunned me. Though my seat belt held, I slammed around as air bags struck me. One minute all was fine, and the next my thoughts scrambled.

I pushed away from the air bags, struggling for clarity. "You okay?"

"I think so." Sage sat back, rubbing her forehead.

Our car jittered. A motor revved. The vehicle behind us reversed and zipped around us. I tried to see the driver, but the car flashed by in a smear of dark blue or green. I didn't catch the license plate. I squinted to focus and nearly passed out from pain in my nose.

I pressed my throbbing temples. "Missed the tag. You get it?"

"African American driver. Four-door sedan. Last part of tag is fifty-eight." Sage's breath hitched. "Don't feel good." She opened her door and vomited.

I held her shoulders until the heaves stopped.

People stared. Car horns honked. We were wedged in the SUV. Were others hurt? Our buckled car hood and trunk limited my view.

Oh no. The rear gas tank. If fuel leaked, we were in danger. We had to go. I tried my door. Wouldn't budge. Had to exit through Sage's door.

Unclicked my seat belt. Pain in my side. Grabbed Sage's arm. "Out of the car. Now."

"What?" Sage managed.

I pushed her. "Move. Could be a fire. My door is jammed."

Hands reached for her as I pushed her out. I scrambled over the console and out her door. The world spun in lazy circles when I stood. Someone drew me away from the car, and I wobbled on legs of dry sand. "I can't . . ."

"Yes, you can," Quig said. "You can do this, by God. Breathe."

At his familiar voice, I closed my eyes in relief. He would make sure we were safe. The bright sunshine beyond my eyelids paled into darkness.

* * *

I awoke to pungent disinfectant smells and machine beeps. Light filled the curtained space. Too bright. I closed my eyes.

"Tabby!"

Quig's voice slid away as I floated into nowhere.

*   *   *

Pressure on my hand drew me to the surface. The constant tension invoked fear: I was trapped. I had to get free. The car. It might catch on fire. I flailed at the restraint.

"Easy," a man whispered. "You're safe. No one will hurt you."

I knew that voice. Quig. There was something I needed to say. Something important. Cotton padded my thoughts.

Quig. His name shaped in my dry mouth, but no sound emerged. My eyelids fought me. I felt his gentle caress. Sleep tugged me under.

*   *   *

Coffee. I smelled coffee. Mmm. I needed caffeine to dispel the fog in my head.

"Tabby, you're okay," Quig said. "Open your eyes. You've got a concussion. Wake up, or they will do brain surgery."

Surgery. Crap. I didn't want that. I battled the weight of my eyelids. Caught a glimpse of a different ceiling, a room shrouded in twilight. I blinked to keep my eyes open. The need to speak overcame everything, and I focused all my attention on uttering a word.

"No," I managed.

Quig leaned down into my field of vision. "Hey, beautiful. Welcome back."

"No," I said again, in case he didn't hear the first time.

His lips twitched before the corners turned up. "No, what?"

"No. Surgery." The effort to speak and the constant throb of pain dominated. If I drifted off, the pain would fade.

"Wait!" Quig said. "Stay with me. Your sister. Don't you want to know about her?"

Sage. She was in the accident too. I forced my eyes open, battled waves of pain, and squeezed his hand briefly. "Tell. Me."

He pushed the call button. "She's here, but she's awake and bossing everyone around. She may get booted today because she's so ornery."

"That's my sister." Ouch. Why was it so hard to talk? "Throat. Sore."

"You had a breathing tube."

I did? "How. Long?"

"About twenty-four hours."

Heavy stubble shadowed his face. "Thanks."

His grip on my hand tightened. "Keep fighting. You must pass a cognitive exam before getting released. I want you out of here."

A nurse bustled in full of questions. I answered because I wanted to be healed by the energy in my apartment. During questioning, I learned it was two days later, and I had a broken rib, a deviated septum, and a nasty gash on my head. They thought the shock and lack of consciousness I'd experienced had been brought on by blood loss from the scalp wound and the concussion from the air bag. The nurse said I could go home with my fiancé if I answered the doctor's questions as well as I'd answered hers.

After she left, I fixed my gaze on Quig. "Fiancé?"

He gave a rueful smile. "I said that to stay with you. However, that's where our relationship is headed. I want to marry you, Tabby. Always have."

"Too much for today," I said, proud I'd managed four words in one breath.

He smoothed my hair. "I know, love. We'll discuss it later. Are you curious about the wreck?"

I nodded my head and regretted it. I froze until the room righted. "Tell me."

"Jurrell Dawson hit Sage's car," Quig began. "A witness who was filming doves at the fountain caught Jurrell's vehicle on the video. Others described him and the car. He's jailed for hit-and-run. He alleges he and his half brother, Rashad Vernon, are on the payroll of a large developer. Jurrell has been on it for months, while Rashad joined more recently. Rashad has cold feet about the development project."

I focused on the most important thing first. "Was Sage hurt?"

"No broken bones. She has a concussion and vertigo. Dizziness and nausea are her main complaints. She's taking something mild for it."

I tried to sit, but Quig gently blocked my efforts to rise. "Get her out of here. Don't let them pump her full of drugs." I ruminated for a few seconds. "Did they drug me?"

"I wouldn't let them."

"Thanks. Please take me home."

"Working on it. Did you hear what I said about Jurrell?"

"Yes. No energy for the case. Just Sage. Very tired."

"You're exhausted. We need to get you home where you'll get some real rest."

I frowned at his comment, wondering how he knew that, then yawned. "Yes."

The doctor entered, and I faked more animation than I felt. I wanted out of there, like yesterday. Eek! Two days of my life were gone. Drawing on my energy talents, I convinced the doc I was much better and earned my ticket out of Dodge. I couldn't wait to be home.

Chapter
Forty-Two

Home turned out to be Quig's place and his bed. "You'll get
more rest here," he said. "Your aunt and her friend are operating the shop."

"Need to bathe," I mumbled, sinking into the soft bedding as
he drew the covers around me.

"Tomorrow," he said. "Rest is your priority. Your aunt will
come in the morning."

A protest welled, but as he stroked my hair, my eyelids closed.
I dozed, dreamed of the crash, and awakened. Each time, Quig
held me and eased me back into sleep. The third time, his kindness
brought tears to my eyes.

He wiped away my tears and whispered assurances. I slept
hard. Then it was broad daylight, and Auntie O joined me.

She bustled around, opening the curtains and blinds. I smiled
at the mug of steaming coffee on the bedside table.

"How's my sweet niece today?" Auntie O asked.

"Better." I sat up, fighting the covers because Quig had tucked
me in tight. Finally, I squirmed free of the bedding, only to discover I wore his T-shirt and nothing else. Mercy! I drew the covers

across my lower half and reached for the coffee, allowing the vapor to fill my head before I drew a sip. "What time is it?"

"About eight, dear. Your young man told us how tired you were last night. He's arranged for our lawyer to bring your sister home, so hopefully we're all under one roof tonight."

I was technically two apartments down the street, but this was not the time to quibble over details. "Wait a sec, What? How come I came home last night, and Sage didn't?"

"She became noncompliant, and the medical team thought it was a delayed reaction, so they kept her longer. Trust me, she's less moody today."

I nodded and felt relieved when the room didn't move with my head. Progress. My nose felt better too, as did my broken rib. I just had to remember not to cough or sneeze until I mended that break. My stomach growled loudly, embarrassing me. "Sorry."

"Quite understandable after all the energy you expended on healing last night. I've got breakfast fixings in the kitchen. You want to shower or eat first?"

"Food, please."

After I set the empty mug down, I texted Quig: *Thank you.*

He called a moment later. "Wish I could've stayed until you awakened. I'm behind on my autopsies and paperwork."

Feeling a stab of remorse, I hurried to say, "It's okay. You've been so kind. I truly appreciate everything you've done."

"Keep that in mind because I asked your aunt to pack a few things so you can recuperate at my place."

"My legs still feel rubbery, so I'm good with that decision if you don't mind the inconvenience of a roommate. Auntie O is making sure I eat and get showered."

"Excellent, roomie. Sweet dreams."

I looked for my clothes, but they weren't here. No suitcase either. Hmm. Looked like I would need Quig's robe when I rose.

My eyes rounded when Auntie O bustled in with breakfast. "I can't eat all of that."

"You can and will eat it. Then you'll shower and spend the day in bed."

"I'm not one to goof off."

"Today you will. Your body needs to heal." She nodded at the food. "Dig in. I'll be right back with mine."

I ate like a hungry mother squirrel. When my aunt perched in the bedside chair, I asked, "What about Gerard?"

"Gerard is in jail. Time is running out. It's urgent that we find Blithe's killer."

"Why did they arrest him? What do they know about Gerard we don't?"

Auntie O took a deep breath and another. "His grandfather was a McAdam. That revelation came from the similar DNA results. The cops discovered Jurrell and Rashad are Blithe's half brothers, and Gerard is her cousin."

"What?" I nearly upended my breakfast tray. The McAdam family tree had expanded while I was out of commission. "Did he know?"

Auntie O finished chewing her toast before she answered. "Nope. Moxley Sr. was as much a womanizer as his son. Maw-Maw's daughter was fathered by Senior. She kept quiet all these years. Gerard's mother never knew."

"I'm stunned." My mind stuck on Gerard's new lineage. "If Gerard never knew, how come he's in jail?"

"They think he knew and that he resented Blithe. Same reason you added Jurrell and Rashad to the suspect pool. Nevertheless, everyone is in the dark as to who this big developer is, some LLC out of Atlanta. Their registered address is a high-powered law firm that isn't talking."

I sipped more coffee, desperate for clarity. "Hmm. One mystery developer marked for investment in Savannah. One dead woman missing a fortune. Putting those together, what if the developer stole Blithe's inheritance?"

Auntie O beamed at me and my empty plate. "Now you're cooking with gas. That makes good sense. We should look for someone who worked at McAdam Investments."

"Or someone he swindled. His pyramid schemes left many unhappy investors. We'll never identify all those people."

"We may not have to. MawMaw and I've been talking. There's someone who hid in plain sight all along."

Oh. Someone who worked with Moxley McAdam Jr. Someone who had access to Blithe's inheritance. Someone who knew how to move money around and hide it. The answer came with a lightning-like bolt of energy. "Brindle Platt's senior partner, Barrett Brendon Cranford III."

"Yep. That's the name we came up with. That man is as slippery as an eel. He and Moxley Jr. did business together. BB must be warped, too, if he stole from his business partner and used his late partner's illegitimate sons for his dirty work. Heck, I wouldn't be surprised if Barrett didn't push his partner off the pier that fateful night. If so, he hated Moxley with a passion."

"Wait. You're going too fast. He killed Blithe's dad too?"

"I think he took what he wanted and left a trail of dead bodies behind."

"None of this is evidence, even if we both reached the same name independently. The cops won't buy it."

"With that thought in mind, we did a little digging. One of my Orlando friends has a granddaughter that's super with computers. Kiana, or The Divine Miss K as we call her at the center, found proof that Barrett was Moxley's silent business partner. The day Moxley Jr. drowned, all remaining McAdam Investment assets were deposited in Cranford's personal accounts."

"Can we take that evidence to the cops?"

"Sadly, no. She, uh, broke rules to get it, but the information is a place to start." Auntie O flashed a bright smile. "She also tracked down Blithe's trust fund. Over the course of several years, her five million dollars went from her trust into Cranford's pocket."

"Wait. Trusts are tough to break. If her father provided for her, and that changed, why didn't the feds go after Cranford?"

"BB was the trustee, and get this: he had Blithe declared incompetent when her father passed. She must've played along to get that new condo. He probably promised to take care of her. Upon her death, Cranford dissolved the empty trust since he'd already helped himself to her money with regular withdrawals marked for Blithe that she never saw."

Poor Blithe. My fingers fisted in the sheets. "Good grief. All that effort we put into investigating Tansie Fuller, Eileen Hutson, Luis Chickillo, Rashad Vernon, and Jurrell Dawson was for naught."

"Nothing's ever wasted. Once you're rested, we'll lean on BB Cranford."

The background ache of my broken rib throbbed, so I moved to ease the pain. "Gotta say he rubs me the wrong way."

"He used to frequent Southern Tea back in our day. People rarely change, so I imagine he still goes there, keeping an eye on his prospective investment, and no one realized his duplicity."

"Why gut perfectly good buildings and create cheap condos?"

"Money. Condos create wealth these days. Retirees from northern cities want big-city services. Savannah has that, but it needs more affordable housing."

"I don't like it."

"Me neither, so you have to stop it."

"Sure. Right after a shower and a nap. Where are my clothes?"

Auntie O gave a sly shrug. "Must've slipped my mind. I've got a shop to run today. See you tomorrow."

Chapter Forty-Three

Early the next day I showered and borrowed another shirt from Quig, a dress shirt this time so that more body parts were covered. He burst out laughing when he realized my aunt had stranded me without any clothes. "I always knew I liked Oralee."

"She's got her own agenda, that's for sure." I sat down on the freshly made bed. "Personally, I think she has her eye on my room."

Quig knotted his tie for work. "Could be, but it's worked out fine for you to be at my place. Why not stay here indefinitely?"

My mouth went dry. "Are you asking me to move in with you?"

He pinned me with an unwavering gaze. "Yes. A hundred times, yes. Please move in with me."

I should've prepared for this. Should've realized he'd push for cohabitation. What if I screwed this up? I wanted to be here, but Winslow women didn't stay with their men for long. We couldn't let down our guard, and quite soon our mates felt our lack of commitment.

I'd break his heart if I stayed.

I'd break mine if I left.

"Tabby! Say something. You left me flapping in the wind."

"I'm not a fan of change," I began slowly, needing him to understand my hesitation. "I do things the same way repeatedly. If you saw me every day, you'd see I'm the most boring person you know."

"Never." He crossed to the bedroom threshold where I stood. "Give yourself more credit. You are the most interesting, most beautiful, most everything woman I know. I'm crazy about you."

My heart fluttered. Heck, my *everything* fluttered. Feeling the nauseating tug of mental quicksand, I hedged. "I'm very fond of you too, but there's so much you don't know." I couldn't explain my energetic side to him, couldn't avoid this approaching train wreck.

He caressed my hand. "That's why we should move in together, to fully explore each other. As it stands now, our orbits barely overlap. We're workaholics."

Tingles spread up my arm from his touch, making it hard to stay focused. However, I had to make my thoughts known too. "Don't be getting any grand ideas about me being at your constant beck and call if I agree. My family's business depends on me, and doing that work satisfies me."

"I understand. Your work completes you. I feel the same way. I'd be miserable if I couldn't do what comes naturally. We'll figure it out."

His insightful comment rocked me on my heels. This made me want to stay even more, and it also worried me that my secrets would destroy our friendship.

I had to say something. "Let me think about it today, okay? I want to be here, but I need to work through my feelings. This is a huge step for me. I've never moved in with anyone before."

"Good," he said leaning in for a kiss. When he broke away, he smiled down at me in that special bone-melting way he had. "I'll help you move your things over tonight."

Alarms blared in my head. Then everything in me pushed at him for crowding me, and he didn't react to my energy blast, which ignited my last nerve. "Octavian Henry Quigsly IV, you will not railroad me into this. You will respect my need for space."

He beamed and stroked my hair. "You know you're going to do it."

How'd he remain unaffected by my energy shove? Another mystery in the world of Quig, one I was determined to solve once I deciphered the pressing murder mystery on my plate. "I know nothing of the sort. Gerard is in jail, and I need to free him."

Quig's lips twitched. "I'll compromise. We'll move a few things over, and you'll stay through the weekend."

My pride wouldn't let me cave. "Maybe. I'll let you know after work."

"You look great in my shirt, but I have to ask. Are you walking next door like that?"

"Yes," I teased, knowing full well I planned to pull on a pair of his sweats before I hiked across the alley. I didn't plan to expose my bare bottom to anyone besides Quig.

"Wait for your aunt to bring your clothes."

I jabbed his chest with my forefinger. "Listen up, roomie, she's never bringing my clothes. She's playing matchmaker, and it suits her for me to be here, with you, without clothes. I'll handle it."

He caught my finger and kissed it. "Okay, *roomie*. Since you're arguing so much about this, I know you're feeling much better. You might as well admit it, my brand of TLC suits you."

I grabbed the pillow and swatted him. Quig ended up being very late for work.

* * *

I let myself in the back apartment door, to the smell of mint wafting through the air. Sage glowered at me over her mug of steaming tea. "What's this I hear about you moving to Quig's place?"

What a morning of surprises. I bustled over to the teapot, poured a cup of the restorative peppermint brew, then sat at the table across from her. Sage looked like she hadn't slept in a week. "I haven't decided yet if I will do it, but I thought you wanted me to move out."

My twin rubbed her temples. "I don't know what I want. I can't get my bearings. I keep getting headaches, and the hospital stay made them worse. They gave me pain pills, but I only pretended to take them."

She needed a booster shot of energy. I pulsed gentle energy her way without her even asking. "I didn't knowingly take any meds there either." I did my game show hostess impression, pointing to each body part as I mentioned it. "I broke a rib, deviated my septum, and nearly got scalped. All that pain didn't disappear overnight. Neither of us is ready for action."

Sage eyed my outfit. "Those aren't your clothes."

"Auntie O swiped my clothes. It was either borrow from Quig or streak over here in my birthday suit."

"Sneaky of her, but she's working on her reproductive plan." Sage's energy grazed against mine and stuck. "You look good. Did you tap into Quig's energy field last night?"

251

"In a manner of speaking. His energy suits me. It somehow reinforces me. Enough about that. Where's Brindle? Thought he'd be here with you."

"Brindle picked me up from the hospital and dumped me at the back stairs yesterday. Said he had to run. Something urgent to do for his boss. I haven't heard from him since."

"Oh." I started to share my suspicions about Brindle's boss, but I hesitated. What if Sage told her boyfriend? He'd surely tell his boss, and we'd be next on the hit list.

"What?" she asked.

Luckily, I'd developed mad skills to shield my thoughts from her. I downed the rest of my tea and rose to stash the cup in the dishwasher. "Busy day ahead. I need to get dressed, pack some clothes, and spring Gerard from jail."

"Brindle says Gerard isn't getting out of jail. Something about his DNA being essentially a criminal indictment. I cut Brindle's explanation short because I wanted to talk about our relationship. Brindle brushed my concerns about us aside, and his callous manner stung. He's a jerk."

Air hissed through my clenched teeth, and I sat to parse my wild thoughts. Had Cranford instructed Brindle to sleep with Sage? If so, shame on him. For now, I would assume her boyfriend was innocent. "I'm sure he was preoccupied with work. Whatever happens, you'll see Brindle's true colors. Back to Gerard. Can he have visitors in jail?"

"I don't know, but I don't see why not. If he's still there tomorrow, let's go see him."

"Yes."

Sage yawned and then gave me a sleepy grin. "I feel much better when you're around."

I'd been happy to give her that energy boost. "Glad you're home too." I headed for my room, opened the door, and stopped short. A man snored in my bed.

"Oh yeah," Sage peered over my shoulder and whispered in our special twin-only voice. "That's Auntie O's guest from Florida. He's staying awhile."

I pulled the door closed to regroup. I needed my stuff and wasn't leaving without it. "Is he a sound sleeper?"

"Don't know. I haven't been sneaking around in there."

"I need clothes."

"I need a car and another day of sleep."

I sighed and dove into problem-solving mode. All Sage had to do to solve her problem was pick up the phone. I couldn't hold it in. "Call your insurance company."

Her eyes narrowed. "Did that. My car wasn't worth three grand."

"You'll find something. Maybe you could lease a vehicle for a year while you look for a bargain car."

"Whatever." She padded down the hall to her room and closed the door.

Now what? I needed clothes. It was my room, and this man didn't have my permission to be there. It would be rude to invade his privacy, but he wouldn't even see me, I rationalized. I went invisible, drawing heavily on the darkness in the shadowed hall. I opened the door again and grabbed my stuff quickly. The sleeping man never stirred.

*   *   *

Suitcase in hand and a backpack strapped over my shoulders, I marched down to the shop and Auntie O, a vision in an ice-blue tunic and leggings. She beamed at me. "You look much better, dear. That young man put pep in your step."

Harley jumped off the chair and trotted over for a cuddle. I held him close, and his purring soothed us both. Oh, how I'd missed this cat.

"Thanks." No way would I discuss my love life while customers wandered our aisles. I changed the subject. "Do I need to make candles today? Feels like I've been gone for months instead of days."

"I made candles yesterday. We're good on everything else, though one of your consignors pulled out. Brenda's Bees said the shop was too notorious, and she couldn't risk that association with her line of wholistic products."

We counted on the steady sales of Brenda's wares. Many of our college student customers swore by her lip balm. Heck, I had a tube of it in my purse right now. This was bad news. "Brenda is leaving?"

"She collected her products, and she's no longer a consigner. Norman called too. He said he appreciates the level of sales here, but he's uncomfortable with the recent bad press for The Book and Candle Shop. He's not leaving yet, but he's on the fence and wanted us to know."

Norman's dragon, unicorn, and pirate sculptures were true works of art. I'd fallen in love with all of them. If his eye-catching sculptures departed, our shop windows would have less visual appeal. I didn't want Norman to withdraw.

"I'll call him, but I can't give him the reassurances he wants yet, not with Gerard in jail and Blithe's killer at large. We must find the killer."

Auntie O nodded. "In other news, Carla came by. She believes in us, and she isn't leaving."

"Great. Her lotions and skin-care line are good sellers, and they partner well with our soaps and candles."

"You could make her stuff, easy peasy," Auntie O said. "She downloads her recipes from a website called Pinterest. Say, what if we included a line of teas? I heard the tea place might close."

"Southern Tea isn't closing to my knowledge, and there's no room for a café in here. Food service is a headache we don't need."

Auntie O's face fell, but she gave a tepid smile. "We'll talk when you're rested."

"I've got time now, but let's change the subject. What's with the man in my bed?"

"Frankie? He followed me from Florida. Just couldn't manage without me, though between us, I'm sure he misses my cooking the most."

I didn't remember her mentioning Frankie before. "Is it serious between you?"

She took a moment. "Frankie Mango's a good friend, but he wants more from me."

"I see." She hadn't sent him to a hotel. She'd stuck him in my room. That shouted more than a friend to me.

Something about my tone must've made her nervous because she made a big sweeping motion with her hand. "Tell me how the investigation is going. I do a lot of my best thinking in my dreams."

Auntie O wasn't prone to gesturing. Clearly, the subject of Frankie was off-limits. I understood that. Relationships were fleeting in our family.

"No progress."

"I hoped a blinding insight occurred as you slept."

"I need to follow up on BB Cranford. I didn't mention his name to my sister because of her relationship with Brindle. Also, Sage and I learned Bristol Street is in a developer's sights. If we don't pay close attention, every building here will soon be a condo with someone else living in it. We should call a neighborhood meeting."

"No need for that. We're in the historic district," Auntie O said. "That developer can't get around the historic designations."

"I heard he could." I explained Rashad's life cycle of urban blight. "This is serious. The pattern of trouble developing around here gives the impression Bristol Street is prone to crime and violence."

"That's not true," Auntie O said.

A wave of pragmatism washed over me. "Money talks, truth walks."

Chapter
Forty-Four

"What's going on down here?" Sage asked, stomping down the stairs into the shop. "I could sense you two going at it from upstairs. I am trying to sleep."

"Sorry," I said, hoping she hadn't heard the part about her boyfriend's villain of a boss. "Auntie O asked me about the investigation, and I shared what we learned about the property-grab plot by an unknown developer. Did you realize how our car accident stopped our investigation into the murder and Bristol Street?"

"Sneaky. I don't like being targeted, but we're safe now. Jurrell Dawson was arrested and charged with felony hit-and-run," Sage said, shooing the words away with her hand. "Don't worry about him."

"He made bail," Auntie O said, her voice serious. "Be careful. That young man is reckless, spiteful, and mean."

"He's out?" I reeled at her words. No doubt, Jurrell blamed us for his arrest, when it had been entirely his fault.

"That does it," Sage said. "For Jurrell to be a free man and Gerard to be locked in jail is absolutely wrong."

"Life isn't always fair or even right," Auntie O cautioned, matching the whisper-soft voices Sage and I were using.

I shuddered at the thought. "That's true, so we'll be on the lookout for Jurrell. Meanwhile, tell us about past Bristol Street land grabs."

My aunt looked off into the distance. "We thought that was behind us. He promised."

"Who promised?" Sage and I asked in unison.

"Blithe's grandfather assured us Bristol Street was safe."

I had this sense of a fishing line from the past reeling us into uncharted waters. The phrase *"Here there be monsters"* came to mind. I would rather be standing on solid ground, but how could I? We had twice as many problems now. "How could Moxley McAdam Sr. back up such a claim?"

"He was the go-to guy for land deals around Savannah for decades. Allegedly, his business partners obtained whatever properties the group wanted, a tradition his son continued."

Powerful figures could move mountains. "But why extend a wide berth to our street?"

"Lots of history on Bristol Street, and long memories in this town. From the start, money men who came knocking here got dead in a hurry. Even so, Moxley Sr. tried to grab the street's properties forty years ago. Marjoram convinced him that he and his investors couldn't build here. She gave Moxley the suggestion that he wouldn't be able to perform, er, romantically, if he even thought of developing Bristol Street."

My eyes widened. Mom threatened the most powerful man in Savannah? The event sounded like a bizarre fairy tale instead of my family history. "I didn't know she was so brazen." I leaned in close to whisper, the cat squirming in my arms. "How did she do that and survive?"

"Don't throw your cat on me, Tabby." Auntie O sniffed and used her extended arm to put space between us. "Harley hates most people, and he barely tolerates me. About your mother—Marjoram had hidden talents and that's all she needed. She sent Moxley Sr. home with a sample dose of what she intended to do to him. Scared him so bad he impressed the same suggestion on his son and bought us forty-some-odd years of peace."

I had never thought about trying to control an instinctive process like that in the opposite sex, but it seemed like an energy spear or an icer blast to the reproductive organ area would knock things offline for a bit. I stepped back with Harley, stroking his head and enjoying his purring. "Wait. As Moxley Jr.'s lawyer and business partner, Mr. Cranford had access to Junior's money when he was alive and then in his estate. He's the money man."

Sage whispered to us. "I could ask Brindle to snoop through his boss's files."

"Please don't," I said. "If Cranford is behind today's land grab, your boyfriend might be forced to make a terrible choice—confide in you or protect his partnership at Cranford, Aldrich, and Platt."

"He wouldn't hang me out to dry," Sage said. "Nor would he force me from my home. He knows how much it means to me."

I had to say it. "He might, to save his job."

Sage fumed while a customer checked out with lotions, a dolphin sculpture, and a Savannah ghost-story book. After the sale, my twin glowered at me. "If Brindle betrays me, he'll be sorry."

"He may not have all the facts," I suggested. "The developer who wants our street must feel invincible. He won't tolerate any resistance to what's best for his bottom line."

Auntie O nodded, and Sage's bad energy ebbed. "What can we do?" I asked Auntie O. "How did Mom command their attention last time?"

"Energetics come and go as the years roll by. Some years the need for action burns brightly, and we join forces to fight for our species. But she delivered her message as powerfully as I'm sure you'll do." My aunt stared right through me before answering. "You need to put a good scare into that man."

"Me?" I pointed to myself. "Sage is the scariest and most vindictive of the two of us. She should do it. I don't want the job."

Auntie O shook her head. "You are a natural leader, Tabby, despite issues with controlling your talent fifteen years ago."

I didn't have to pretend bafflement. "Why do you say that?"

She shook her head and dealt with another customer. I fiddled around until she was done, feeling uneasy about where this was headed. All these years I'd bottled up my energy talent, and now I was supposed to use it to bring a powerful man to heel? By myself? My energy flared with each breath, and I felt antsy.

All my life I'd been taught to behave in a way that didn't draw notice. It went against the grain to be front and center of anything. However, I wanted to clear Gerard's name and stop the land grab from happening. Standing up to Cranford was the only way to save our shop, but it was also downright scary. Why was Auntie O so sure I had to spearhead this activity?

She believed in me. That fact came through loud and clear, and it rang with the resonance of truth. Auntie O believed in me. Mom would believe in me if she were alive. I could do this. I would do whatever it took to stop Cranford.

The happy customer left, and a mother-daughter pair entered and browsed. Harley squirmed out of my arms and darted up the back stairs. I wasn't out of control, but powerful currents moved within me.

Certainty mounted. No one could take our street. I couldn't let them. I *wouldn't* let them. The energy in and around my body pulsed with wild fury, demanding release, so I let it go. Immediately, a sense of peace bathed the space where that frenetic energy had been.

Auntie O nodded my way. "Good. Pick up the phone and call Cranford. Invite him to come to the shop today."

Reaching deep for my wild-woman vibe, I called his receptionist and invited the man over to talk, then I hung up without ever talking to Cranford. "Now what?"

"Now we wait. I need to rest first." Auntie O went in the still-room and shut the door, her rapid departure leaving us in the lurch.

Sage shared a look of astonishment with me. We closed the shop and tromped upstairs to do a little preparing ourselves.

"This is downright bizarre," Sage said, flopping down on the sofa with her kitty, Luna. "What will you say? Something like 'You can't have our shop'?"

I took the rocking chair, needing motion to work off the edginess inside me. "I guess so."

"Shouldn't you sound more assertive? Auntie O says you're the one to do it. I'm not sensing a confident vibe from you."

"I'm not confident. I want to save the shop, but I don't want to threaten his manhood. Did Mom plan that in advance? How did she even come up with that? Seems like I should start with zits or fat ankles or something minor."

"Nope. Mom had the right of it, I'm sure. If you want to make an impression, go big. Zits and fat ankles won't do."

I sighed. "How big?"

"Hit him where it hurts, in the heart."

Sadly, I knew how to do that. It's what I'd accidentally done years ago when that creep tried to rape me. I'd sworn never to do that again, but to save our family I'd make an exception to that blanket policy. "The heart it is." And I'd make sure not to do anything irreparable.

Sage nodded. "You're a force to be reckoned with, Tabs. I've always known it. About time you realized it."

Confidence and determination flowed together in a vibrant energy current, filling me to the brim. With it came the knowing that this was meant to be. That *I* was meant to be. I wasn't a freak of nature. I was powerful and protective. Best of all, I was whole for the first time in a very long time.

"Don't worry about me, Sis," I said. "I'm all in."

"What would be the point otherwise?" Sage stacked her ankles on the coffee table. "You're more like me than you admit. Nothing halfway about your talent."

"This isn't the pep talk I envisioned, but it's working. I swear to stop Cranford. I will threaten his heart, and I will give him a taste of what I can do and hopefully buy us another forty-something years of safety. We're in a fight for our lives and Gerard's freedom. Y'all are depending on me, and I won't let you down. Cranford will learn not to mess with the Winslows."

Chapter Forty-Five

Frankie Mango joined us in the living room a few minutes later. Strands of his thinning hair flew in all directions, and he'd dressed in trousers and a polo shirt. He walked straight to my chair and introduced himself. I rose and shook his hand, feeling a pulse of strong energy pass between us. That explained a few things. Frankie was an energetic.

"At your service, dear Tabby." Frankie glanced over his shoulder. "And your service too, Sage. Glad you're both improved after the accident. I'm delighted I met your aunt in Florida. You have no idea how alone I felt in Orlando before your aunt arrived."

"Why did you go there?" Sage asked.

"Needed to simplify my life. Had no kids or siblings. Wife died twenty years ago from cancer. Tired of yardwork and my own cooking . . . The main reason was to seek companionship with people my age, and it worked. I'm not alone any longer. I have your aunt, and now I hope I you girls will welcome me into your pod."

Wary, I asked, "What are you, and what's a *pod*?"

263

"I'm an energy reader. In my other-vision I see a person's energy field, very much like I assume both of you do. Pods are groupings of energetics. Like whales, we school together for safety. I haven't had a pod since my parents were alive."

"O-kay," I said, drawing out the words. "We've never met other energetics or heard of pods."

"Oralee mentioned that. Your mom and aunt isolated you two for your protection. Energy talents exist in small pod clusters throughout the world, though our kind is nearly extinct. Most find it impossible to bond with someone else long enough to have a family. We seek solitude." He glanced at his shoes. "My 'normal' wife was on the verge of divorcing me for my secretiveness, when she became ill. Then she became resigned to my company, and at the end she clung to me." His chin quivered. "Her loss hit me hard."

His story touched my heart. Somehow he'd married and kept his energetic secret from his wife. They'd stuck it out for years. That boded well for me and Quig. "I'm sorry about your wife, and I understand how hard relationships are for you. For us, I mean. Sage and I have boyfriends now, but that's rare for us. It's hard to find men who understand our need to keep a large chunk of our lives private."

"Don't I know it. The same issue repeats with every generation. You're the only energetics I know who are young enough to have kids. Most are older and childless. I hope you will meet energetics your own age." He cleared his throat. "Oralee woke me with a text message, said she's getting ready. Is something about to happen? Tabby's energy looks positively fierce."

Oh goody, I thought at first. Another adult who wanted Sage and me to reproduce. The fate of our species wasn't relying on us, was it? That was too much pressure. I was just starting to understand more about the energetic world. Then I realized he'd called me fierce. It fit. I'd totally recharged and more. Cranford wouldn't stop me. I would defend my family with everything I had.

"Auntie O says Cranford will accept our invitation. Tabby will take point on the discussion with him," Sage said.

Frankie gestured toward me. "That explains the energy storm I see around you. If he's powerful, you'll need it. Oralee and I will be there and share our energy if needed."

"Thanks," I said. "I'm ready for the meetup, and I'm deadly serious about keeping our property. That man has no right to it. Our family has had this place for three generations. I won't let him steal it from us."

"Good. Your grounded nature and heritage will guide you well," Frankie said. "This place feels amazing. I can tell people like me have lived here. There are energy sparks all around me, and you girls too. You're positively glowing."

I looked at him and then Sage. They both looked normal to me.

"Your auras, I mean," Frankie added. "Your auras are amazing—zesty even. Neither of you look like the world beat you down. You'll notice that on most energetics. They are barely hanging on because they don't have resting places like this for their pods."

I hadn't gotten used to the word *pod* yet, but he had a point about Sage's energy. I always knew when Sage was nearby. Sight unseen, my energy recognized hers. I assumed that was because of our twin link. No doubt, though, that her energy was stronger than anyone else's I'd ever met. Perhaps there was something to what Frankie was saying. If I went down that rabbit hole, the next thought that followed was the importance of saving our Bristol Street home.

"Yeah, we'll send that guy a strong message today so he'll stay away forever. I'm excited to be at the epicenter of the confrontation," Frank said.

Glad he was excited. I'd set this in motion at Auntie O's prompting. No doubt in my mind that Cranford would waltz in here and try to intimidate us. I couldn't let him control the narrative. I had to be strong.

"Yessiree. You'll neutralize the threat and all will be good," Frank continued.

Neutralizing was a worrisome term. It was close kin to *rubbing out*, which was something mafia people did. Was that why we had to keep everything so close to our chest? Though I was fully charged and physically ready, I hated not knowing exactly how this would proceed. I had to blindly trust everything would work out, whatever happened. "We're not killing anyone, are we?"

"No killing is needed, most of the time. The object of the focus quickly realizes it's in his best interest to leave us alone."

I gripped the arms of the rocker in alarm. "BB Cranford barely knows us. He's coming here thinking I will hand him the shop on a fancy platter."

"It will play out as I've said. Of that I'm certain. You have the energy chops, Oralee has the experience. No need to worry at all."

Easy for him to say. His part involved showing up for the meeting and lending energy if needed. I had to change our enemy's mind and save the day. Daunting tasks for an introvert. "I wish it were over."

"Nonsense. You'll relive this day in your dreams for the rest of your life. This will be awesome. *You* will be awesome."

"Are we in danger?" Sage asked, chewing her thumbnail.

A muscle twitched in Frankie's cheek. "No more so than you were thirty minutes ago."

"How soon will Cranford arrive?" I asked.

"I guarantee he will be here in the next hour. You have something he wants very much, Tabby. Power, pure and undiluted. We have an early warning system, in any event. Oralee will know when he's coming."

Only an hour. That seemed an eternity to wait, and at the same time felt much too soon. "Good to know." Crap, maybe we were witches after all. Maybe Mom had denied we were witches all these years to protect us. It was another odd notion in a bizarre day.

Frankie nodded. "All right then. I'm headed down to see Oralee, but first, is there anything I can get for you ladies?"

"I'm good," I said.

"Nothing for me, thanks," Sage said.

After he left, I looked at Sage. "You understand all this?"

She grinned. "Not even a little bit, but I'm behind you every step of the way."

I choked out a laugh. "Yeah, because who else would stand in front of a category five storm?"

Chapter
Forty-Six

Unsure how long I'd be sleeping at Quig's, and with about an hour to kill, I hurriedly grabbed a second bag of clothes, shoes, and books. I lugged everything over, hoping Quig was right about his smart lock. He hadn't given me a key, saying the lock would recognize my hand and I didn't need a key.

I'd never heard of such a lock, but it worked as he claimed. I waved my hand over the sensor. There was a click, and the doorknob turned in my hand. The approaching dark clouds suggested we'd have a thunderstorm in the next hour. Probably arriving at the same time as Cranford, the way things were going.

I rolled the suitcases to the master bedroom and unpacked. I hung up a few blouses and pants, stacked my shoes in the bottom of the closet, and consolidated my undergarments and nightgowns in one suitcase, as no drawers were available, nerves jittering the whole time. The books, I tossed on his living room bookshelf.

I was standing on tiptoe, to squeeze my empty suitcase in the top of Quig's closet, when he burst through the door. "There you are." He hurried over and hugged me tight, trembling. "I was frightened when the shop was locked."

"You were?" I had a blinding realization that left me breathless. "What gave you the impression something was wrong?"

"I don't know. I was finishing my notes on an autopsy, and I suddenly needed to be with you. I was so worried I couldn't focus on work. Thought for sure something awful had happened."

His intense reaction to my upcoming showdown with BB Cranford suggested Quig might be an energetic, but maybe his ability to amplify my powers made him sensitive to my needs. "I'm fine, but I appreciate your concern."

"Concern? It's more than that. My sense of dread is growing. Something is very wrong. You are in danger. I feel it in my bones. I will protect you."

I blinked and leaned close to study his expression. "You know what's about to happen?"

Puzzlement flashed like sheet lightning across his worried face. "I tried to call you, but you didn't pick up. I nearly lost it. Babe. You aren't that long out of the hospital. Tell me you're all right."

My rising hopes crashed. Quig couldn't be an energetic—that was wishful thinking on my part. I wouldn't lie to him, so I went with the flow. "I feel much better today, but you're right. Something is happening in just a bit at the shop. A developer is coming after Bristol Street. We believe it's connected to the Blithe McAdam murder. Everything is interrelated." I stroked his cheeks, wanting him to be safe from whatever happened. "You must be busy, and I shouldn't keep you from your work. Look." I gestured to the suitcase, and my stuff hanging in his closet. "My clothes are here."

His grip on my arms tightened. "Don't distract me with cohabitation. Neither of us is going anywhere until I know what's going on."

I shared most of the truth. "My family and I are meeting with BB Cranford very soon, and I'm going to convince him to look elsewhere for property. He can't have ours, and we aren't moving."

"I've never trusted that man."

His sour tone made me smile. "You have good instincts. Now, I must return to The Book and Candle Shop."

"I'm coming too."

The need to keep him safe intensified. "What about your job?"

"I'll sort that out later."

I fisted my hands together and hoped this wasn't the beginning of the end with Quig. "It would be best if you didn't accompany me."

His gaze narrowed. "Why?"

"I can't tell you."

"No secrets."

"I . . ." The words wouldn't come. I turned my head to hide my flaming cheeks.

"You're scaring me."

"You should be scared, Quig. I'm not like you. There are hidden parts of me you shouldn't know about."

"I doubt that. I want to know everything about you."

Thoughts whirled in my head. I wanted to tell him. I needed to be in the shop. I feared he'd reject me if he knew about the woo-woo stuff. I dreaded what Quig might witness when Cranford arrived. If things went wrong, I could lose my home, the shop, and my boyfriend in one fell swoop.

This was the worst day of my life.

"Tabby! Don't shut me out," Quig implored, cradling my hand in his. "Whatever it is, we'll deal with it together."

If Quig came with me, what repercussions would follow? Would I be strong enough to do whatever it took to keep him from telling anyone else?

I tried again. "I'm different. My family is different. We sense things others don't. We see things that aren't visible."

He stared at me through narrowed eyes. "You're a psychic?"

I wrenched away from him. "Not exactly. I didn't want you to find out. I don't want you to hate me. I must go. I invited Cranford to come, you see."

He followed and caught my hand again. "Whatever you are doesn't matter to me. I've loved you since grade school. I've lived for the day you'd be here. With me. For better or worse, we're in this together. I'm coming with you, love."

My breath hitched in my throat. If there was fallout, I'd deal with it later. "Let's go."

Chapter Forty-Seven

The Book and Candle Shop was empty except for my aunt. I sidled up to Auntie O. "Is the door still locked?"

"I unlocked it, but the "Closed sign" is up," she said, eying Quig attached to my hand. She made an open-palmed gesture of welcome to us. "Now I need to get Frankie so he'll be with us when BB Cranford arrives."

"About time you returned," Sage said, handing me Harley.

It took both hands to hold the squirming cat. Undeterred at losing his grip on me, Quig wrapped his arm around my waist. "Together," he whispered.

I nodded, though I wished I had a plan. It felt like I stood on a tall windswept dune, gazing over a vast beach inundated with violent thunderstorms. Actual lightning arced across the dark sky outside our shop every few minutes, followed by cracks of thunder. The storm was here.

"You scared?" Sage asked.

I nodded. "Terrified he'll have a new threat up his sleeve. Rest assured, I will do whatever it takes to beat him. He can't have our place."

"Just speak from your heart. The right words will come to you."

My aunt returned and nodded toward the closed door of the stillroom. "Frankie will be out in a minute. As for Cranford, he's on the way."

Her words renewed my resolve to win at all costs. It was as if the atoms inside my bones spun faster.

"What's happening?" Quig asked. "Your body feels tingly."

He was right. My entire body tingled. In my gut, energy pulsed and surged like the volatile surface of the sun. "Auntie O?"

She patted my other shoulder. "Stay strong and remain open to possibilities, dear. Let the meeting unfold naturally, and all will be well."

"Okay." Sage stood behind me, her fingers clenched in my belt loops. Frankie Mango entered and drew Auntie O to the wall behind us.

"You should go," I whispered to Quig. "I don't want you to get hurt."

"I'm right where I need to be," he said. "I'm not leaving."

Sage gasped, and I turned toward the front door. Under leaden skies, BB Cranford loomed outside our entrance. Behind him stood Alderman Rashad Vernon and his half brother, Jurrell Dawson. How they came to be here, I didn't know. But they'd come, and now I had to be the best version of myself I'd ever been. Instead of one enemy, I faced three.

I summoned my courage front and center. This showdown in our shop would be as memorable to my family as the gunfight at the OK Corral. Every nerve in my body snapped and crackled. I felt warrior fierce and battle ready. This meeting would determine our future in Savannah.

In my other vision, the three men were shrouded in darkness, with the densest, vilest aura around Cranford. He motioned for the brothers to follow him inside. The door opened, and Cranford strode in, flanked by his minions.

"Ms. Winslow," Cranford said in a commanding theatrical voice. "You can't stop what's coming. I will own this street and everything on it. Today is your last day of business. No one can halt progress. The plans are drawn. The die is cast."

His dramatics didn't impress me. I gripped Harley tighter. Power amped in my core higher and higher. My vision sharpened until the shop lights blazed with stark ferocity. The brightness battled Cranford's darkness. Candle fragrance enriched every breath, centering me on my home turf.

This man was an outsider, a carpetbagger, trying to steal what was ours. I wasn't having it. "Not on my watch, Cranford. This shop has been in my family for generations. You can't have it. We're staying put."

"We'll see about that." He nodded over his shoulder. "Knock everything off the shelves, then set this place on fire."

Neutralizing his lackeys took priority. Energy coiled and surged inside me until it streamed through my pores, and a seemingly endless cascade of compressed power crackled in the room. Dawson set his ball cap on the counter and circled around to the book nook. I shot invisible energy out of both hands, one stream toward Vernon and the other to Dawson, both shaped into lassoes.

Vernon ducked down so I could no longer see him. I canceled his beam. Jurrell bobbed, and I missed as he took a swipe down a shelf of glassware. The items wobbled, then fell in a splintering crash. I tried again to capture him. Got him. Jurrell didn't bat an eyelash after I trapped him. My energy lasso held him in thrall. Satisfaction hummed in me.

"Move, dammit," Cranford said, his voice roughening. "What happened to Vernon?"

Another stream of electric current arced from my body and circled Cranford. It didn't confine him for long. His face clouded with anger as he incredibly shook off the binding force. "You can't stop me. I am the game master. I own this town, and these old shops on Bristol Street have to go."

The authority amplifying his words implied he was hot stuff indeed. Personally, I thought he was a puffed-up frog. Harley hissed at him, and his feline warning encouraged me. This was our place. Cranford didn't belong here. Words boiled out of my mouth. "Wrong. We're staying. You're not welcome here, now or ever. If you ever set foot on these premises again, your heart won't be right."

His aura throbbed with darkness and evil. "You don't scare me, little girl. My heart is fine. Never better. I have the might of wealthy investors behind me. Our millions will make these shops and you Winslows disappear. If you won't vacate, I'll take you out of the game."

"Like you made Blithe McAdam disappear?" I challenged.

He snorted. "That woman didn't realize I stole her inheritance. I was due that money, by the way. Her father swindled me with his investment schemes, and I took her estate as payback with interest. She complained constantly about the money, so I shut her up permanently. How poignant that her father's seed money and her death will be the undoing of Bristol Street. Old Man McAdam pronounced this street untouchable decades ago. Now that the legitimate bearers of the McAdam name are dead, I will build where I please. Bristol Street is prime real estate, and it will be mine. My attorney is preparing offers for everyone in this three-block area of Bristol Street."

"This property is not for sale." Whispers assailed me as time flexed, then one voice rose above the fray. Auntie O's words flowed into my head, and I voiced them. "Blithe's grandfather, Moxley Sr., came after this street once, but never again. You will not build condos here, Barrett Brendon Cranford. Leave Bristol Street alone or suffer dire consequences."

"You *people* can't stop me!" he said. "I have wealth and author-ity. Once I crush The Book and Candle Shop, other shops will close. What's so freakin' special about this street anyway? It's one more decaying avenue in a city built on the dead."

He referred to the yellow fever victims who centuries ago had been buried in Savannah. As the city later expanded, unmarked graves became covered by structures. I had reason to believe the land under our building had been a mass grave. That made sense, considering how much good energy the candle shop had showered into the earth for nearly a century. Those spirits felt gratitude and recharged our energy talents.

Even as I thought of the dead beneath us, more energy welled in my core, expanded into my aura. I glanced down and gulped. My body fluctuated between visible and invisible. Omigod. No shadows nearby to draw energy from. There'd be a huge pay-back for using true white light invisibility, even though I stopped the cycling process and stayed visible. Couldn't think about my energy budget now. With Cranford's confession, I had the answer to Blithe's murder and maybe another. Time to push him a bit. "You killed Blithe's father too."

Cranford laughed like only a psychopath could. "Everyone believes Moxley Jr. fell off the pier. He had some help, but I'll deny helping him along with my dying breath. That fool tried an end run around me. After he discovered I'd bled him dry, he began stealing it back. Got him plastered, took care of business, and the rest is history."

He took a menacing step toward me, and I zapped his heart with a laser-focused micro energy spear from my right hand, as if I did it every day. No time to marvel about my surgical efficiency right now. The darkness in his aura sizzled like bacon in a hot skillet, and like that breakfast meat, shrank to half size. Since his survival wouldn't stop what he'd put in motion, I knew what had to be done. Using a delicate touch, I focused on the walls of the vein by his right atrium. The extra energy created a storm of current, disrupting the heart's performance. Immediately, BB clutched his chest, dropped to his knees, and gasped for air.

"What are you doing to me, witch?" Cranford snarled, his face scarlet with anger, sweat glistening on his forehead. "You'll pay for this outrage. *I. Control. Savannah.*"

With my entire focus on BB Cranford, Jurrell Dawson jerked free and bolted out the door. Good riddance, I said silently. Cranford shuddered and clutched his chest. I knew the erratic energy was painful, but I couldn't stop yet.

Auntie O's words vectored straight through me again. "Your life is ours, Cranford. If you consider Bristol Street in your plans again, you will feel ill like this, and your heart will race. You will be fine if you never bother us again. Understood?"

"Understood," he gasped, the color gone from his face. "Make it stop."

"Do you want to buy Bristol Street?" I asked, keeping the energy storm centered on him.

He moaned in pain. "No. Make it stop, please—make it stop."

"How do you feel about Bristol Street?" I asked.

He shivered violently and vomited on his shoes. "I hate this place. My chest. It hurts. I'm dying. Call 911."

I glanced at Auntie O. She nodded. I shut off the energy instantly, and Cranford fell to the floor, unconscious but alive. Tears dripped off my cheeks, tears I was crying. I felt sick to my stomach for inflicting pain on another human. Harley jumped out of my arms, and my legs buckled. The colors in the room merged into a river of rioting watercolors until everything faded to black.

*   *   *

I woke up on Auntie O's Murphy bed in the stillroom, Quig and Sage flanking the bed and Harley resting on my belly. "What happened?"

"You stopped BB Cranford two hours ago," Sage crowed. "Our home and Bristol Street are safe, thanks to you."

I didn't do any of that alone. "Where is he?"

"Hospital," Quig said, holding my hand. "Apparently Cranford had an undiagnosed and very serious A-fib problem. They tried to stabilize the electricity in his heart, but he didn't make it. The electrocardiologist said he'd never seen anything like those alternate rhythms."

Details returned in awful clarity. I'd fought Cranford. I'd zapped him with energy to get his attention. But I hadn't *killed* him outright. I couldn't be a killer. Like him. "We saved Bristol Street. But Gerard is still in trouble. Cranford killed Blithe and her father, but we can't prove it."

"Your shop's security camera recorded his confession. At your aunt's urging, Detective Nowry copied the silent video footage and used a lipreader to interpret what Cranford said."

"But not what I said?"

"The camera pointed precisely at Cranford, so only his side of the conversation is available to the police. His confession proves his guilt. Don't worry—he will never bother you again. Nothing they tried brought him back. It was his time to go."

I couldn't breathe. "He was alive when he left here. He should not be dead."

"He's dead," Quig said. "The man wasn't as healthy as his boast, not by a long shot. He had multiple undiagnosed health issues, and apparently his ticker was already failing before he came here. Once they opened him up, it was lights out for Cranford. The surgeon said the man's heart was a walking timebomb. He is gone like the wind."

Quig could think that all he wanted. He hadn't aimed an energy spear at Cranford's heart. He hadn't battled a primitive urge to crush the man who threatened my very existence. He hadn't pulled back because he didn't want to be a killer.

My God.

I'd killed someone.

My stomach lurched.

"It's okay, Tabby." Sage placed her hand on my shoulder and switched to our silent twin-speak to communicate with thoughts. *"It wasn't your fault."*

"How can you say that?" I asked silently. *"I buzzed him. On purpose. To give him a potent reminder of who he was dealing with. Now he's dead."*

"Lucky you. I wish it had been me zapping that loser. I'd have barbecued the man."

"Careful what you wish for. I thought I was ready to face the consequences, but I'm appalled at what happened. I'm not cut out for punishing bad guys."

"Auntie O says we all get dealt different cards in life. Anyway, you pulled back. I felt it. He was alive when he left here. Everyone in the shop knows that, even the emergency responders. Especially them. No one believes you killed him, not your family and certainly not the cops."

"I didn't want him to come after us again, but I couldn't purposefully kill him. That goes against who I am. I wanted to teach him a lesson, and now I feel sick that he died due to my actions."

"It worked out for the best. He didn't die here. Why did you bring Quig?"

"He felt my distress and knew I needed him. I tried to shake him, but he insisted. The only thing I can figure is Quig has some sensitivity, but that's a guess. I think I'll have a panic attack now. Or two. This day definitely rates multiple panic attacks."

"Pull yourself together before Quig figures out we're keeping secrets."

Message received loud and clear. "Where's Auntie O?" I asked aloud.

"Upstairs cooking with Frankie," Sage said, then blushed. "I mean the two of them are upstairs cooking our dinner tonight."

I glanced from her to Quig. "Are we having dinner here?"

"We're taking it easy tonight," Quig said with a gentle caress to my hand. "I thought eating here was what you would prefer. Did I guess wrong?"

"You guessed right." There was so much more I needed to know about what happened, and I needed to be around my family, to feel they were truly safe.

Quig smiled. "Once you're fully recovered, we'll invite your family over for dinner at our place."

Our place. I guess it was. I shot an anxious glance to Sage, unsure of how much I should ask in Quig's presence. "What is the deal with Rashad? I noticed he didn't trash our shop."

"Rashad was working undercover with the cops. He knew BB Cranford was bad news, and he set out to prove it," Sage said with a barbed gaze Quig's way.

I got the message to keep further questions to myself. Except for Quig and our enemies, everyone else in the shop had been energetics, so our secrets were safe. "There's a lot to consider about what happened today."

Chapter Forty-Eight

After a filling dinner of homemade tomato soup, cornbread, and grilled cheese sandwiches, I felt human again, even though I bore the weight of the day on my shoulders. With such dark knowledge, would I ever feel lighthearted again? Perhaps Mom had been right to shield us so heavily. "Thanks, Auntie O and Frankie, for a delicious meal. Your cornbread is a winner every time, but tonight it truly hit the spot."

"I'm so glad to be home with my nieces," my aunt said. "We don't know how soon it will work out, but Frankie and I are moving to Savannah full-time. Is that okay with everyone?"

What wasn't to love about that? "I'm delighted. We'll figure out the logistics."

"Frankie and I are buying the building next door. Consolidation of energetic ownership on this block will keep the land sharks away from our turf. Anyway, we'll fix up the living space over there. I'll continue to help in The Book and Candle Shop, and since the lease of the decor shop is up and they want to move closer to their kids on the West Coast, Frankie plans to open a custom T-shirt shop over there."

Sage started to say something, probably about our dire finances, but I privately shushed her. Aloud, I said, "What a great idea for the whole unit. We'll be next-door neighbors. Only, no one has lived in that upper space for a very long time. It will take serious renovation before it's livable."

Auntie O beamed. "That's why it's so nice you and Quig are a couple now. There's room for us here with Sage in the meanwhile. We can take our time and truly create a home there."

This place. A building most likely constructed atop an unmarked graveyard. How was it such a hospitable home to us? Why didn't the despair and misery of the dead burnish our every thought? It made no sense that this was a good space. And yet it was. I'd seen and done strange things today. This day would haunt me forever, even though I'd accomplished what I set out to do. Victory came at a very high cost.

Aware that everyone was looking at me, I tuned back into the conversation. "What about the money you two used to buy into the place in Florida?"

"I'm still in the deposit refund window, so no problem for me," my aunt said. "Frankie has a few strings to untangle before he can pry his money free, but it's all good."

Her answer made sense, but the energy resonance felt off. Given her penchant for secrets, I wondered what she wasn't saying. Would moving back financially overextend her? Despite my misgivings, I accepted her answer for now. I was running on fumes this evening. "I hope so. We deserve peace and quiet after Cranford's vendetta against us."

"You can't relax your guard," Auntie O cautioned. "Not even for a minute. Evil never sleeps."

I didn't know how to phrase my next question, with Quig at the table. I tried something very generic. "Did our *meeting* work as well as the last one?"

"Yes, but we can never rest on success. Power always fills a void."

Reading between the lines, soon there'd be another developer gunning for us. I hoped it wasn't right away. I had serious concerns about wrestling bad guys every week or two. The practicalities of what had happened earlier seemed surreal and a bit fantastical now. When I'd confronted Cranford this afternoon, I'd gathered human and natural energy for our defense. Possibly even pulled energy from the dead. Except for Cranford's unfortunate death, which was likely helped along or started by my interference, I'd handled the invasive energy manipulation as if I were a pro. I made a solemn vow to myself. Focusing energy to protect family and friends is something I would do gladly when needed.

Glancing around, my entire family was none the worse for wear, and while I was running low on energy, I wasn't knee-knocking exhausted either. How was that possible? I burned tons of energy, and yet I still had enough onboard to eat and manage a polite conversation. My physics education bordered between rusty to nonexistent. However, burning energy required refueling—even amateur athletes knew that.

Another puzzle to solve later.

With the property grab quashed, my thoughts turned to the original reason for our investigation. Our shop clerk was still behind bars for a murder he didn't commit. "Is Gerard's name cleared?"

"According to Detective Belfor, he'll be released early tomorrow," Auntie O said. "If not, MawMaw and I will stage a sit-in at the jail."

Quig laughed out loud. "That should be interesting."

"What about Jurrell Dawson?" Sage asked. "He was in this land-grab plot up to his neck."

"He's an accomplice. He came here with intent to destroy the shop," Auntie O said. "The cops will haul him in for questioning as soon as they locate him. Jurrell Dawson is a loose cannon. I'm sure he'll crack and tell all. That will tie up any remaining loose ends."

I felt a nudge in my brain, twin-speak from Sage. *"Don't worry about Jurrell. I caught up with him an hour ago at the Moonlight Fishing Hole and made sure he knew what would happen to him if he crossed us again."*

That was expedient of her, but Jurrell didn't strike me as a reasonable sort. The alderman wouldn't be a problem, but Jurrell was a powder keg of walking contradictions. Maybe he wouldn't be so vocal once he wasn't on Cranford's payroll. Maybe he'd have to get a real job and work like the rest of us. Bottom line, we'd saved our home and Gerard. That mattered.

"Amen to that," I said aloud, and we toasted our victory.

* * *

Afterward, Quig escorted me to our apartment two doors down. Once inside, he drew me in his arms. "You've been through hell today. Cranford planned to burn you out of house and home. I should've punched him in the face, but you needed me at your side. That meeting with him felt intense."

His comment puzzled me. We had never experienced mutual telepathy, and yet he'd come and contributed his energy to the showdown. "What do you remember about this afternoon?"

"My intuition kicked in and told me you needed me. I came home to be with you. Cranford arrived, threatened you. He collapsed because of his undiagnosed A-fib and later died in surgery."

"That's what I remember too." Saying his intuition brought him to me covered a lot of gray area. I'd become sensitive to his moods and emotions, so it was nice to realize the vibe went both ways. That had to be why he'd joined us, and yet, there was another remote possibility, even more out there than his intuition.

Had Quig and I bonded like my twin-bond with Sage? Had my sleeping with him somehow tuned our energies in a deeper way? I sent him a mental image of a sea turtle to see if he'd mention it. A yawn slipped out, though it was barely nine. I covered it with my hand, but Quig noticed how sleepy I was.

"Bedtime," he stated firmly. "But first tell me how you went invisible before Cranford dropped to the ground."

"Must've been a trick of the light," I suggested.

He tapped his glasses. "No trick, and my corrected vision is perfect. You were invisible, but my arm still bound us together."

Suddenly the weight of the day hit me like gale force winds. True white light invisibility always came at a steep cost. I was thankful I'd only used the invisibility umbrella to cover myself for a few seconds. Two-person coverage would have been twice the energy drain. The nap I'd taken immediately afterward had worn off. I needed at least six hours of deep sleep to regenerate my energy. "I can't explain now. I've got about ten minutes worth of go left in me, and then I'll crash hard."

"Long as you crash here, I'm good, and I'm hanging onto you so I can find you if you go invisible again."

"Works for me," I said, caressing his face.

"Let's get some rest."

"Perfect."

* * *

The next day Auntie O and Frankie made an offer on the adjoining property. Quig went to work, as usual, at the morgue. Sage and Brindle drove to the jail to pick up Gerard, so it was just me and the cats running The Book and Candle Shop. Customers arrived at a steady pace all morning.

A little before noon, Sage strolled in with Gerard. He ran to me and swung me around in a circle. "You and Sage are my absolute heroes. I am a free man, and after I get cleaned up and check on MawMaw, I'm partying all night. You in?"

"I'm thrilled for you," I said, "but I'm drained from all the excitement. No partying for me. You'll have to drink my share."

"Will do. When they told me who killed Blithe, I nearly dropped my teeth. How did you come up with BB Cranford? I wouldn't have guessed him in a million years."

"Pretty sure he counted on his reputation protecting him." I drew in a deep breath and let it out. "Once we discovered his unlimited access to the McAdam fortune before and after Moxley's death, all roads led to him."

Gerard grinned. "Follow the money, eh? Good strategy. I'm thrilled to be walking around Savannah and breathing fresh air. This is amazing! Y'all are amazing!"

Sage tugged on his arm. "Okay, Mr. Amazing. Let's get you home."

287

"You partying with me tonight, girlfriend?"

She looked at him full on, questions bright in her eyes. "You want me to be there?"

"You know I do."

"Let me check with Brindle first." Sage turned to me, a bit red-faced. "Brindle would've come in with us, but he had another appointment at noon. He and Aldrich are scrambling to reposition Cranford, Aldrich, and Platt now that Cranford is gone."

Her embarrassment puzzled me. I wasn't concerned about Brindle. But Sage—I was concerned about her. "It's all good."

They left, both walking on air. People ebbed and flowed through our shop the rest of the day. I sold candles and books. I chatted up customers. Nevertheless, I had the unsettling feeling the proverbial other shoe would drop any minute. That premonition proved correct when an unmarked cop car parked in front of the store.

Detectives Nowry and Belfor sailed in on a gusty wind. "There you are," Belfor said with a grin.

I nodded, knowing the less I said to cops about yesterday, the better. "Here I am. What can I do for you?"

"Thought we'd touch base with you about Cranford's video confession. Any idea what brought him to your shop?"

"He's a repeat customer." I was proud that was a truth.

Nowry pulled out a notepad and pen. "We don't understand why he voluntarily confessed to you about the McAdams murders."

"Didn't make sense to me either." Darn, I was good at this half-truth stuff. "Guess he heard I'd been asking around in an effort to clear my employee's name."

Nowry tapped the pen on the pad and scowled. "Try again. We're not buying that story, and neither are our superiors. What did you have on the man?"

I pulled a few more truths from the data pile. "BB Cranford was the executor of Blithe's father's will, and he'd been Moxley's silent business partner. Once we realized how much money was involved, it wasn't a leap to figure out he also stole Blithe's inheritance and her life."

Nowry and Belfor exchanged a concerned glance before Nowry continued speaking. "If not for Rashad Vernon coming forward and agreeing to wear a wire, we wouldn't have suspected a thing about BB Cranford. He looked golden. He was a big deal in Savannah, with more money than God, and even judges jumped to do his bidding. Why jeopardize his prestige with theft, vandalism, and murder?"

"Revenge on the McAdam family guided his actions, as I see it. He came here to teach me a lesson for trying to stop him from destroying the reputation of our block of stores. He instructed Dawson and Vernon to trash and burn our shop to punish my family. Bad luck for him that our security camera taped his confession."

Sharmilla Belfor's gaze tightened. "Even worse luck for his heart to fail on the operating table. We had a lot of questions for him."

I gestured broadly with my hands. "Karma. It bites you in the butt every time."

"What about his bizarre claim to be the 'game master'?" Belfor continued. "What brought that on?"

I nodded, glad to be on another subject. "It was very strange. I looked it up because I wasn't certain what it meant. According to the internet, a game master organizes the play in a game. My guess is because he planned and orchestrated the end of the McAdam family, he thought he called all the shots. I've never heard the game master term applied to anyone, much less Cranford. Considering his own wealth and clout, he likely thought he could buy and sell anyone in Savannah. Turns out he didn't control the game or Savannah. Now he's not even in the game."

"Game over for him," Belfor said with a wry smile.

Nowry ignored his younger partner and leveled his notepad at me. "Perhaps, but why did he think a young shopkeeper such as yourself could thwart his plans? No offense, but you don't have his millions."

"None taken. The thing that comes to mind is this: with his bad heart, he wasn't thinking clearly." I took a considering breath as I chose my next words. "Given my interest in Blithe's murder, he fixated on me. He didn't want me to keep digging and learn he was her killer. Maybe more answers about his death will show up at the autopsy. What does Quig say about the man's heart?"

"Due to his *personal* involvement, Dr. Quigsly is too close to this case, so Cranford's body went to the Georgia Bureau of Investigation lab for autopsy. We don't have those results at this time."

Just then the blue-haired art student and her pals entered the shop. Blue Hair circled around the cops to my side. "Is Gerard here? We heard he was released."

I tried not to smile at Nowry and Belfor's dour expressions over the intrusion. "He stopped by earlier, but he's off for the rest of the day."

"Bummer that we missed him," Blue Hair said. "We'll browse a bit and come back tomorrow to talk to him."

Once they headed to their hangout in the book corner, I turned back to the detectives. "My apology for the interruption. Anything else?"

Nowry shook his head and stormed out.

Belfor leaned across the counter and spoke confidentially. "Good job on solving the case. Nowry's upset because he wanted it to be Gerard. Also, you were right about Eileen Hutson."

She had my full attention. "How so?"

"She has Blithe's dog, Boo Boo."

"What happens to Jurrell Dawson?"

"Jurrell's still facing the hit-and-run charge on your sister's car. As for his violent behavior at your shop when Cranford confessed, he claims Cranford blackmailed him into helping with the Bristol Street acquisition by making it a war zone. Nowry and I will take another run at him this afternoon."

Interesting. "I hope he stays behind bars. He destroyed shop merchandise and violated that restraining order. He's not supposed to be near me or this shop. Those behaviors and his striking our car were fueled by malicious intent. He is not a good person."

Belfor laughed. "You're a natural at this, Winslow. Ever thought about becoming a cop?"

"Nope." I gestured to the shop. "Sticking with the family business. Candle making is my jam."

"Good deal. I better scoot before Nowry lays on the horn."

*   *   *

As I brushed my teeth that evening, I reached several conclusions. Quig knew about my extra abilities, but he cared for me and protected me in spite of my baggage. He felt like family. My feelings for him were so deep I didn't dare examine them in the light of day, but maybe that was the point.

We were good together—better than good. Our relationship felt shiny and bright, like sunlight on the sea, and oh so happy. We had good synergy and possibly were developing a deeper communication. Quig was a mystery that I could take a lifetime to solve, and I hoped he felt the same way about me.

It'd been a good day despite yesterday's craziness of BB Cranford attempting to destroy us. Karma took Cranford and Jurrell Dawson out of the game, and now Gerard cherished his freedom. I'd accomplished my goal of clearing my employee's name.

With Auntie O and Frankie moving to Bristol Street, I'd have my entire family nearby and a new family member to boot. No longer would I deny my energy manipulation abilities. Sure, there was darkness with this ability, but there was light too. I could wield my talent and still dwell in the light.

At the end of the day, I had my family, home, and now Quig. Whatever nasty weather blew in tomorrow, we'd stand together against the storm, united in love and good energy.

I finished and climbed into bed with the man I loved and hugged the plush stuffed sea turtle he'd surprised me with tonight.

Enjoyed the read?

We'd love to hear your thoughts!

crookedlanebooks.com/feedback

Acknowledgments

No person or book is an island, and that's certainly the case for this new series. I am forever indebted to my critique partner Polly Iyer who gets the first pass on my pages, and also to my freelance editor Beth "Jaden" Terrell who adds her keen insights. Thanks also to my agent Jill Marsal of the Marsal Lyon Agency for taking a chance on this series, and for Tara Gavin, my editor at Crooked Lane Books for loving the story.